Black Ice

OTHER WORKS BY THOMAS KING

FICTION

Medicine River
Green Grass, Running Water
One Good Story, That One
Truth and Bright Water
A Short History of Indians in Canada
The Back of the Turtle
Indians on Vacation
Sufferance

DREADFULWATER MYSTERIES

DreadfulWater
The Red Power Murders
Cold Skies
A Matter of Malice
Obsidian
Deep House
Double Eagle

NON-FICTION

The Truth About Stories
The Inconvenient Indian

POETRY

77 Fragments of a Familiar Ruin

CHILDREN'S ILLUSTRATED BOOKS

Coyote Sings to the Moon, illustrated by Johnny Wales
A Coyote Columbus Story, illustrated by William Kent Monkman
Coyote's New Suit, illustrated by Johnny Wales
Coyote Tales, illustrated by Byron Eggenschwiler
A Coyote Solstice Tale, illustrated by Gary Clement
My Lala, illustrated by Charlene Chua
The Green Baby Swing, illustrated by Yong Ling Kang

GRAPHIC NOVELS

Borders, illustrated by Natasha Donovan

THOMAS KING

Black Ice

A DreadfulWater Mystery

HarperCollins*PublishersLtd*

Black Ice

Published by HarperCollins Publishers Ltd

First edition

HarperCollins Publishers Ltd
Bay Adelaide Centre, East Tower
22 Adelaide Street West, 41st Floor
Toronto, Ontario, Canada
M5H 4E3

www.harpercollins.ca

Library and Archives Canada Cataloguing in Publication

Title: Black ice : a DreadfulWater mystery / Thomas King.
Names: King, Thomas, 1943- author.
Description: Series statement: A DreadfulWater mystery
Identifiers: Canadiana (print) 20240413555 | Canadiana (ebook) 2024041411X |
ISBN 9781443474061 (hardcover) | ISBN 9781443474078 (softcover) |
ISBN 9781443474085 (Ebook)
Subjects: LCGFT: Detective and mystery fiction. | LCGFT: Novels.
Classification: LCC PS8571.I5298 B53 2024 | DDC C813/.54—dc23

Printed and bound in the United States of America
24 25 26 27 28 LBC 5 4 3 2 1

For the other living creatures who share this planet.
All things considered, I've given up hope for humans.

1

Spring on the high plains was a magic act. Now you see it. Now you don't. Today, spring was back again, and this time it had brought summer with it.

Last night, Thumps DreadfulWater had made the mistake of watching a round-table discussion on global warming.

The usual suspects.

A university professor in a gold and green tunic dress (made of recycled plastic, according to the caption) argued that the melting ice caps and rising ocean levels would create cataclysmic weather events, which would overwhelm social and political orders around the world.

An older man, who had been melted down and poured into a business suit, suggested that higher temperatures could have the benefit of opening new areas for the exploration of much-needed natural resources. He had figures on the amount of oil and gas that would be available as the ice at the poles retreated, figures he tossed into the audience like treats from a float. Thumps was pretty sure the man had made the numbers up on the spot.

The café was long and skinny with a run of scruffy, red Naugahyde stools bellied up to a lime-green counter, and a row of plywood booths jammed against the wall for any tourists who might wander in.

Not that many did.

First, Al's was hard to find. There was no sign to mark the spot, just a turtle shell that Preston Wagamese had glued next to the door, with the word "Food" written on it.

Second, the café wasn't particularly inviting. The place was dim, the light from the window by the grill filtered through a thin film of grease, the air thick and moist, with hash brown highlights and a sausage finish.

Thumps got to the café just as Al was opening the door.

"Come back in fifteen minutes."

"You open at seven." Thumps held out his watch. "It's seven."

"Okay, early bird. You get to exercise Lucy." Al reached under the counter and came up with a long piece of orange string on the end of a stick. "Make sure you make her sweat."

"What am I supposed to do?"

"Sheriff such as yourself should be able to figure that out."

"Deputy sheriff." Thumps found his favourite stool and sat down. "Temporary deputy sheriff."

The cat appeared out of nowhere, jumped on the counter, sat down next to the salt and pepper shakers.

"Her impression of an Egyptian figurine," said Al. "Don't know how many times I've told her not to do that."

"Pretty sure a cat on the counter is a health-code violation."

"Don't let me stop you," said Al. "Read her her rights. Slap the cuffs on. Night in jail might do her some good."

Thumps flicked the stick. Lucy was off the counter in a flash, hit the end of the string like a ten-pound bass on a two-pound line.

"Mind you," said Al, "I do like a strong-willed woman."

Lucy let go the string, waited for it to move, and then pounced on it again.

"She's wiped out the café's mouse population, and now she's bored." Al set a cup in front of Thumps. "How's Duke holding up?"

"Okay."

"Funeral was only a month ago," said Al. "A month ain't okay."

Alzheimer's. The disease had come on gradually. Macy had been staying at her sister's in Missoula. She'd been seeing a specialist when she died. Suddenly and unexpectedly. Duke had rushed over, but he was too late to do anything except make arrangements for her body.

"Stas and Rawat said they went by the office to pay their respects." Al wiped at a spot on the napkin dispenser. "Left a bottle of vodka and flowers. I hear that even Morris Dumbo stepped up. A dozen chocolate-coated doughnuts? And a sympathy card?"

"That was Fancy's doing."

"Boys said Duke wasn't there."

"He's taking time off."

"You seen him since he got back?"

"Going to stop by later today."

"Sitting on grief can be dangerous," said Al. "Empty house. Long nights. Loaded gun."

"That's not Duke."

"Death changes people," said Al.

Thumps pushed his coffee cup forward.

"You want coffee?"

"I do."

"Think I should give you preferential treatment? Because you're sheriff and all."

"A hungry temporary deputy sheriff," said Thumps. "Who would like to be fed."

"You want to hear about Wutty's new idea or do you want to eat your breakfast in peace?"

"Door number two."

"As deputy sheriff," said Al, "you're obliged to keep up on current events."

"The usual," said Thumps. "Extra salsa."

"And Wutty is generally a current event."

Wutty Youngbeaver was more properly a continuing event. Sometimes a successful event. More often a disaster. But neither success nor failure dampened the man's enthusiasms.

"He still taking tourists across Red Tail Lake in his Little Otter?"

"Had to give that up," said Al.

"He drown someone?"

"Nope. Had to sell it. Insurance costs. Evidently, an amphibious van is not a good risk."

"Grill hot yet?"

"Rush, rush, rush." Al ambled back toward the front. "Whatever happened to comradery and companionship?"

Thumps cupped his mug, imagined that it was filled with coffee.

"Thumps, my man."

Wutty Youngbeaver had come into the café when Thumps wasn't looking. With Russell Plunkett and Jimmy Monroe in tow.

Wutty ambled down the line of stools, whacked Thumps on the shoulders, began massaging his neck. "This is your lucky day."

Thumps couldn't recall exactly how many lucky days he had had with Wutty. Certainly more than his fair share.

Wutty sat down on the stool beside Thumps. "What do you know about the U.S. Open?"

"Not talking tennis," said Russell.

"Talking golf," said Jimmy.

Al arrived with the coffee pot. "Now there's a game in need of extinction."

"Sport of kings," said Wutty.

"That's horse racing," said Jimmy.

"Breakfast of Champions," said Russell.

"That's Wheaties," said Wutty. "Pay attention. There's going to be a qualifying round for the U.S. Open right here in Chinook."

Thumps opened his eyes.

"PGA normally uses the Missoula Country Club," said Wutty, "but it's being renovated, so they're going to hold it at Shadow Ranch."

"A qualifying round?"

"That's right," said Wutty. "And guess who's going to qualify for the big show?"

"That's baseball," said Jimmy.

Thumps knew better than to ask. "You?"

Wutty smiled, nodded his head as though he were trying to snap it off at the neck.

Thumps hid his smile behind the cup. "You know, you can't just sign up to play. You have to be a professional golfer or have a USGA Handicap Index not exceeding 1.4."

Wutty gripped an imaginary club, took an imaginary swing. "Index of 1.0."

"Probably don't want to encourage him," Al shouted from the grill.

"You're a scratch golfer?"

Wutty threw his arms around Jimmy and Russell. "What you're looking at," he said, "is Team Wutty."

"We're getting T-shirts made," said Russell.

"Red with gold lettering," said Jimmy.

"Sponsorship," said Wutty. "And there's still opportunity."

Thumps could see Al coming his way with breakfast.

"And you know what they say about opportunity," said Wutty. "It only knocks once."

Al slid the plate in front of Thumps. "Doesn't mean you have to open the door."

"Al's is the official café of Team Wutty," said Wutty.

"I paid for a couple boxes of balls," said Al. "Moment of weakness."

"So, can I sign you up?"

Thumps worked his fork into the eggs. Perfect.

"I think what Thumps is trying to say," said Al, "is that as an officer of the law, he can't show favouritism."

Thumps cut the sausage into pieces.

"Understood," said Wutty. "I've got my clubs. Rocky is letting me use the facilities."

Thumps stopped his fork in mid-air. "Rocky?"

"You know. Vernon Rockland. The big man. I got free use of the golf course. So, I'm all set."

Thumps put the sausage in his mouth. "Good luck."

"All I need is a caddy."

"Rocky said you used to play golf," said Jimmy. "Said you were pretty good."

"Not as good as me," said Wutty. "But caddies aren't supposed to be as good as the player."

"Me and Jimmy volunteered," said Russell, "but we don't know the rules of the game."

"I get through the qualifying round, make the cut at the Open, and I'm in the money. At least forty, fifty thousand."

Thumps put his fork to one side. "Do you know how hard it is to make it all the way through qualifying? Do you know how hard it is to make the cut at the Open?"

Wutty smiled. "Caddies get ten percent. Seeing as we're friends, I'll cut you in for twelve."

Russell looked at his watch. "Got to get going."

"Breakfast at Shadow Ranch," said Jimmy. "Part of the sponsorship. Then it's on the course for a practice round."

"Shot two under, the other day," said Russell.

"Knock, knock," said Wutty. "Knock, knock."

Al waited until the boys were all the way out the door. "Okay," she said. "Coast is clear."

"You could have warned me."

"If you had come in at your regular time," said Al, "you would have missed them altogether."

"He hasn't got a prayer in hell."

"But you got to admire his enthusiasm." Al topped up Thumps's cup. "You really going to go by Duke's?"

Thumps nodded.

"If you wait until after I close, I'll go with you."

"Probably should go alone."

"So the two of you can watch a little baseball, talk a little football?"

"I can do grief counselling."

"Man doesn't need grief counselling," said Al. "Man needs a friend who will sit with him in the dark. I'd tell you to hold him, but you guys get all wiggly about that sort of stuff."

"Probably take him out and feed him."

"'Cause nothing says I love you," said Al, "like a cheeseburger and a beer."

Thumps pushed off the stool. "I was thinking of pizza."

"Close enough," said Al. "Close enough."

2

Deanna Heavy Runner was standing by the filing cabinet, a coffee cup in her hand.

"You got any idea how to make coffee in this antique spittoon?"

"You put coffee in the basket."

"I did that," said Deanna.

"Water in the pot."

"Duh." Deanna rolled her eyes. "And I plugged it in."

"Wiggle the plug. Bang it on the table."

There was a tower of wood blocks on Duke's desk that hadn't been there the day before.

"How about I just shoot it? Throw the body in Deep House. Leave a suicide note."

There was a soft hissing sound, and the percolator began its smeltering bubble.

"It's alive." Deanna held her arms out, staggered around in a circle. "It's alive."

"When Duke comes back to work," said Thumps, "it's the first thing he'll check."

"So, don't hurt it?"

"Don't hurt it." Thumps picked up a pile of messages. "These the overnights?"

"They are."

"Another stolen car?"

"Number six," said Deanna. "Five have been recovered."

"Repaired and detailed?"

"Yeah," said Deanna. "It's a little weird. Who steals a car and fixes it? Oil change, tune-up, vacuum, shampoo, wash and wax, and then returns it?"

"Cooley around?"

"Probationary Deputy Cooley Small Elk is interviewing the latest victim. Although 'victim' is probably the wrong word."

"Stealing cars is still a crime."

"I got a Chevy with a wonky air conditioner and an interior that looks like a landfill. Tempted to just leave the keys on the dash and hope White Quiver grabs it."

"White Quiver?"

"I forget. You're Cherokee."

Thumps waited.

"If you were Blackfeet, you'd know who White Quiver was." Deanna gestured to the filing cabinet. "And the doughnuts in the sympathy box that Fancy dropped off? They're all gone."

"Any other good news?"

"Oh, and I'm to remind you that we need to hire another deputy," said Deanna. "ASAP."

"Duke'll take care of that when he returns."

"You sure he's coming back?"

Thumps went to the filing cabinet, checked the box.

"Not being mean," said Deanna. "My dad took me to a rodeo

over in Great Falls when I was ten. Saw a cowboy get trampled by a bull."

"You're going to tell me that Duke looks worse."

"Duke looks worse."

"He'll be fine."

Deanna slid one of the blocks out from the centre of the tower. "You want a turn?"

"What is it?"

"Jenga." Deanna cocked her head. "You never played Jenga? I found it when I was cleaning out a closet."

"And you brought it here because?"

"Sitting around, waiting for crime to happen can be boring. A game of skill will keep us sharp."

"Okay."

"You stack the blocks up into a tower, and then you remove a block, one at a time. Each block you remove, you place on top of the structure."

"And you do this until . . . ?"

"Until someone pulls out the wrong block, and the whole thing collapses."

"That's it?"

"It's a lot of fun." Deanna grabbed her hat, headed for the door. "When Probationary Deputy Small Elk gets back, make sure he takes out the garbage."

THERE WAS LITTLE Thumps remembered of high-school Latin. *Tempus fugit. Carpe diem. Veni, vidi, vici. Carthago delenda est. Morior Invictus.*

Along with *annus horribilis* and *annus mirabilis*.

Which neatly summed up the last year.

On the *horribilis* side, Moses Blood had gotten sick, had nearly died. Claire had almost lost custody of Ivory. Macy Hockney had succumbed to Alzheimer's, and the domino effect had thrown Duke into a dark place. Whether he would survive intact was in question.

On the *mirabilis* side, Cooley had decided to become a cop, had taken the twelve-week Law Enforcement Officer Basic Course through the Montana Law Enforcement Academy and was now on probation with the sheriff's office. Even better, he and Scoop Macleod had gotten together, were living with Moses, looking after the old man. Archie's restaurant was a big hit, and Beth Mooney and Gabby Santucci had gotten married.

But maybe all years were like that. Bad. Good. Rain and sunshine. Maybe life and the weather had much in common. Maybe what mattered was where you were standing when the storm broke.

THUMPS PICKED UP the phone, listened as it rang, but he didn't think Duke was going to answer. Thumps had tried several times in the last few days and each call had gone to voice mail. He knew the sheriff was back in town, pictured the man in an empty house, sitting in a dark room, staring at a wall.

Thumps knew that room all too well. He had sat in that room after Anna and Callie had been murdered, had stared at that same wall.

He could just drop by. Someone on your porch, knocking on

the door, was harder to ignore than a phone. That's what a friend would do.

Or just leave him alone. Let Duke find his own way back. Thumps had tried that. Without much success. When Anna and Callie had been murdered, he had pulled back into himself, shut everyone out. He couldn't remember much of those first weeks, the first months. And then one day he quit, packed what he needed in his car, and headed east.

He made it as far as a small town in Montana, where his car broke down. The fuel pump had to be ordered, was slow in arriving, and by the time the car was repaired, Thumps realized there was nowhere he could go to outrun the exhaustion and the sorrow.

He hadn't chosen Chinook. The town had simply been at the bottom of a long fall.

THUMPS WAS STILL falling when Cooley banged in through the door.

"Hey, chief."

"Temporary."

"Right. Temporary chief." Cooley held up a box. "Guess what."

"Doughnuts."

Cooley smiled. "The logo on the side gave it away, right?"

Cooley Small Elk was one of the largest men Thumps had ever known. And one of the gentlest.

"Hey, Jenga." Cooley carefully slid a block out and placed it on top of the tower. "Where'd you get this?"

"There any old-fashioned plain in there?"

Cooley set the box on the filing cabinet and raised the lid.

"Appears that there are four. The rest are chocolate-coated cake."

"In case Duke shows up."

"*Semper fidelis*," said Cooley. "Always prepared. Boy Scout motto."

"*Semper fidelis* is the Marine Corps motto," said Thumps. "'Be prepared' is the Boy Scout motto."

"Mottos sound better in Latin." Cooley took a doughnut out of the box and placed it on a napkin in front of Thumps. "Do we have a motto?"

"For the sheriff's department?"

"I mean, there's the 'Serve and Protect' on the side of the cruiser, but that's kinda lame."

Thumps tried the doughnut. Delicious. Easy to ignore that you were eating flour and sugar, salt and eggs, boiled up in fat.

"Latin is a dead language." Cooley helped himself to a chocolate-coated doughnut. "We should do the motto in a living language. Like Blackfoot."

Thumps leaned back in the chair. "In the meantime, how about bringing me up to speed on our car thief."

Cooley took out his notebook. "We got seven cars that have been stolen."

"I thought it was six."

"It was six last night," said Cooley. "It's seven this morning."

"But some have been returned."

"Five," said Cooley. "If the pattern holds, I expect that the rest will show up soon enough."

"Serviced and cleaned."

"Got to admit it's a little weird." Cooley flipped a page in his notebook. "What do you want me to do?"

"You've interviewed the owners?"

"Have."

"Before and after their cars were returned?"

"Bunch of happy people," said Cooley.

Thumps could feel the doughnut begin to screw with his blood sugars, making him sleepy.

"People who got their cars back don't want to file a complaint." Cooley smiled. "Deanna wants to leave her Chevy out with the keys on the dash, but that might be seen as aiding and abetting."

Thumps pushed himself out of the chair, took his hat off the hook. "I've been meaning to ask, how was the academy?"

"Fine," said Cooley. "Lot of physical stuff, lectures, stuff to memorize, bunch of tests, filling out forms. Long hours. Hardest thing was staying awake."

Thumps chuckled. "So, how you like being a cop?"

Cooley took a moment. "I like helping people. Paperwork is boring. And if I'm careful, I won't have to shoot anyone."

"Don't forget the doughnuts."

"One of the requirements of the job," said Cooley.

Thumps bumped knuckles with the big man. "How about you hold the office down for the next while?"

"You going to see Duke?" Cooley put four doughnuts in an evidence bag. "Tell him Scoop and me said hi."

"Probably give him space. Probably just leave the doughnuts on the porch."

Cooley handed Thumps the bag. "Tough being sad. Only thing worse is having to watch."

Cooley went to the tower. "You bring this in?"

"Deanna," said Thumps. "Thinks it will help keep us sharp."

Cooley pushed on a block. "You want to give it a try?"

"I can take out any block I want?"

"You can," said Cooley. "But if you take out the wrong block, the whole thing collapses."

Thumps smiled. "This supposed to be a commentary on life?"

"Don't think so," said Cooley. "With Jenga, no matter how many times the tower falls apart, you can always put it back together."

3

The house was a bungalow in the older part of Chinook, about a block from the river. For all the years that Thumps had known Duke, he had only been inside once.

A birthday party.

Hockney's fiftieth. Macy had arranged it as a surprise. Thumps remembered the look on Duke's face when he walked in the door and everyone leaped out of hiding places, screaming, "Happy birthday."

It was such a surprise that Duke's first reaction was to reach for his service revolver. At the time, Thumps figured that it was a toss-up between shooting the well-wishers and shooting himself. Gone was the peaceful evening Hockney had envisioned, sitting in front of the TV with a beer, watching *Monday Night Football*.

Thumps hadn't expected to find the sheriff sitting on the porch, enjoying the day. And he wasn't. The house was dark and quiet. Thumps casually peeked in the front window. Nothing.

"Those doughnuts?"

Duke came around the side of the house, dressed in work clothes. Work hat. Work gloves. A shovel in his hand.

Thumps held the sack out. "Dumbo's best."

Duke set the shovel against the side of the house. "If you're trying to think of something sympathetic to say, don't bother."

"Okay."

"And I don't need a hug."

Duke came onto the porch, sat down in the chair, took off the hat and gloves.

"Yardwork?"

"Macy had been after me to dig up a section by the garage for years. She wanted to plant rhubarb." Duke opened the bag, took out a doughnut. "Better late than never."

"You can make jam."

"What?"

"Rhubarb jam," said Thumps. "Anna made it once. It was good."

Duke nodded. "Anna Tripp. Your woman in Northern California. The one who was murdered. This your way of letting me know that you know how I feel?"

"Maybe."

"Beats another one of those 'I'm sorry for your loss.'" Duke took a deep breath. "You want a beer?"

"Beer and doughnuts?"

"Who the hell cares."

Thumps sat on the porch railing, watched the breeze rattle the lilacs in the side yard.

"You here to give me the Chinook crime report, or you here because you're worried I'm wallowing in grief and depression and might do something stupid?"

"The first one."

"Liar." Duke bit the doughnut in half. "There a pool?"

"What?"

"A pool. You know, bets on whether or not I'll come back to the job."

"No pool." Thumps took his hat off, put it on his lap. "I figure you'll come back if you want to come back."

"That one of those tautologies?"

"Not sure."

At the very least, Thumps had expected to find a gaunt and exhausted Duke, but the man sitting in the chair was clean-shaven and bright-eyed, as though he had passed through the anguish of Macy's death unscathed.

"You're probably wondering why I'm looking so chipper."

"Glad to see it."

"Macy's sister thought I was heartless, thought I should have broken down, thrown myself into her grave." Duke finished the doughnut. "Except there wasn't a grave. The two of us had already decided on cremation when the time came."

Thumps fished a doughnut out of the bag.

"That didn't sit well with Joan. She's a staunch Catholic. Believes in god and the soul and all that. You bury bodies. You don't burn them. Asked Joan what difference it made, and she reminded me that Jesus wasn't cremated. That pretty much settled it."

"Would have come to the funeral."

Duke shook his head. "Wasn't any funeral. Joan organized a memorial for the family."

"Chance for people to say their goodbyes, share stories, come to terms with death."

"Wouldn't know." Duke stretched his legs out, leaned back. "I wasn't invited."

The breeze had picked up. There was a dark line of clouds on the horizon. A storm in the distance.

"I miss her, you know. You live with someone for that many years and you sort of get rolled up into one person. Don't even realize it's happened. Then suddenly, you're torn in half."

Maybe the storm would sneak into Chinook to see how Duke was doing. Maybe there would be a little rain for the rhubarb.

"Ragged edges. Every time I turn around, there's another ragged edge."

"You had anything to eat?"

Duke licked his fingers.

"Besides this."

"You want to feed me?"

"Was thinking about it."

"What were you thinking?"

"Pizza and beer?"

Duke stood up in one motion. "Do I have to change?"

BADA BING PIZZERIA was one of the new restaurants that had risen out of the ashes of COVID. Thumps had taken Claire and Ivory to the grand opening. Which hadn't been all that grand. A power outage shut down the ovens for the first part of the evening. The server got the order wrong and arrived with a medium vegetarian when they had ordered an extra-large sausage, onion, and hot pepper special.

The correct pizza arrived forty-five minutes later, during which time Thumps had to follow Ivory up and down Main Street, as the seven-year-old skipped along the sidewalk, looking in the store windows and shouting, "I'm hungry," at the top of her voice.

But the pizza was good. And in the end, that's what mattered.

DUKE LEFT HIS WORK GLOVES and work hat at home. He even changed out of his boots and combed his hair.

"Let's sit at the back."

"So no one can see us?"

"Hard enough losing Macy," said Duke. "Don't need a bunch of well-wishers reminding me she's gone."

"People don't know what to say."

"That's just it. They don't need to say anything."

The server was a young woman with half her hair dyed blond and the other half a bright magenta.

"We have several specials."

Duke smiled, shook his head. "Extra-large pepperoni and sausage. You got any Westvleteren 12?"

"Is that beer?"

"Or Sapporo Premium Black?"

"We have Bud," said the woman. "And something that starts with an *H*."

"The pizza and two of the *H*s." Duke jerked his thumb at Thumps. "My friend here is paying."

Thumps watched the woman retreat to the kitchen. "Probably Heineken."

"Probably."

"Westvleteren 12?"

"Saw an article about expensive beers on the internet."

"So, you were just being a jerk."

"Aren't you supposed to be lifting me out of my depression?"

"Yeah," said Thumps, "I am."

"Well, you're doing a shitty job."

Thumps would have preferred to sit at a window, so he could look out onto the street. There was something luxurious about lounging in a café over a meal and watching people as they went about their business. You could make up stories about who they were, what they were doing, where they were going. A bit voyeuristic, if he was being honest with himself.

"So, fill me in." Duke laced his fingers, leaned forward on the table.

"Nothing much. Our car thief is still at large."

"It's been six months," said Duke. "Before Macy went to her sister's."

"More like seven," said Thumps. "And we've got the tournament at Shadow Ranch. Vernon Rockland has requested that we have a couple of deputies at the ready, in case someone has too much to drink and decides to skinny-dip in the pond at the eighth hole."

"You tell Vernon we don't do resort security?"

"I did."

"And that we don't have a couple of deputies to spare."

"Two deputies is all we have."

"Three, counting you," said Duke.

"I'm the sheriff," said Thumps.

"Temporary," said Hockney. "Temporary deputy sheriff."

"Nothing much else shaking," said Thumps. "I thought we were going to have problems out at the Mustang after the town pushed the city limits to the turnoff to Glory, but so far so good."

"Lorraine and Big Fish got their own security."

"You talking about Lorraine's temper and Big Fish's mouth?"

"I'll be back in the office tomorrow."

"You sure?"

"Binge-watched *Justified* and *Death in Paradise.* Cleaned out the garage. Took the snow tires off the car. Joan is coming by to take Macy's stuff. Family gets first shot. The rest goes to the Goodwill."

Duke tapped out a quick rhythm on the table. "So, what's happening with you and Claire?"

Thumps shrugged.

"That's not really helpful," said Duke. "I heard the two of you were looking at houses."

"We were."

"And?"

"We stopped looking."

The pizza and beer arrived just in time.

"Heineken," said Duke. "Where's the imagination?"

Thumps wouldn't have seen her, if he hadn't been looking.

Ora Mae Foreman.

Chinook's realtor extraordinaire. Standing on the sidewalk, peering in. But it wasn't Ora Mae who caught his eye. There were two other people with her. An older woman whom Thumps didn't recognize. Probably someone in the market for a house. The other was a man, dressed in black, looking as though he had stepped out of a bad spy novel.

Cisco Cruz.

Duke was saying something about wheat beers versus dark malts, when he realized that Thumps wasn't listening.

"Shit," said the sheriff. "That who I think it is?"

Cruz and the two women were locked in a discussion of some sort. Ora Mae pointing down the street, the woman shaking her head, Cruz shifting his weight back and forth, his hands in his pockets.

"You didn't tell me he was in town."

"Didn't know."

And then Ora Mae turned and headed down the street, with the woman and Cruz in her wake.

"You do realize," said Duke, "that every time he comes to town, someone dies."

"Not really his fault."

Duke helped himself to another slice. "True enough. But some people are catalysts for trouble, lightning rods for disaster. Just standing next to them voids your warranty."

"I should get back to the office."

Duke tapped the table. "You only had one slice of pizza."

"Not really hungry."

"You not going to finish your beer?"

"Help yourself."

"You mind if I pack up the rest?" said Duke. "Take it home. Save me the trauma of what to eat for dinner."

"Go for it."

"Macy never much liked pepperoni. Said it gave her gas."

"You really coming back tomorrow?"

"Tell me that Deanna hasn't broken my percolator."

"It's still in one piece."

"Okay." Duke stacked the pizza slices, wrapped a couple of napkins around them. "See you tomorrow."

"Okay."

"Maybe by then, you can find out why Cisco Cruz is wandering our green and pleasant land."

Thumps wiped his hands. "Last time he was in town, he said he was thinking of moving here."

"Which would explain Ora Mae."

"Which would."

"The ninja assassin as a neighbour." Duke got to his feet. "I feel a tremor of concern coming on."

"You need another deputy," said Thumps. "Maybe he'd be interested in the job."

Duke laughed all the way out of the restaurant. And all the way back to the car. He was still chuckling when Thumps dropped him off in front of his house.

Duke opened the door but stayed in the car.

"When your woman in California and her daughter were killed, where did you spend that first night?"

"I should get back to the office."

Duke nodded. "I'd invite you in," he said, "but I don't want to."

4

The plan had been to go back to the office, and now the plan had changed. Thumps pulled into the Cash & Carry, parked at the far end of the lot. How *had* he spent that first night? At the Humboldt County Sheriff's office? At the beach where Anna and Callie had died? Working the scene?

No.

He hadn't even been in town. He had been at a forensics conference in San Diego, staying in an upgraded room with a view of the ocean, eating shrimp, drinking red wine, watching cable TV and a pay-per-view movie.

A morning breakfast buffet with food piled high in hot trays.

He didn't find out what had happened until he got back to Eureka. Much too late to do anything other than bury that part of his life. The days and nights, after that, all ran together, a blur of anger and frustration.

And sorrow.

That was what Thumps could remember most vividly. The dark, burning sorrow. And the intense and uncomplicated urge to kill the man who had left his lover and her child on a moonless beach in front of a running tide.

Macy hadn't been murdered. And maybe that was worse. No one to blame, nowhere for the rage to go. Thumps had gotten the satisfaction of ending the man who had massacred Anna and Callie. Duke knew his wife's killer, but what was he supposed to do with a disease?

Arrest it?

Shoot it trying to escape?

Everywhere you looked, there was no satisfaction. No peace.

THUMPS HADN'T REALIZED how long he had been sitting in his car in the parking lot, until he looked at his watch.

An hour?

Impossible.

Next time he was at the mall, he'd take the thing to the watch store and have it checked out.

Thumps fished his cell out of his pocket. Cooley answered on the first ring.

"Chinook Sheriff's Office."

"Cooley."

"Hey, boss."

"Who's got the evening shift?"

"I do."

Thumps let the silence settle in around him. "I thought I had graveyard."

"You did," said Cooley, "but I figure if you have to ask, you've got business needs attending."

"You mind?"

"Naw. I got coffee and doughnuts, and Scoop is bringing over some stew."

"I'll see you in the morning."

"Scoop may stay over. That okay?"

Thumps smiled. "As in, sleep in the holding cell?"

"Cleaned it out good. Fresh sheets, quilt, painted over the graffiti on the walls. Doesn't smell like sweat and vomit anymore."

"Woman must really love you."

"Hope to hell you're right," said Cooley. "Bought the quilt with my own money."

Claire Merchant lived on the reservation, on a section of land above the Ironstone. You could see the river from her living room window, and the mountains to the west from the kitchen.

Thumps had two distinct impressions concerning the house and the location. Beautiful and isolated.

Rather like Claire.

There was a late-model van parked next to the Russian olive that guarded the driveway. The tree was doing its "just about to die" routine, the same routine it had been doing since it was planted. In all likelihood, it would outlive the lot of them.

Thumps turned toward the shout. People. On the high ground beyond the barn.

Great.

He had come to see Claire, to talk to her, and instead had stumbled on a party.

"Thumps!"

Big Fish Patek. And Lorraine Chubby.

Thumps hiked up the long rise. Little Hack and Ivory were chasing each other in the prairie grass. Big Fish and Lorraine and Claire were holding down a blanket. There was food spread out, a cooler off to one side.

Claire shaded her eyes. "Didn't expect to see you."

"Spontaneity," said Thumps. "The spice of life."

"Thought it was salt," said Big Fish.

Lorraine gave Big Fish a whack on the shoulder. "Don't listen to him. He thinks a romantic evening is shooting pool while watching a football game on the big-screen."

Claire moved over, made a space for Thumps. "How's Duke?"

"Hard to say."

"But you've seen him since Macy died, talked to him."

"Took him to lunch today," said Thumps. "That new pizza place on Main."

"Should have brought him out to the Mustang," said Lorraine. "Eat with friends. Yo-Yo would have cooked him up one of his famous cheeseburgers."

Ivory came charging onto the blanket with Little Hack at her heels. Both kids slid into the cooler.

Claire put a hand out to protect the food. "Careful."

Little Hack made a face. "She told me I had to eat a grasshopper."

Ivory rolled up against her mother. "Indians eat grasshoppers all the time."

"No, we don't," said Claire.

"And then she threw grass at me."

Lorraine shook her head. "Well, then I guess Sheriff Thumps is going to have to arrest you."

"Deputy sheriff," said Thumps. "Temporary."

"You think Duke is going to come back?" said Big Fish.

"There a reason you came out?" Claire's voice was flat, with no apparent emotion. She didn't sound annoyed. She didn't sound happy. And she didn't sound curious.

"Just in the area."

Claire smiled. "Picnic. So the kids could get together."

"Think dog park," said Big Fish.

"You two should stop screwing around and get married," said Lorraine.

"We could be your model," said Big Fish.

"And then again . . ." said Lorraine.

"Mommy," said Ivory, "are you going to marry Dog?"

"What Mommy is going to do," said Claire, "is eat another sandwich."

"Are we going to have to eat sandwiches for supper?"

Little Hack raised a hand. "Ivory went all funny again."

"Did not."

"Did so." Little Hack froze, his arms hanging at his sides, his eyes staring off across the land. "Like that."

"Eat grasshoppers," said Ivory.

"They're not bad if you dip them in chocolate," said Thumps.

"Eww," said Ivory.

Claire rolled up, got to her feet. "You have time?"

"Sure."

"Problem with the barn," said Claire. "Now that you're out here, maybe you could have a look."

"We'll watch the kids," said Lorraine. "You two lovebirds take your time."

• • •

THE SUN WAS on the horizon, throwing long shadows across the land. Thumps followed Claire down the slope. She walked around to the shady side of the barn and stopped.

"There's nothing wrong with the barn."

Thumps nodded. "Okay."

"Thought we should talk," said Claire. "Might as well be now."

The day was working its way to evening. Up on the rise, Little Hack and Ivory were on the move again, chasing each other.

Big Fish was right. Dog park.

"Remember when we were looking at houses?" Claire folded her arms, leaned against the barn. "When we were thinking about living together?"

Ivory had found a stick somewhere, was waving it around, trying to knock the clouds out of the sky.

"And then we stopped?"

"You want to start again?"

Claire turned away for a moment. "It helped to settle some things for me."

"You don't want to live together."

"I don't."

"So, I suppose marriage is out as well."

It wasn't a smile, but neither was it a frown. "You're a good man," said Claire.

Now Little Hack had the stick and was beating the grass for tigers.

"I got pregnant young. Stanley's father stayed around for the first few months. After that I was on my own. I was young, stupid, and scared. There was no time to enjoy a baby, no time to ease into motherhood. Those years are a blur."

"And now you're a mother again."

"And now I'm a mother again. Now I'm smarter. I don't have to worry about money. I'd like to enjoy the second time around."

Thumps waited.

"But I don't want to have to depend on anyone. And I don't want to have to negotiate with another person when it comes to Ivory."

"Okay."

"We can still spend time together," said Claire. "But you can't be my husband, and you can't be Ivory's father."

"Not much left."

"A friend," said Claire. "To me and my daughter."

Thumps couldn't see Big Fish or Lorraine now. Or the kids for that matter. He imagined the adults stretched out on the blanket, Ivory and Little Hack curled up next to them like a tumble of puppies.

"You think that's possible?"

Thumps pulled his hands out of his pockets, hitched his pants. "I should get back."

Claire nodded. "When you see Duke, tell him I said hi."

"I will."

"I'm no good at sympathy," said Claire. "Don't even do it for myself."

5

It was dark by the time Thumps got back to town. Not the "black at the bottom of the well" dark. More a joyless gloom that comes from sitting by yourself in a windowless room.

He considered going back to the office and taking the shift, but Scoop would be there by now, and she and Cooley would be playing house in the holding cell. Which left him behind the wheel of his car, going nowhere.

The impromptu visit to Claire's had not ended according to plan. The plan having been dinner, play with Ivory, cuddle with Claire, stay overnight, more cuddling, sex, wake up together with the morning sun.

Okay. Life was like that, he supposed. Something in the distance that looked to be an oasis with palm trees and fresh water and turned out to be a landfill with toxic waste and used appliances.

Thumps grimaced. A bit dramatic, but that's what you got when you were dumped and hungry. Cooley had Scoop and her stew. Claire had Ivory and leftover sandwiches. Who was going to feed him?

• • •

Archimedes Kousoulas. Archie to his friends. Proprietor of the Aegean, Chinook's only authentic bookstore, and owner of Pappous's, an eclectic restaurant that blended understated elegance with casual dining. Featuring a menu of Old World dishes such as calamari alongside local favourites such as mac and cheese.

Thumps understood that coming to the restaurant, hat in hand, was a bad idea. Archie would want to know about Duke, about Claire, why the sky was blue, and whether pigs could fly. On the surface, trading information for food seemed a reasonable exchange, but Thumps knew that he would pay dearly for the privilege of being fed.

"Mr. DreadfulWater."

Fancy Whelan was at the restaurant podium. Fancy was Morris Dumbo's niece. She was looking after Dumbo's Doughnuts while her uncle was on an extended world tour with his new love, a Puerto Rican movie makeup artist.

"Archie said you might arrive." Fancy picked up a menu. "Said I was to look after you if yourself wandered in."

Archie had hired a Frenchman named Henri Dubois. Tall, austere, aloof, Dubois was the perfect maître d', the maître d' you saw and heard in every old black-and-white movie that needed a maître d'.

"Where's Dubois?"

"Fired," said Fancy. "Archie found out the gom wasn't French. Couldn't even spell 'croissant.' Yeah."

"Okay."

"Might not have mattered, but our lad was helping himself to the gargle."

"Gargle?"

"The wine."

"Ah." Thumps found himself nodding. "And now you're the maître d'."

"You daft? Do I look like a maître d'?"

There was an empty table at the back in the corner. The perfect place to hide away and eat.

"That one available?"

"It is," said Fancy.

"And maybe you could neglect to tell Archie that I'm here until after I eat."

"Man's got the second sight, he has. No need to tell him anything." Fancy led him to the table. "I'm just helping out until Archie can find another wanker."

"And then back to Dumbo's?"

"To be decided," said Fancy. "Stay away from the octopus. Creepy shite, it is."

Thumps moved the chair back, so he could lean against the wall, opened the menu. There would be a couple of specials, dishes that would have at least three ingredients that he would not recognize. He could always check the internet with his phone. He had to admit the World Wide Web was a handy way to discover that "pangrattato" was fried bread crumbs, and that *friarielli* was broccoli, more or less, and that "toum" was garlic sauce.

And if *paidakia*, or *stifado*, or *papoutsakia* made an appearance as a special, enlightenment was only a click away.

Thumps was trying to decide between the *yemista* and the elk meatloaf when he felt the floor move and the table shake.

"There you are."

Archie considered himself a force of nature. Certainly, he could be as annoying as the weather, mosquitoes, blackflies, but somewhat less intimidating than cornered wolverines and bears just out of hibernation.

Most of the time.

"You're sheriff now." Archie plopped himself down. "Which means you have obligations."

"Temporary deputy sheriff." Thumps tapped the menu. "What's this?"

Archie leaned over the table. "A Greek delicacy."

"*Trahana*?"

"Try it."

"What's in it?"

"What is it with North Americans? Always with the 'What's this?' and the 'What's in it?' Try it, you'll like it."

Thumps had his phone out and was thumbing in the letters before Archie realized what he was doing.

"What? You don't trust me."

Thumps read the description on the screen. "Made from fermented ewes' or goat's milk that's left to go sour?"

"Google," said Archie. "What does it know about Greek cooking? I'll bring you some. On the house."

Thumps kept reading. "A kind of breakfast mush?"

"Stop reading. Tell me about Duke."

There was a site that told you how to make *trahana* from scratch. Thumps read the first sentence, put the phone in his pocket.

"Duke's fine."

"Sure, sure. Man loses his wife, and he's fine. My head looks like it zips up the back?"

Thumps was tempted to take out his phone again. Just to annoy Archie.

"I had lunch with him. He seemed okay."

Archie made a face. "Why didn't you bring him here?"

"You don't serve lunch."

Archie scowled. "I can always make lunch for friends."

"You were at the bookstore."

"Ten-minute walk away," said Archie. "Seven, if I jog."

"I think Duke just wants to be left alone."

Archie stared off into space for a moment. "That's a sure sign of depression. But that's not why I called you here."

"You didn't call me here. I came here to get dinner."

"You ever check your texts?" Archie shook his head. "No wonder crime is rampant in town."

"Archie . . ."

"Cars being stolen in broad daylight. Ninja assassins walking the streets . . ."

"You know about Cisco Cruz?"

"Came into the Aegean," said Archie. "Bold as brass. With an older woman, not his mother."

"You get a name?"

"She bought a couple of books." Archie looked at Thumps over the top of his glasses. "Unlike others, not to be mentioned."

"You get a name?"

Archie rolled his eyes. "I forget. Seeing the ninja assassin walk into my bookstore was a shock to my memory."

"And Ora Mae wasn't with them?"

"Ora Mae?" Archie pushed his glasses up his nose. "What's Ora Mae got to do with you-know-who?"

Thumps sat back. "Last time Cruz was in town, he talked about settling here."

"Better we have an earthquake that swallows us whole," said Archie. "Or another flood."

"He's a decent guy once you get to know him."

"How many times has he been in town?"

"I don't know," said Thumps. "Three, four."

"And which of those times didn't include a dead body?"

"Not really his fault," said Thumps. "He didn't kill anyone."

"What about Graham Chandler, Carl Mobley, and Oliver Parrish?"

"He didn't kill Chandler, and he only shot at Carl Mobley to keep him from killing me and the sheriff."

Archie took his glasses off for a moment, wiped them with a tissue. "And Oliver Parrish?"

Thumps leaned forward on his elbows. "Oliver Parrish was a really bad guy. And I'm really hungry. You think I could order dinner?"

"I'll bring you some special dishes," said Archie. "Otherwise, you'll order the cheeseburger."

"Cheeseburgers aren't on the menu."

"It's a metaphor." Archie headed back to the kitchen. "You need your taste buds expanded."

"No octopus," Thumps called out after him. "I'm not going to eat octopus."

THERE WERE CANDLES on all the tables. Thumps supposed that they were there to lend atmosphere to the restaurant, but he didn't see the point. You couldn't read by them, and the flickering lights were more annoying than they were romantic.

But a problem easily solved. Thumps leaned forward and pinched his out. That was better. A dark and peaceful refuge. Temporary to be sure, but a shelter nonetheless.

At least Archie hadn't asked him about Claire. Thumps wasn't sure what he would have said. Last he checked, he and Claire and Ivory were motoring along, a nuclear family on the go.

And then an abrupt left turn into a dead-end alley. Without signalling.

This wasn't the first such manoeuvre that Claire had made. In the years that they had known each other, had been lovers, there had been other traffic infractions.

U-turns. Sudden stops. Unexpected lane changes.

But today had seemed more decisive, final. Had something happened when he wasn't looking, wasn't paying attention? Had his love life been the plot of a novel, Thumps would have to conclude that the author did not have his best interests at heart.

"Here's how we start." Archie was back. With a small bowl of something in hand. "*Trahana*."

"It looks like mush."

"It's not mush." Archie handed Thumps a spoon. "It's *trahana*."

"Sour ewes' or goat's milk."

"Less complaining," said Archie. "More eating."

The *trahana* looked singularly unappealing. Thumps caught a small lump of the stuff on the end of his spoon.

"See?" said Archie. "Good, yes?"

Actually, it wasn't bad. Sort of nutty with a hint of lemon.

"It's okay."

"Okay?" Archie did his huffy face. "I grew up on *trahana*. The trick is to make it with chicken broth rather than water. And then you add in just a little grated Parmesan cheese and some lemon juice."

"I'm going to need more to eat than this."

"Yes, sure. But first you have to tell me why Cisco Cruz is in town."

"How should I know?"

"He's your friend."

"He lies to me." Thumps finished the *trahana*. "He lies to me a lot."

"What happened to the candle?"

"It went out."

Archie took a book of matches out of his pocket and relit the wick. "And Claire," said the little Greek. "When is the wedding? I want to be best man. We'll have the reception here in the restaurant."

"My blood sugars are dropping."

Archie pushed out of the chair. "Sure, sure. This is what I live for. Feeding you."

Thumps waited until Archie disappeared. Then he leaned over and pinched the candle out again.

6

Thumps didn't get out of Pappous's until late. The meal was excellent, small portions of adventurous and, for the most part, tasty food. He particularly liked the orzo and lamb pilaf, would have it again, but would pass on the lumps of bread soaked in garlic sauce.

Who would think such a dish was a good idea?

However, the price of the meal was putting up with Archie and the little Greek's helpful analysis of Thumps's personal life. Along with a refresher course on Greek philosophy and the Socratic method.

Archie was particularly distressed over not having been invited to Macy's funeral. Thumps explained that there hadn't been one, just a gathering for family.

"Duke wasn't invited?"

"The sister organized it."

"This sounds like a Greek tragedy," said Archie. "They never end well."

• • •

THE HOUSE WAS DARK. Thumps reminded himself once again that he should leave a light on, so it wouldn't look as though the place had been abandoned. Given past experience, he half expected to find Cisco Cruz's car parked at the curb and the man from Pie Town sitting on his porch.

Or in his living room, on the sofa, watching TV, eating his food.

Freeway and Cookie were waiting for him. Both cats were standing next to their empty bowls. As soon as Cookie saw him, the big male rolled over on his back and began licking his butt.

"Charming."

His mother was more restrained. Freeway simply stared at him without blinking, waiting for him to figure out the crisis on his own.

"You want to be fed."

Both cats began a low trill, a pleasant sound designed to elicit, Thumps supposed, an extra portion of Nature's Bounty Dry Feline Rabbit Feast. There was a can of wet food in the refrigerator as well, a recommended brand that smelled like dead fish and old potatoes. It was an every-other-day treat that he might have to stretch out to every third day, so that the house and his taste buds could recover from the stink.

Okay. Claire didn't want to move in together. And she didn't want to get married. Which left what exactly? Friends? Good friends? Casual friends? What was the phrase? Friends with benefits? Thumps had never understood how that was supposed to work.

Normal relationships were difficult enough.

In the days when ships made their way by sail, there were particular areas in the ocean where the wind would disappear.

Sometimes for days. Sometimes for weeks. Where all forward progress stopped. Where nothing happened and time stagnated.

The doldrums.

DreadfulWater of the doldrums. Floating on the sea of life. No wind in his sails. Thumps didn't think he'd use the phrase to describe his situation. It sounded prosaic and vaguely scatological at the same time.

Thumps's father had had plenty of wind in his sails. One day Eugene DreadfulWater was there, the next he wasn't. Sudden and complete. Blown over the horizon. Never to be seen again.

Better to describe his situation as becalmed. As opposed to marooned or stranded. Waiting. That was it. A perfectly acceptable condition. He was good at waiting. Waiting meant he didn't have to wrestle with choices, didn't have to make decisions. Doing nothing. Going nowhere. Waiting to see if the wind would pick up.

In the meantime, he would stay offshore. Anchored just beyond the reef. In case Claire or Ivory needed him. Ready to sail to the rescue when the tide turned.

Some people might consider this attentiveness, this vigilance, a form of stalking. Others might see it as sad and pathetic. Thumps didn't see why it couldn't be both.

THE PHONE IN his pocket went off like a bomb. Thumps was going to have to figure out a way to mute the damn thing or at least turn down the volume.

"Hey, boss. This an okay time?"

"What's up?"

"Scoop was worried that it might be awkward. You know, if you and Claire were . . ."

"No," said Thumps, "it's not awkward."

"Because if it is, I can call back."

Thumps tapped the phone against his head.

"Course, I can handle it myself," said Cooley, "but I haven't done many dead bodies."

Thumps stopped tapping.

"Just came in," said Cooley. "You want me to call Dr. Mooney?"

Thumps rubbed his face. "Where?"

"I'll text you the address. You know how to text, right?"

THE ADDRESS WAS on the outskirts of town, a new development along the river. Ironstone River Estates. An enclave for folks with disposable incomes who wanted the things that disposable incomes could buy.

Thumps had seen a brochure for the place. Glossy pictures. All the buzzwords. All the amenity boxes ticked.

Exclusive. Expensive. Enormous.

Along with surveillance cameras, a guard at the main gate, an armed mobile security force to patrol the property.

Or at least that was the promise, once all the McMansions were sold. But after the initial rush, sales had stalled. It turned out that almost half the houses had been built on the flood plain, and when the county discovered the problem, they slapped an injunction on the sale of the remaining properties.

Until such time as the developers built a water wall to deal with spring runoff and hundred-year floods.

But a water wall was an expensive solution and not one that Conan & Fallon Ltd. were keen on pursuing. Nor was the corporation interested in a protracted court case. So, the captains of industry quietly closed out the remaining escrow accounts, declared bankruptcy, and scampered off to find less contentious opportunities.

All of which left the development stuck in a legal limbo, the front gate open, the security cameras and the roaming bands of paramilitaries in armoured golf carts no more than an idea whose time would never come.

THE HOUSE AT 1492 River View Road was ablaze in lights, a lump of stone and glass that sat on the river's edge like a boil. The landscaping had been started and then stopped and then abandoned completely. There were remnants of a lawn by the front door along with several dead trees. The runoff from the rains, with nothing to slow it on its way to the river, had begun to erode the west side of the property and to undermine the interlocking brick driveway.

A skirmish that the driveway was losing.

Thumps parked his car next to a mound of dirt covered in weeds. Topsoil, he supposed, waiting to be spread and levelled. At the side of the house was a deep hole formed up with planks and rebar and wire mesh.

A swimming pool in the raw.

With construction halted, the sides of the hole had begun to slump and slide, nature's way of filling in an annoying mistake. At this pace, by fall, the wound would be healed over and the land made whole again.

Thumps was coming up the driveway when the front door opened and an older woman stepped out.

"Selling or the law?"

Thumps opened his jacket, so the sheriff's star twinkled in the light of the porch.

"Last time I saw a tin star like that," said the woman, "was on *Gunsmoke*."

"Thumps DreadfulWater. Deputy sheriff. Temporary."

"I believe you're serious."

"I am."

"Nora Gage," said the woman. "Might I ask what flavour of a name DreadfulWater is?"

"Cherokee."

"If I remember my history class, the Cherokee were in the Carolinas and Georgia until they were forced out by the U.S. government and dumped into Indian territory which later became Oklahoma."

"You had an enlightened history class."

You wouldn't notice the woman in a crowd. She wasn't tall, she wasn't short. She wasn't thick, she wasn't thin. Short hair, glasses. If Thumps had to come up with a single word to describe the woman, it would have been "ordinary."

Except for her eyes. They were clear and sharp, as though they spent their time burning holes in steel.

Thumps touched the brim of his hat. "I understand there's a body."

"Down by the river. Appears he fell."

Thumps was lousy at guessing a woman's age, and he knew it was a fool's errand to try. But hold his feet to a fire, and he'd put Gage somewhere in her early sixties.

"Appears we have more company."

Behind him, Thumps heard a car door open and slam shut. Angry footsteps coming up from behind. He didn't bother to turn.

"Damn it, DreadfulWater. Why can't you and dead bodies keep business hours."

"Evening, Beth."

Apparently, Cooley had gotten Beth out of bed. Or something more awkward.

"Hi, yourself. You know what time it is?"

Thumps turned to the woman. "This is Dr. Beth Mooney. Doctor and county coroner. Beth, this is Nora Gage."

"I'm guessing you're not the dead body," said Beth.

"Not today," said Gage.

THUMPS GOT THE hand-held spot from the cruiser. Gage got a flashlight from the house, led the way down the slope to the river.

"Howdy found him."

"Howdy being . . . ?"

"A dog," said Gage. "Golden retriever mix. Thought about calling him Potus 'cause he's big and orange and dumb as a post. Spends most of his time licking his doodle."

"Lovely," said Beth.

"So, Howdy found him?"

"Began barking like hell," said Gage. "Running back and forth. Thought it might be a skunk or a coyote. Or a Republican. You got Republicans in this neck of the woods?"

"So, you went to look."

"I went to look."

• • •

After it left the mountains, the Ironstone ran out across the high prairies, twisting and turning like an enormous snake, doubling back on itself in places. But here, the river ran through a basalt canyon where the sloping edges of the coulees gave way to hard cuts, low cliffs, and ledges.

In the daylight, the area was a geological delight, all craggy and prehistoric. At night, the broken ground and the drops made it forbidding and treacherous.

The man was lying on a lower ledge, slumped on his side, his face buried in his arms.

Beth peered over the edge. "Borrow your light, deputy?"

"You see something?"

Beth played the beam across the rocks. As the light hit the man's face, he moved, raised a hand to shield his eyes.

"About fucking time." The man rolled up on his side, groaned in pain. "I've been shouting for hours."

Beth had her cell out and was dialing. "This is Dr. Beth Mooney. Need an ambulance and a rescue unit out at Ironstone River Estates. We're down the slope behind number . . ."

"1492 River View," said Gage. "My bad. When I found him, he wasn't moving."

Beth sighed, turned to Thumps. "Come on. This just gets better and better."

It took the two of them longer to work their way down to the man than Thumps would have expected.

"I'm Deputy Sheriff Thumps DreadfulWater. What's your name?"

"Jim Brown," said the man. "Christ, but it hurts."

"What happened?"

"Out for a walk." Brown paused between mouthfuls of air. "Minding my own business. Was attacked by a bear."

Thumps looked up at Gage.

"Came out of nowhere." Brown tried to shift position, moaned. "Knocked me over the cliff."

"Just stay still, Mr. Brown," said Beth. "We've got a rescue unit and an ambulance on the way. Are you married?"

"What?"

"Deputy DreadfulWater could call your wife," said Beth. "Let her know you're all right."

"I'm not all right. Fucking bear tried to kill me."

THE RESCUE UNIT and the ambulance arrived at the same time in the same vehicle. Chinook being a small town, they were one and the same. It was a standing joke. The Sifton twins were rescue when rescue was called for and ambulance when one was needed.

"What do we got?"

Thumps had worked with the two men on several occasions, but he still couldn't tell them apart.

"You're Justin?"

"I'm Jason. He's Justin."

"No, he's not. I'm Jason."

Beth whacked one of the twins on the shoulder. "This is Justin. The one with the red hair is Jason."

Thumps could feel a small surge of annoyance. "They both have red hair."

"Keep up," said Beth.

It took the twins the better part of an hour to climb down, rig a basket, drag Brown up, and load him into the ambulance.

Thumps stood by the door as Jason locked the gurney in place. Or maybe it was Justin.

"I'll stop by the hospital," Thumps told Brown. "Get your statement for the accident report."

"Nothing to report," said Brown. "I was out walking, minding my own business, and this huge bear attacked me. You find it, you need to put it down. Animal is dangerous."

"I think it was a dog," said Thumps.

"A dog? I know a bear when I see one."

"Did it bite you?"

"Bite me? Damn thing knocked me off the edge of a cliff. Could have killed me. Isn't that enough?"

Brown was about to launch into another round of complaints when Jason or Justin shut the door.

"Which one are you?"

"Jason," said the twin.

"How's he look?"

"Cuts and bruises," said Jason. "Nasty head wound. Could have a concussion. What sort of numbnuts goes walking around here at night?"

THUMPS STOOD AT the edge of the driveway and watched the tail lights of the ambulance disappear in the distance. Then he turned, walked back to the house.

Beth and Gage were waiting for him.

"You buy his story?" asked Beth.

"Out for a walk along the river?"

"Wouldn't go for a walk out there in the daylight," said Gage.

Thumps felt it before he saw anything. Moving fast, coming out of the night. A large something that clipped his thigh on the first pass.

Gage clapped her hands. "Howdy!"

The dog came to a skidding stop, turned, stumbled over his own feet, came romping back, his whole body shaking with joy. Thumps always wondered what dogs found so delightful about life.

Gage began rubbing Howdy's sides. "Has you been a frisky doggy? Has you been a frisky doggy?"

Howdy hadn't come back alone. He had something in his mouth.

"Drop it," said Gage, in a motherly tone. "Drop it now."

Which Howdy wasn't about to do. The dog crouched down and then sprang away, tossing the backpack about.

"Howdy!" Gage took a rawhide bone out of her jacket pocket, held it high.

The dog disappeared into the night, but Gage was patient. She stood still as a statue, the bone in her hand. And then Howdy was back, the backpack hanging from his mouth like a dead rabbit.

"Drop it."

Howdy chewed on the pack, looked at the bone, chewed on the pack, looked at the bone.

"Drop it now."

Thumps was prepared to try to snatch the pack from the jaws of the hound of the Baskervilles, but the rawhide bone and Gage's voice worked their magic. Howdy dropped the pack, sat down at Gage's feet, quivering with anticipation.

"Go!" Gage shouted, and flung the bone into the night.

The dog was off like a shot, the ground shaking with his going.

Thumps picked up the pack. It was wet with dog slobber.

"That," said Beth, "is disgusting."

"He's still a puppy," said Gage. "Doesn't know his own strength."

Thumps held the pack out at arm's length. "You got gloves?"

Beth took a step back. "Little dog spit isn't going to hurt you."

"Gloves? Please?"

Gage stepped in with her flashlight. "You thinking this belongs to our Mr. Brown?"

Thumps worked the zipper. Inside was a wallet, two energy bars, a bottle of water, along with a monocular and a camera.

"Exactly what I'd pack for an evening's stroll," said Beth.

Inside the wallet was a driver's licence for one Stan Greeley. The picture on the licence was of the injured man, Jim Brown.

Thumps handed the licence to Beth. "Appears our Mr. Brown has a hitch in his giddyap."

Gage shook her head. "You people actually talk like that?"

"No," said Beth, "we do not."

"Monocular's a Duovox," said Gage. "Night-vision model. Camera's a Sony. Super telephoto."

Thumps and Beth looked at Gage.

"Mr. Brown–cum-Greeley's clothes are low rent," said Gage, "but the monocular and the camera are high-end goodies."

Beth zipped her jacket, jammed her hands in her pockets. "And exactly what is it you do for a living, Nora Gage?"

"Isn't the big guy supposed to ask me that?"

Thumps was beginning to feel like piggy in the middle. "The big guy is asking."

"U.S. Customs," said Gage. "Retired."

"Fixed income?" asked Beth.

"'Fixed' makes it sound as though it was working at some point."

Beth nodded. "For a retired federal employee on a fixed income, you seem to know a lot about high-end goodies."

"Occupational hazard," said Gage. "You'd be amazed what people try to smuggle into the country."

"Nice house," said Beth, "for a retired federal employee on a fixed income."

"Renting," said Gage. "Surprisingly cheap, but I should have specified no dead bodies in the agreement."

"Injured," said Beth. "Not dead."

"Point taken."

"Okay," said Thumps. "We got a Mr. Brown who may in fact be a Mr. Greeley, who is found behind your place with a night-vision monocular and a camera."

"Don't forget the water and the energy bars," said Beth.

"Before you ask, I never saw him before in my life." Gage crossed her arms. "I'm thinking he's a Republican, but I'll leave the thinking to those who get paid for doing that sort of work."

"Deputy Sheriff DreadfulWater is in charge of thinking," said Beth. "I just do the how."

"Speaking of which," said Gage, "I better go find Howdy. Before the big dummy gets lost and winds up in Idaho."

"I'm going to have more questions," said Thumps.

"You know where to find me," said Gage. "Kinda quiet out here, so I'd welcome the company."

Cisco Cruz. That's where Thumps had seen Gage. On the sidewalk outside the pizza place. With Cisco Cruz.

"I'm going home," said Beth. "Try to salvage the night."

Thumps watched Beth trudge back up to her station wagon. He waited until she was on her way to the main road. Then he turned to Gage.

"Cisco Cruz."

Gage's face stayed flat and quiet. "Who?"

"Give him a message," said Thumps. "Tell him to be at the sheriff's office first thing tomorrow or I'll find him, tie him to my bumper, and drag him through a patch of prickly pear."

"That some kind of cactus?"

"It is."

"You know," said Gage, "I think I'm going to like it here."

7

The first thing Thumps did when he got to the hospital was find a bathroom. Yes, he had been wearing gloves when he rummaged around in the day pack. Yes, dog slobber wasn't going to kill him. It probably wouldn't even make him sick. But just remembering the slimy, pus-like feel of the drool made the hair at the back of his neck quiver.

He washed his hands twice. Then he went down the hall to emergency.

Gina Tucci looked as though she had pulled a double shift. There were bags under her eyes and a slump to her shoulders that suggested that everything below her neck had gone to sleep.

"Morning, Gina."

"DreadfulWater." Gina looked up, tried a smile, failed. "You injured?"

"Nope."

"Sick?"

"Exciting night?"

Gina faked a yawn. "Think 'breaking news' on Fox."

"The Siftons brought in a Mr. Brown. Multiple injuries. Took a nasty fall out at Ironstone River Estates."

"You know," said Gina, "I still can't tell those two apart."

"One has red hair," said Thumps.

"Funny," said Gina.

"Where'd you put Brown?"

Gina pursed her lips. "Didn't put him anywhere. Came in on a gurney. The boys took him to triage. I went to get his vitals and personal information . . ."

"Such as insurance."

"Place isn't a charity." Gina leaned forward on the counter. "But when I got there, he was gone."

"Gone? He check himself out?"

"Nope," said Gina. "Did a runner on us."

"Anyone see him go?"

"Nope," said Gina.

"Well, hell." Thumps started to turn away.

"And you're not the first one to ask."

Thumps turned back. Stood there for a moment, allowed the new information to flow over him. "Let me guess. Good-looking Latino. Black leather. Nice smile."

"Best thing to come through here all night," said Gina. "No offence."

"He say anything?"

"Said I reminded him of Sophia Loren." Gina smoothed her hair. "You know him?"

"I do."

"Tell him he can come back anytime."

• • •

It was well after three before Thumps got home for a second time. Freeway and Cookie were stretched out across the bed, as though they owned the deed to the mattress.

"My bed," Thumps told the cats. "My bed, my house."

Thumps picked Cookie up, carried the enormous cat to his basket in the living room, wondered, not for the first time, if Freeway had found a lost cougar kitten and brought him home by mistake.

Thumps was carrying Freeway out to her basket when Cookie passed him on his way back to the bed.

Normally, Thumps liked to get at least eight hours of sleep. Given the night's activities, that would mean he should be allowed to sleep in until noon that morning.

At seven, the phone rang.

"I have four questions for you."

Thumps rolled up on his side. "Morning, Duke."

"One. Why does my holding cell look as though it's been attacked by the home decorating channel?"

"You at the office?"

"Two. Why are Cooley and Scoop playing house in my holding cell?"

"You know what time it is?"

"Three. What the hell is this pile of blocks on my desk?"

"It's called Jenga. It's a game."

"Christ, DreadfulWater," said the sheriff. "Office isn't a daycare."

"You said you had four questions?"

"Yeah," said Duke. "Why are there no doughnuts waiting for me?"

• • •

THUMPS TOOK HIS time. Shower, dress, breakfast. There was little point in getting to the office before Duke had a chance to find his happy place.

If such a place existed.

The sheriff was standing by the filing cabinet with his back to the door. The old percolator was hissing and grumbling, in the throes of a coronary.

"Coffee's almost ready," said Duke without turning. "You better have doughnuts."

Thumps set the box on the desk. "A dozen of Dumbo's finest."

"Chocolate cake?"

"Half the box."

Duke lifted the percolator, banged it down on the table a couple of times. "Helps to stiffen the taste."

Whatever it was that Duke's coffee needed, stiffening was not on the list.

"Coffee's not coffee until it has time to stiffen." Duke gave the pot a sniff. "Hear we caught a dead body last night."

"Not dead," said Thumps. "Just injured."

Duke poured himself a cup of coffee. It looked normal. More or less. Black and heavy as tar with iridescent oil-on-water flashes. A rotten cabbage bouquet that reminded Thumps of the Samoa pulp mill across the bay from Eureka on the Northern California coast.

"How bad?"

"Sifton twins took him to the hospital."

"I hear a 'but' on its way."

"There was a problem with his ID. I went to the hospital to straighten it out."

"And?"

"He wasn't there. Walked out of emergency and disappeared."

"The problem with his ID?"

"Said his name was Jim Brown." Thumps took the driver's licence out of his pocket. "But here we have one Stan Greeley. Different name, same man."

Duke turned the licence over. Looked at the photograph.

"Along with these."

Thumps put the monocular and the camera on the desk.

"Sweet." Duke picked the camera up, racked out the lens, aimed it at the coffee pot. "Macy would have liked this."

"Good to have you back."

"Who says I'm back?" said Duke. "Maybe I just stopped by to address the troops."

Thumps didn't bother to hide the pained look.

"The minute I come back to work," said Duke, "you're going to try to quit."

"I won't just try."

"You can't quit," said Duke. "You know how many deputies I got?"

Duke didn't wait for an answer.

"I'm supposed to have four," said the sheriff. "But until I can find two more to hire, all I got is Heavy Runner and Small Elk."

"Deanna is first-rate," said Thumps. "Cooley is getting better every day."

"You make three," said Duke. "Which means I'm still one short. And since I'm on compassionate leave, for the time being, you're me."

Thumps closed his eyes. When he opened them, the sheriff was still there.

"You trying to play on my sympathies?"

Duke took another doughnut, broke it in half. "Who's looking after the stolen cars?"

"Cooley."

"Maybe you want to toss Brown-cum-Greeley to Heavy Runner. Give her something tasty to chew on."

"Speaking of which, how about I buy you lunch?"

"You bought me lunch yesterday."

"We could go to the Mustang."

"You still feeling sorry for me?"

"Do you care why?"

"Not in the least." Duke took his feet off the desk. "So, what's with this Jangle thing?"

"Jenga," said Thumps. "You remove blocks one at a time. If you remove the wrong block, the whole thing falls over."

"Easier way to do that." Duke gave the tower a gentle push. It tipped over, scattered the wood blocks across the desk. "Let's eat."

AT ONE POINT in its life, the Mustang had been a Texaco gas station. Delroy "Hack" Chubby bought the property at auction and turned the place into a biker bar. He left most of the station intact, brought in a beat-to-shit double-wide and spliced it onto the back of the service bays. Ingenious and cheap, Hack built the bar out of old doors and zinc roofing panels.

He saved the Texaco sign, hung it from the ceiling behind the bar and nailed the grille of a 1965 Mustang to the wall just below an old neon sign for the 'Big Chief Motel.'"

Back in the day, the Mustang was a dark, dank cave, famous for its fist fights and arm-wrestling contests. And for the motorcycles lined up in the parking lot like horses at a hitching rail.

In those days, the bar was just beyond the city limits of Chinook and was a country unto itself with its own code of conduct, which included, but was not limited to, shouting matches, races along the shoulder of the road, and target practice with beer cans, road signs, tires, windshields, and the occasional radiator.

Hack was killed when he tried to pass a semi on the grade just north of Glory. His wake was held at the Mustang, ran through the weekend. And when the sun came up Monday morning, Hack's daughter, Lorraine, moved the Texaco sign out of the bar along with the jukebox, the pool tables, the '65 grille, and the 'Big Chief' neon, and burned the place to the ground.

Lorraine had her mother's looks as well as her brains, and before the ashes of the old Mustang cooled, she brought in a bulldozer and levelled the site. The next week, she put up a new prefab building, bright red with a herd of wild horses on the side.

Along with free WiFi, satellite TV, and video gaming.

Lorraine was of the opinion that a twenty-first-century biker bar didn't have to look and smell like a porta-potty, and that cowboys and bikers should be able to enjoy all the amenities that the modern world had to offer.

The Mustang was still the rough-and-tumble place it had been when Hack was alive, but now there were rules. Three to be exact. If you wanted to fight, you did it outside in the roped-off sand ring that Lorraine had built behind the building, a nouveau gladiator arena complete with a first aid station to deal with the various injuries that might result from a difference of opinion.

Lorraine's second rule was no puking in the bar. Puking was to be done in the bathroom or in the parking lot. Puke in the bar, and you were gone for the rest of the evening.

Her last rule was simple enough. There was to be no excessive talking or yelling when she was on stage singing karaoke. Not because she had a great voice. It was only okay. But she liked to sing, and since she owned the bar, when she sang, she expected people to shut the hell up and pay attention.

BIG FISH PATEK was behind the bar.

"Hey, Duke, Thumps. Long time."

Big Fish's real name was Patek Carpenaux, the story being that his father had named him after Patek Philippe, the famous watch manufacturer in Geneva. Wutty Youngbeaver thought Carpenaux sounded French (which it was) and needlessly pretentious (which it was), and shortened Carpenaux to Carp.

And Carp became Big Fish.

Duke made his way to a table in the corner.

"You guys here for lunch?"

"We are," said Thumps, "if Yo-Yo's cooking."

"Hey," said Big Fish. "What am I? Stale beer and chip nuts?"

"Yo-Yo?"

"Yeah, yeah," said Big Fish, "Yo-Yo's in the kitchen."

"Cheeseburgers for two," said Duke, "large fries, onion rings, couple of milkshakes. Thumps is buying."

"Lorraine made her lemon meringue pie," said Big Fish.

"That as well," said Duke. "Thumps is diabetic, so I'll eat his piece."

"Meal's on the house." Big Fish grinned. "Lorraine's orders. Good to see you back, sheriff."

Duke waited until Big Fish had disappeared into the kitchen. "Where the hell does everyone think I'd go? Don't remember ever leaving."

"You got a bunch of friends," said Thumps. "Everyone's been worried about you."

Duke leaned back in the chair. "So, we got a car thief, a peeping Tom with a phony ID, and Cisco Cruz, the ninja assassin. I miss anything?"

"There's the woman staying out at Ironstone River Estates. A Nora Gage. Found the guy behind her place. Appears he was watching the place."

"We know why?"

"Nope."

"This Gage the woman we saw with Cruz and Ora Mae?"

"She is."

Thumps hadn't heard the door to the Mustang open, but he felt the shadow that fell across the table.

"Miss me?" Cisco Cruz slid into a chair, all smiles and good cheer.

"Mr. Cruz." Duke set his hand on the butt of his gun. "So good of you to join us."

"I'm guessing you want to talk to me."

"Actually," said Duke, "I'd prefer to arrest you."

Cruz held his hands out, wrists together. "For what?"

Duke turned to Thumps. "Can you think of something with which we can charge Mr. Cruz?"

"Not offhand," said Thumps.

"Then let's do lunch." Cruz picked up the menu. "You guys order yet?"

8

Cisco Cruz had come into Thumps's life in the guise of a bodyguard for one Randall "Boomper" Austin, billionaire and emperor of Austin Resource Capital, a conglomerate of companies and corporations that manufactured money.

According to Cruz, he was just a working stiff who had spent seven years as an MP in the military and ten years in San Francisco homicide.

Which might have been true, whole or part. Or not.

Thumps had always suspected that Cruz worked for one or more of the alphabet agencies. Langley, Virginia. Washington, D.C. Fort Meade, Maryland. But he couldn't prove it, and Cruz hadn't been particularly forthcoming. What Thumps did know was that the man was an enigma who kept popping up from time to time to complicate Thumps's life and leave dead bodies in his wake.

"I was very sorry to hear about your wife, sheriff."

"Cisco Cruz." Duke nodded his head, tapped his fingers on the table. "Is there a dead body in the vicinity that we should know about?"

Cruz smiled. "Yo-Yo cooking?"

"Nora Gage." Thumps watched Cruz's face.

"Lovely lady. I hear you met her last night. Under somewhat unfortunate circumstances."

"What might you know about those unfortunate circumstances?"

"The bit about the cactus drag? A mite theatrical." Cruz shook his head. "I was going to stop by. Say hello."

"And here you are," said Duke.

Cruz set the menu to one side. "Here I am."

The doors to the kitchen swung open. Big Fish came out with a large tray. Halfway to the table, he stopped dead in his tracks.

"Holy shit."

"You drop that tray," said Duke, "and I'll arrest you for involuntary something or other."

"The ninja assassin."

"You know," said Cruz, "that's really getting old."

"Talk to Archie," said Thumps.

Duke leaned forward on his elbows. "Oh, I'm sure Mr. Kousoulas is going to be delighted to discover that you're back in town."

"He knows already," said Cruz. "Nora and I stopped by the bookstore. We had a nice chat."

Big Fish set the tray on the table. "You in town to kill someone?"

Cruz fished an onion ring out of the basket. "Just helping a friend get settled."

"You want a burger or something?"

"I'll just graze," said Cruz. "Talk with my pals here."

Big Fish picked up the tray, began backing up to the safety of the kitchen. "Okay. You want something, just yell. No need to shoot the place up."

Cruz turned to Thumps. "You want to split that burger?"

"If I ask you why you're in town," said Thumps, "will you tell me?"

"Sure."

"So, I'm asking."

"So am I," said Duke.

"Like I said. Helping a friend."

"Nora Gage."

"That's right."

"And you know her from . . ."

"Here and there," said Cruz. "Here and there."

"I love the smell of bullshit in the morning," said Duke.

"Movie was overrated," said Cruz. "I much preferred Kubrick's *Full Metal Jacket.*"

"And back to Nora Gage," said Thumps.

"Nora used to work for U.S. Customs," said Cruz. "We'd run into each other from time to time. She retired. Wanted to get off the East Coast. I suggested Chinook. Open spaces. Big sky. Friendly people. Cheap real estate."

"And here you are."

"Here I am."

"I take it you plan to stay," said Duke.

"For a while. Thought I'd take in the PGA qualifier out at Shadow Ranch."

"You play golf?"

"Doesn't everyone?" said Cruz.

"I don't," said Duke.

"Okay," said Cruz, "so not everyone."

"Jim Brown," said Thumps. "Stan Greeley. Stop me when you hear a name you like."

Cruz cut Thumps's burger in half, took the larger piece. "You know, I've never had a better burger. Been thinking about these since the last time I was in town."

"Then why don't you order one?"

"This will do me," said Cruz. "Trying to watch what I eat."

"Jim Brown? Stan Greeley?"

"Who are they?"

"You saying you don't know?"

"No idea," said Cruz. "Is there any ketchup?"

THE REST OF the meal was spent in small talk. Big Fish stuck his head out of the kitchen a couple of times but didn't come any closer than the swinging door.

"Morris Dumbo has a girlfriend?" Cruz stuck a straw in Thumps's milkshake.

"Makeup artist from Puerto Rico," said Thumps. "We haven't met her yet."

"Always thought the man was a racist."

"He is," said Duke, "but evidently love conquers all."

Cruz helped himself to a fry. "Hear you and Claire are thinking about moving in together."

Thumps thought about it for a moment. "Ora Mae."

"Ora Mae," said Cruz. "Woman knows her real estate."

"And everything else that happens in Chinook," said Duke.

"She found Nora the rental," said Cruz. "Really good deal."

"And you're staying with Gage?"

"Naw," said Cruz. "I like my own space."

"And your own space would be . . . where?"

"Here and there," said Cruz. "Here and there."

The cellphone in Thumps's jacket began vibrating. It was always a bit of a startle to feel the buzz against the side of his chest, as though a bee had snuck in under his shirt. Or that he was on the verge of a heart attack.

"DreadfulWater."

"Hey, boss."

"Cooley."

"Yeah, it's me. Is this an awkward time?"

"What is it?"

"When are you going to be back at the office?"

"Something wrong?"

"Probably should see it for yourself," said Cooley.

"Serious?"

"Naw," said Cooley. "Not going anywhere."

Thumps put the phone back in his pocket. He didn't much like mysteries. Cooley wouldn't have called him just to check in.

Duke pointed his chin at Cruz. "He ate your burger."

Cruz wiped his fingers with a napkin. "Thought you were finished. Didn't want good food to go to waste."

"So, you eat my lunch and now what? You ride off into the sunset?"

"Just wanted to check in." Cruz stood, brushed off his pants. "Say hello."

"And maybe tell us why you're in town?"

Cruz floated to the door. "*Cabrón*. You got to learn to relax. Smell the roses."

• • •

Duke took the last onion ring. "You smell many roses?"

"No."

"Me neither. Macy liked roses, but they're too hard to grow in this part of the world."

Thumps was debating ordering a replacement burger when Big Fish slipped out of the kitchen.

"He gone?"

"He is."

"He seems nice enough," said Big Fish, "but the guy gives me the creeps."

"Can I get a burger to go?"

"The ninja assassin ate his," said Duke.

Thumps took his phone out, brought up the photo of Stan Greeley, a.k.a. Jim Brown. "This guy come in here in the last bit?"

Big Fish looked at the image. "Nope. This the dead guy you found out at Ironstone River Estates?"

"He's not dead."

"Lucky duck," said Big Fish. "Only an idiot would be wandering around out there after dark."

The burger sat on the seat between them. Every so often, Duke would cast a glance in its direction.

"Don't even think about it."

"You're not going to eat the whole thing," said Duke.

"I'm going to try."

"Who was that on the phone?"

"Cooley." Thumps moved the burger closer. "Got something at the office for us."

"Why don't you drop me off at my house," said Duke. "I feel some compassionate leave coming on."

"Don't you want to know what Cooley has?"

"Sure," said Duke. "And if it's important and complicated, don't call me."

9

Thumps took Duke back to his house. Hockney sat in the car, looked straight ahead through the windshield. Thumps waited. And then he waited some more.

"Don't ask me how I'm doing."

"Okay."

"Everyone asks me how I'm doing. It's annoying, and it's rhetorical."

"It's not rhetorical," said Thumps. "No one knows how you're feeling."

"Hell," said Duke, "*I* don't know how I'm feeling."

More silence.

"That's why I'm sitting in a car with you, staring at an empty house. I don't even have a dog."

"I've got a cat I can give you," said Thumps. "He's as big as a dog."

Thumps wondered if Cookie could manage on his own in another household, suspected that the cat would have a hard time without his mother close at hand. Still, Thumps was willing to give it a try.

"Macy wanted to travel. I kept putting it off. Couple of nights a week, we'd watch a walking tour of a city she wanted to visit. There's a bunch of them on YouTube. Some guy wanders a city with a camera on his head. It's not the real thing, but it's pretty good. You ever been to Venice?"

"Sure," said Thumps, "Venice, California."

"I liked the one on Barcelona," said Duke. "That crazy church is something else."

"You be okay?"

"Absolutely," said the sheriff. "Have a couple of beers, get a pizza delivered. There's an *NCIS* marathon on tonight. The ones with the old cast."

"Okay."

Duke opened the door. "What's the cat's name?"

"Cookie," said Thumps. "He's a big suck."

COOLEY WAS STANDING beside the filing cabinet. The old percolator was rattling about on the table, and there were little puffs of steam coming out of the spout.

"Don't think it's going to explode," said Cooley, "but I'd keep my distance."

Thumps walked over to the pot, picked it up, slammed it back down on the table.

"Wow," said Cooley. "That's impressive. Sort of like rebooting a computer."

Thumps looked around the office. Everything seemed exactly the same. Filing cabinet, coffee pot, desk, chairs. Someone had rebuilt the Jenga tower.

"You said you had something for me?"

• • •

Jim Brown or Stan Greeley was in the holding cell, looking somewhat the worse for wear. As soon as the man saw Thumps, he was on his feet.

"About fucking time. Now let me out of here."

"He's been like this since I found him," said Cooley. "Grumpy."

"Found him?"

"Yeah, I came back to the office, and here he was."

Thumps rubbed the back of his neck. "Let's start with the easy stuff. Name?"

"You got no reason to hold me."

"Name? Please."

"Greeley," said the man. "Stan Greeley. Shit. I got a splitting headache."

"Kinda cool having a couple of different names," said Cooley. "Just like in the spy movies."

"And Stan Greeley is your real name? As opposed to Jim Brown?"

"You find my car?" Greeley pushed his hand through his hair. "Damn thing was stolen. I get out of the hospital, go back to pick it up, and it's gone. What kind of a town you running?"

Thumps went with the patient face. "Private detective?"

"What?" said Greeley. "No."

Thumps waited.

"I'm a private *investigator*," said Greeley. "Big difference."

"Private detectives normally work cases where there are legal issues." Cooley kept his voice steady, as though he was reading the answer from a book. "They're normally attached to an attorney.

Private investigators work the non-legal side of the street. Lost relatives, cheating husbands, background checks."

"Exactly," said Greeley.

"It was in a lecture at the academy," said Cooley.

"Okay." Thumps leaned into the bars. "You want to tell me what you were doing out at Ironstone River Estates?"

"Client confidentiality."

"Fine," said Thumps. He turned away, headed to the office.

"Wait. Where you going?"

"Back to work," said Thumps.

"Come on. You need to let me out."

"No, I don't."

"My head hurts like hell." Greeley grabbed the bars as though he thought he could bend them. "I'm the victim here."

Thumps came back to the cell. "Here's how it's going to work. You tell me what's going on, and maybe I let you out. Right now, I have you for lying to an officer of the law, trespass, fleeing police custody, unlicensed camera—"

"I wasn't in custody, so I couldn't flee anything." Greeley opened his mouth, shut it, opened it again. "I know my rights. You can't make any of this stick."

"Maybe not," said Thumps. "But I bet I can hold you for the better part of a week."

Greeley's shoulders slumped. "You guys are real assholes."

"Yes," said Thumps, "we know. Let's try this again. What were you doing out at Ironstone River Estates?"

"Okay, okay. I was hired to watch the place."

"Why?"

"They didn't say."

"All right," said Thumps. "Who hired you?"

"No idea."

Thumps looked at Cooley. Cooley looked at Thumps. They both looked at Greeley.

"It's the truth. Week ago, I get a text message. Was I available."

"And you were?"

"You kidding? A thousand dollars a day plus expenses. Five days guaranteed? Plus a bonus?"

"But you don't know who you were working for."

"Everything was done via text message."

"And the money?"

"Wire transfers," said Greeley. "Right to my bank account."

"You normally work for people you don't know?"

"You know how tough it is to make a living in this state as a private investigator? You check our population lately? A bus stop has more people."

"So, what were your instructions?"

"We got a deal? I tell you everything I know, and you let me go?"

Thumps turned his back to Greeley. "What do you think?"

"We could keep him here." Cooley lowered his voice. "But then Scoop couldn't sleep over when I'm working graveyard."

Thumps turned back to Greeley. "Everything from the beginning."

EVERYTHING WASN'T ALL that much. Stan Greeley was indeed a private investigator. Out of Great Falls.

Cooley looked him up on the internet. "He's got a website. My ten-year-old niece could do a better job, but it's him."

"Hey, you know how much web design costs?"

"The job?"

"Surveillance. Pretty straightforward. Come to Chinook. Watch the house."

"At 1492 River View."

"Yeah, easy to remember. Same year that Columbus discovered America."

"Columbus didn't discover shit," said Cooley.

"Jesus," said Greeley. "You people are sensitive."

"Watch the house 24/7?"

"No, just the evenings until about two in the morning or until all the lights went out. See who came and went. Take photos."

"Of Nora Gage?"

"Who?"

"The woman who's living in the house."

"Didn't get any names. My only instructions were to watch the place."

"That's it?"

"Swear to god."

"So, you drive in from Great Falls . . ."

"Flew," said Greeley. "Prepaid ticket waiting for me at the airport. Prepaid car, prepaid motel. Prepaid, prepaid, prepaid."

"The monocular and the camera?"

"In a day pack in the car. Shit. Whoever hired me will probably want them back, seeing as I blew the job." Greeley held up his hands. "Don't you want to know how I got here?"

"I can barely contain myself."

"I was kidnapped."

Thumps felt his patient face slipping.

"It's the truth. I get back to the motel, step in the door, and someone sticks a gun to my head. Before I know it, I'm handcuffed, my mouth duct-taped, bag over my head. I'm the victim here, and I want to press charges."

"Do you know who jumped you?"

"No."

"Did you see his face?"

"No."

"How about his voice? Did he speak with an accent?"

"Didn't say a word."

"He didn't ask you any questions?"

"Weird, right? Just tossed me into the trunk of a car. Brought me here and dumped me."

"Pretty efficient," said Cooley. "Sort of like *Mission: Impossible.*"

"That's everything," said Greeley. "So let me out."

Thumps turned to Cooley. "You working graveyard tonight?"

"Not tonight," said Cooley. "Deanna's up."

"Then Scoop won't be needing the space."

"Guess not," said Cooley.

Thumps turned back to Greeley. "Okay, Mr. Greeley, we'll check your story. See if the cuffs and collars match."

"When?"

"In the morning."

"Come on." Greeley rubbed the side of his head. "You're just being shitty."

Cooley patted the bars. "Look on the bright side. It's a nice holding cell. Easy chair. Even has a TV."

Greeley retreated to the chair, sat down with a thud. "Does it get cable?"

10

Scoop says that doughnuts are not really all that good for you." Cooley poured himself a cup of coffee. "Even though they taste great."

"You make the coffee?"

"Duke left instructions." Cooley tapped an index card thumbtacked to the wall above the pot. "Pack basket to top. Cook overnight."

"Overnight?"

"My mother used to do that with turkeys," said Cooley. "You should go home and get some sleep. Deanna and me can handle things here."

"May just do that."

"Claire called. Asked if you were free for dinner tomorrow."

"Okay."

"Buffalo Mountain. Around six. You're to call if you can't make it. I would have checked your appointment book, but you don't have one."

Thumps took a long look at the percolator, decided against it. "Call me if anything comes up."

"You know who did it?" Cooley glanced back at the holding area. "Grabbed Greeley?"

"Maybe."

"Cool delivery service," said Cooley. "Sort of like FedEx for criminals."

WILD ROSE REALTY was at the far end of Main Street, an ordinary storefront with large windows. Most of the glass was papered with real estate listings. Houses for sale. Houses sold. Ora Mae Foreman was behind her desk, staring intently at the two monitors.

Thumps walked to the middle of the office, stood there as though he were waiting for an audience with the queen. "What happened to the rest of your team? Your niece and nephew?"

"Sent the rascals back to their mother to enjoy an expensive university education." Ora Mae didn't look up. "Convinced them that they didn't want to go anywhere near real estate."

"Scare the children, frighten the horses."

"He said you'd show up sooner or later."

"I'm supposing the 'he' you're referring to is Cisco Cruz?"

"Only white man I know looks as good in black as me."

"He's Latino."

"Point is, he ain't Black, and that's the end of it." Ora Mae pushed back from the monitors. "So, the answer to your question is . . . client confidentiality."

"I haven't asked a question yet."

"When you do, the answer will be . . . wait for it . . . client confidentiality."

"Pretty sure it doesn't apply to real estate."

Ora Mae lined Thumps up in her crosshairs. "It does if I say it does."

"Don't worry," said Thumps. "Not going to arrest you. Don't have any room at the jail right now."

"But, as it turns out, this is your lucky day," said Ora Mae. "My client has waived her rights and has advised me to answer any and all of your questions."

"That would be Nora Gage."

"Should you have any."

"I know she's renting a place out at Ironstone River Estates."

"Renting to buy," said Ora Mae. "To be precise."

"Which means exactly?"

Ora Mae flashed a smile. "She's renting right now, until I can convince her to buy."

Thumps smiled back. "Why would anyone buy a house in Ironstone River Estates?"

"You talking about the flood-plain hiccup?"

"Bit more than a hiccup."

Ora Mae stood, went to a large map on the wall. "That's going to be resolved."

"The developers going to build a water wall after all?"

"Conan & Fallon Ltd.?" Ora Mae snorted. "You know what the 'Ltd.' stands for?"

"Limited?"

"As in limited liability, maximum profit. Last time anybody saw those boys, they were running for the jungle."

"I'm just surprised they were able to sell any of those houses."

"Then you'd be surprised by who bought them."

"So, surprise me."

Ora Mae pressed her lips together, made a zipping motion with her fingers.

"You know house sales are public record."

"Then you can look it up. What I can tell you is that folks who own property in that particular part of the world have hired a nasty old law firm. Going to file suit against C & F, the town, the county, and most likely the state and all the saints in heaven. Six months, a year at the most, the whole thing will be settled."

"And just how do you settle something like that?"

Ora Mae ran her finger on the map. "This is the line of the flood plain."

"Okay."

"The lawyers will run up a whack of billable hours. There'll be depositions and geological studies enough to sink Manhattan, and in the end, the line will be moved."

"Moved?"

Ora Mae moved her finger. "Presto chango, no more flood plain."

Thumps didn't try to mask the indignation. "Which won't keep the area from flooding."

"Not my problem," said Ora Mae.

"You going to sell those houses?"

"If I get the listings."

"That's immoral."

"Unethical," said Ora Mae. "It *might* be unethical."

Thumps stared at the map.

"You and Claire should grab a place while the grabbing's good."

"On the flood plain?"

"Prices in Ironstone River Estates are depressed at the moment," said Ora Mae. "But as soon as they move the line, values are going to shoot back up. Do you know the last time that part of the Ironstone flooded?"

"Global warming," said Thumps. "Severe weather. Climate change."

"Eighty-two years," said Ora Mae. "People want to be on water, and living on water has its risks."

"Nora Gage and Cisco Cruz?"

"Don't you want to know the prices? There's a really nice lot overlooking the rapids."

"Nora Gage? Cisco Cruz?"

AS IT TURNED out, Ora Mae didn't have a great deal of information. Nothing much on Cruz that Thumps didn't already know. Even less on Nora Gage.

"Cruz called me. Said he needed a rental, someplace secluded and quiet. Upscale with a view. Ironstone River Estates was perfect."

"Gage's rental is on the river. I thought people couldn't live in those houses."

"At present, it's what we in real estate call a 'grey zone.'"

"As in, don't ask, don't tell?"

"As in."

Thumps was on the sidewalk outside Wild Rose Realty, trying to remember the distinction between "immoral" and "unethical," when he felt his cellphone vibrate.

"Hey, boss. I wake you?"

"What's up?"

"I wasn't going to call 'cause you were going home to get some sleep. So, I didn't want to disturb you . . ."

"Cooley . . ."

"Right. You should probably get back to the office."

"Because?"

"Greeley," said Cooley. "I already called Dr. Mooney."

Thumps started back up the street to the sheriff's office at a quick walk. Now that he thought about it, "immoral" and "unethical" were pretty much the same thing. Both were tied to a set of agreed-upon standards. The word he had been searching for in his discussion with Ora Mae and dynamic flood plains was "amoral."

BETH AND COOLEY were waiting for him when he cantered into the office.

"You can slow down," said Beth. "He's dead."

Thumps stood up straight, tried to slow his breathing. He could feel the sweat pooling up on his shirt, armpits, and back.

"It's hot out there."

"No, it's not," said Beth.

"What the hell happened?"

"Don't know," said Cooley. "Took his order for supper. The choices were a cheeseburger or vegetable lasagna. He went with the cheeseburger, hold the onions and mayo."

"Cooley . . ."

Cooley gave a low snort. "I can see the onions, but who doesn't want mayo?"

"Cooley . . ."

"So, when I got back with the food, he was on the floor."

The door to the cell was open. Stan Greeley was lying face up next to the chair.

"I tried to revive him," said Cooley. "You know, CPR, but nothing happened, so I called Dr. Mooney."

"Turns out the dead guy who turned out to be alive is the alive guy who is now dead." Beth shook her head. "You're going to have a lot of fun with this one."

"Any idea what killed him?"

"Nope," said Beth. "You want me to speculate?"

"Sure."

"When he got knocked over that cliff, he messed himself up pretty good. If he had stayed in the hospital, they might have caught something on a scan."

"But he didn't stay," said Thumps. "He walked away as soon as he got there."

"I'm guessing he was hurt more than he knew. Probably cerebral edema."

"English?"

"An intracranial hematoma."

"Not helpful."

"He hit his head," said Cooley.

"He hit his head," said Beth.

"Enough to kill him?"

"You hit your head," said Beth. "You think you're okay, but the brain doesn't like the trauma, and it starts to swell. Could take minutes. Could take hours. Days, in some cases."

Cooley nodded. "He said his head hurt."

"I rest my case."

"He sort of looks like we beat him up," said Cooley. "In the autopsy report, you might want to mention the fall he took out at the river."

Beth nodded. "Is that Jenga?"

Cooley went to the desk, took a block out of the centre of the tower. "You want to give it a try?"

Beth shook her head. "Have enough annoyances in my life already."

Thumps held up a hand. "Greeley?"

"Sure," said Beth. "I'll take him back to my kitchen, open him up, see what's cooking."

"You mind if I eat his cheeseburger?" said Cooley. "No point it going to waste."

11

Thumps got a body bag from the storage room, and the three of them loaded Greeley into Beth's station wagon.

"Waste of gas," said Beth. "The morgue isn't that far. We could carry him there."

Thumps tried to imagine walking down Main Street with the private investigator from Great Falls slung over his shoulder. What might he tell people he met along the way? *Yes, it's a dead body. No, it's not a problem. Thanks for asking.*

Cooley closed the tailgate. "Hate to say it, but that burger wasn't very good."

Beth cocked her head to one side. "That's because fast-food burgers aren't good for you."

Standing next to Beth's station wagon and a dead body didn't seem a proper place or time to be discussing food, but if Thumps had had to choose, he would have gone with the vegetable lasagna.

"You kidding?" said Cooley. "Burgers have most all your essential food groups. Meat, vegetable, dairy, fat, salt, and condiments."

"Don't forget the sugar," said Beth.

Cooley looked stunned. "Burgers have sugar?"

"The bun is all carbohydrates." Beth slid in behind the wheel. "And don't get me started on ketchup."

THUMPS AND COOLEY stood outside the office, watched Beth drive the body down the street to the old Land Titles building.

"What do you want me and Deanna to do?"

"Be nice to know more about Greeley's mystery employer."

"He didn't seem to know much."

"Let's gather up the pieces," said Thumps. "See what we have."

"Like a puzzle," said Cooley.

"Greeley is hired anonymously to surveil a house. Watch the place. Have to assume this is about Nora Gage."

"That's why he had the monocular and the camera."

"But things don't go as planned. Gage lets her dog out, and the pooch either attacks Greeley or tries to play with him."

"I vote for play," said Cooley. "Dogs are generally friendly."

"Okay, the dog knocks Greeley over the edge of the cliff or Greeley stumbles trying to get away. Whatever happens, he winds up on a ledge somewhat the worse for wear. The dog goes barking back to Gage, she comes out to see what the ruckus is about, and finds Greeley."

"She thinks he's dead," said Cooley. "So she calls the office. You go out there and discover that he's just hurt. You ask him about the monocular and the camera?"

Thumps shook his head. "Didn't have the pack when we found him. The dog had run off with it. Turned it into a chew toy. We found the gear after Greeley was in the ambulance headed for the hospital."

"No phone in the pack?" said Cooley. "No car keys? No motel keys?"

Thumps shook his head. "Must have had them in his jacket."

"You didn't ask him where he was staying?"

That had been a rookie mistake. Except Thumps knew a rookie wouldn't have made it. Rookie one, DreadfulWater zero.

"I already called all the motels in the area," said Cooley. "No reservations for Greeley or Brown."

"Had to be staying somewhere close," said Thumps. "So, the reservation is in a different name."

"That's what I figured," said Cooley. "And most of the motels are completely booked 'cause of the PGA qualifier."

Thumps went back to the narrative. "Greeley slips out of the hospital, takes a cab back to where he left the car."

"And discovers it's been stolen."

"So, what does he do?"

"Goes back to the motel," said Cooley.

"No car. Only one taxi company in town." Thumps felt a little better. Rookie one, DreadfulWater one.

THE WAGON WHEEL Motel. That's where the taxi had taken Greeley the night before.

"Was really hoping it would be the Holiday Inn or the Tucker," said Cooley.

"Eleanor Lake still own it?"

Cooley sighed. "Didn't you find a dead body in one of her rooms a couple of years back?"

"Actually," said Thumps, "Eleanor found the body, called Beth instead of Duke. Figured it for a suicide. Didn't want to have the place locked down. Was hoping Beth would just take the body away."

"Sort of like garbage collection."

"Sort of."

"I'm guessing that didn't work out," said Cooley.

"Eleanor's her own woman," said Thumps.

Cooley pulled the cruiser up to the motel office. "You think two of us are enough?"

The Wagon Wheel had been built in the late 1950s, and, in all the preceding years, little had changed.

"The neon sign that looks like a wagon wheel is pretty cool," said Cooley. "You don't see stuff like that anymore."

"It's called nostalgia," said Thumps.

A split-rail fence surrounded the property. Each year there was less split rail and more bailing wire to hold the pieces together.

"Panel sign is a bit tacky," said Cooley. "Free cable, high-speed internet, whirlpool tubs, free coffee. None of that stuff is much of an incentive anymore."

"Probably don't want to share that with Eleanor."

"I hear the rooms have vibrating beds."

The office was dark and somewhat oppressive. Dark wood panelling, yellowed popcorn ceiling, a registration counter that might have originally been in the Bates Motel.

Eleanor Lake was nowhere in sight, which Thumps took to be a good omen. The sign in the office window said "No Vacancy," which should have put her in a happy mood.

She might even be agreeable.

"You."

One minute Eleanor wasn't there, and the next she was.

"What the hell do you want?"

"Afternoon, Eleanor."

"And who's the moose?"

"Cooley Small Elk," said Cooley.

"You Roxanne Heavy Runner's nephew?"

"I am."

"I like her," said Eleanor. "Woman has iron."

"That she does," said Cooley.

Eleanor was just over five feet tall with steel-grey hair that had been cut short and at angles, so her head looked like an axe.

"What's a nice boy like you doing with a photographer?"

"Thumps is the sheriff," said Cooley.

"Deputy sheriff," said Thumps. "Temporary."

"Got no dead bodies for you today."

Thumps held up a hand. "Not here about a body. Need to talk to you about one of your guests."

"You ever hear of confidentiality?"

"Doesn't apply to motel guests."

"And what would a photographer know about that?"

Thumps bit down on his tongue. Gently. "I believe my office called you, asked if you had a Jim Brown or a Stan Greeley registered."

"Maybe."

"And you told my officer that you did not have a Jim Brown or a Stan Greeley here at the Wagon Wheel."

"Maybe."

Thumps held out his phone. "Does this man look familiar?"

Eleanor squinted at the photo. "Maybe."

Thumps turned to Cooley. "Maybe we'll search the motel,

room by room, check all the guests, maybe fingerprint everyone."

"That ain't Brown or Greeley," said Eleanor. "That's George Banks."

"George Banks?"

"The man who rented the room."

Thumps put the phone back in his pocket. "The man who was staying here was Stan Greeley."

Eleanor put her hands on her hips, widened her stance, as though she were going to take a run at a brick wall. "Name on the reservation was George Banks."

Thumps made a small, pained noise in his throat. "Room?"

ROOM 8 WAS a close cousin to the office: Dark and depressing. Thumps tried to remember whether this was the same room where James Lester had been killed.

Eleanor read his mind. "It was number 10," she said. "Room's never been the same. Don't believe in ghosts, but 10's been unlucky. Air conditioner breaks down, it's number 10. Television won't work. Number 10. Toilet overflows. You get the idea."

Cooley went to the bed, patted the mattress. "This thing work?"

Eleanor took a quarter out of her pocket, put it in the slot, turned the knob. "Knock yourself out."

Cooley lay down on the bed as it hummed and shook. "Really cool."

"If this was number 10," said Eleanor, "the bed wouldn't work."

Thumps walked the room. There was a table at the far end. On the table was a set of car keys, a motel key, and a cellphone, neatly arranged in a line.

"Hey, boss," Cooley called out, "you should give this a try."

Thumps checked the closet. There were two shirts on hangers along with a sports coat and a pair of slacks. The dresser next to the bed had four pairs of underwear and three pairs of socks.

Greeley had planned to stay a while.

The bathroom was home to the man's toothbrush, toothpaste for sensitive teeth, floss, a deodorant stick that was supposed to smell like Tuscan leather, and an electric razor.

Thumps checked under the sink, opened all the drawers, removed the cushions from the chair, looked in the refrigerator.

The bed stopped shaking. Cooley rolled off.

"You find anything?"

Thumps gestured to the table. "Missing car keys. Motel key and cellphone."

"All laid out nice and neat." Cooley stretched, rolled his shoulders. "Like someone wanted to make sure we found them."

"I suppose you're going to lock down my room," said Eleanor. "I suppose you're going to tell me that I can't rent it 'cause it's a crime scene."

"The room was prepaid. Correct?"

"So?"

Getting answers from Eleanor Lake was like pulling a cranky badger out of a hole.

"How long?"

"None of your business."

"A week? Two?"

"Maybe."

"Deputy Small Elk." Thumps stood up straight, so the sheriff's star on his chest flashed in the light. "Let's lock down this room and the rooms on either side. We'll get a full forensics team in from Helena. Shouldn't take much more than—"

"End of the month," said Eleanor. "Room was paid to the end of the month."

"Then if we hold on to it for a few days," said Thumps, "you won't lose any money."

"This Greeley guy dead?"

"Ongoing investigation."

"So, when you're all done, I can rent it again?"

"As in double rent it?"

"I tell you how to play sheriff?"

COOLEY GOT A couple of crime-scene stickers from the car, stuck one on the door, the other across the door and the frame.

"You think there's anything left to find?"

"Doubt it," said Thumps. "Whoever searched the room was thorough."

"So you're just doing this to annoy Eleanor."

Thumps handed Cooley the evidence bag. "Check the phone. See whom Greeley called. See who called him."

"I'll swing by the airport," said Cooley. "Check on the rental."

"Cisco Cruz, Nora Gage, Stan Greeley." Thumps closed and locked the door, just as a wave of weariness broke over him. "Next thing you know, we'll have a partridge in a pear tree."

12

Deanna Heavy Runner was behind the desk, a cup of coffee smouldering in front of her, a doughnut on a napkin. Someone had been working on the Jenga tower. There were holes in the structure, and the whole thing looked about ready to fall over.

"Hear our dead guy is really dead."

There was a fresh box of doughnuts on the filing cabinet. Thumps lifted the lid. There were several plain old-fashioneds.

"Thought we were cutting back on doughnuts."

Deanna raised her cup, gave it a shake. "Can't drink this shit without something to kill the taste."

"Cooley made it," said Thumps.

Cooley helped himself to the coffee, tapped the index card thumbtacked to the wall.

"Per Duke's instructions."

Deanna scowled. "Would you jump off a cliff if the sheriff wrote it out on an index card?"

Roxanne Heavy Runner was a boulder of a woman who

enjoyed falling down mountains and crushing innocent trees. Deanna Heavy Runner was not the same physical menace as her famous older sister, but she had the same quick mind and bear-trap mouth.

Thumps held up a doughnut. "Who wants to exercise their little grey cells?"

Both Cooley and Deanna waited.

"Hercule Poirot?"

More waiting.

"Really?"

Thumps took a moment to reflect on the dictum that getting old was, in part, the running out of recognizable allusions.

"I need one of you to run a background check on Nora Gage."

Deanna took a pad of paper out of the drawer. "Social security number? Driver's licence? Last address?"

"All I have is a name," said Thumps. "Retired. U.S. Customs. At least that's what she says."

"Not much."

"And while you're at it, I want a similar check run on Cisco Cruz."

Cooley smiled. "The ninja assassin?"

"Thought he was your friend," said Deanna.

"He may not like that," said Cooley.

Thumps headed for the door. "And see if you can find Greeley's car."

Deanna faked a salute. "So, which one of us is Captain Hastings?"

• • •

THUMPS STOPPED BY the house to pick up the gear he would need and drove out to the dirt parking lot on the edge of Ironstone River Estates. Just beyond the lot was the public access trail that ran out along the river and down into the canyon. Thumps supposed that this was where Greeley had left his car. You couldn't see the houses from here, which meant that the houses couldn't see you.

If Thumps was right, Greeley had hiked in along the river trail and then climbed up the rocks, until he was level with the house. It was the easiest, most direct route, and Greeley hadn't struck Thumps as someone who was drawn to the difficult.

It was still early, the sun still above the horizon, but the house at 1492 River View was a blaze of lights, inside and out. Thumps grumbled silently to himself about the waste of electricity. Had Gage not gotten the memo on conspicuous consumption and global warming?

Thumps put the binoculars on the house. The wall that faced the river was all glass, floor to ceiling, and he could see into every room.

What had Greeley been watching? Nora Gage? The house? Anyone who came and went? What was he supposed to do? Take photos? Keep a log?

Thumps checked the outside perimeter, then swung the binoculars from room to room. No Nora Gage. No movement. All in all, the place looked deserted. Which was when he remembered the dog.

Howdy.

Where was the dog? He didn't appear to be in the house. Was he romping loose on the prairies? The mutt had surprised

Greeley, was probably responsible in no small part for the man's death. Thumps held his breath, listened for the sound of a small elephant heading his way.

Nothing.

The sun dropped below the horizon. The house remained silent. Nothing moved in the rooms. Maybe Gage had gone out for dinner. Thumps tried to remember if he had seen a car during his first visit.

No. No car. Though it could have been in the garage.

Well, he wasn't about to stay here all night. He was already stiff. His back and knees ached. A mental note. He was too old for this sort of nonsense. He wouldn't mention this to anyone, and he'd try to remember not to do it again.

He stood up, waited for his body to realign itself, began walking toward the house. Maybe the direct approach was the best option. Knock on the door, ask a bunch of law enforcement–type questions. See if the answers would make him any smarter.

Thumps knew something was wrong before he got all the way to the house. The front door was open. He stood just outside, put his hand on his gun.

"Ms. Gage! It's Deputy Sheriff DreadfulWater. Are you all right?"

There were a number of possibilities. Nora Gage could come to the door. Howdy could come to the door. Cisco Cruz could come to the door. Or any combination thereof.

Thumps waited, called out again.

"Ms. Gage. Sheriff's office."

None of the above.

"I'm coming in."

Thumps pushed the door wide open and waited some more, listened for any sounds.

More nothing.

Thumps took his time, checked the two floors of the house. The place was empty, showroom sterile. No foodstuff in the cupboards. No crumbs on the kitchen counter. Nothing in the refrigerator. No clothes in the closet.

A house that had never been lived in.

He was standing in the living room when it hit him. Not only was Nora Gage missing, but so was the dog and any sign of the dog.

Thumps checked the laundry room and the outdoor patio. No food dish. No water dish. No sign that Howdy had ever been in the house. This wasn't the way someone leaves in a hurry. This was a calculated departure, as though there were already a plan in place before Greeley fell off the cliff and the sheriff's department arrived on the scene.

So, why had Nora Gage disappeared? Where had she gone? And if she knew she might have to leave, why add the complication of a large dog?

He didn't know how, but Thumps was sure that the linchpin in all of this was one Cisco Cruz.

Thumps turned off all the lights. Except for the security floods at the corners of the house. From all indications, Gage was not going to return. Still, he'd have Cooley do a drive-by tomorrow afternoon, just in case. For now, the first order of business was to find Cruz and squeeze answers out of him. The only thing Thumps knew for sure was that the explanation, whatever it was, would be curious and complicated.

Greeley's car was another missing piece of the puzzle. If it had been stolen, as Greeley claimed, Thumps wondered if that could be the work of their car thief. If that was the case, then they could expect the car to reappear in the fullness of time, repaired, with any and all forensic information washed and waxed away.

Thumps walked back to his car, slid behind the wheel, watched the world go dark. Everywhere he looked these days, there was darkness. Claire and Ivory. Duke and Macy. Moses Blood and the unkindness of old age. Sorrow. It was like the night. You couldn't really see it. But you could feel its presence. Hear worry in a word. Recognize grief in a gesture.

How long could he sit here staring out at nothing? Going over a past he couldn't change? Quite a while, he imagined.

Anna Tripp. Callie Tripp.

Even now, after all these years, that moment could rise up out of the depths of memory and stagger him. Mother and daughter murdered on a lonely beach on the Northern California coast. On a night much like this.

Quite a while, he imagined.

But not as long as before. Not anymore. By the time Thumps pulled up in front of the sheriff's office, the memory had receded, leaving only an undercurrent of melancholy in its wake.

Thumps expected to find Deanna Heavy Runner sitting at the desk, watching TikTok videos on the computer. Deanna was an excellent deputy, albeit one with questionable viewing habits. Thumps had watched a couple of the offerings over Deanna's shoulder.

A fat man in a cow suit, standing in a shower, pouring chocolate milk all over himself.

A guy trying to break a motorcycle helmet with his elbow.

A lunatic jumping up and down in the middle of a restaurant, screaming that he smelled like a candle.

Along with a medley of filmic moments involving toilets.

To be fair, there were a couple of amusing segments. But all in all, the unavoidable conclusions were that nothing TikTok had to offer could make up for time lost, and that the advent of the internet had much to answer for.

Thumps came around the desk, looked at the monitor. Not TikTok. On the screen was a website on the ten best ways to commit suicide. He was reaching for the mouse when he heard a toilet flush and a door open.

"Well, shit."

Sheriff Duke Hockney walked out of the back, fixing his belt as he came.

"I can see you're about to get the wrong idea."

Thumps looked at Duke and then back at the screen.

"I'm not looking to kill myself." Duke bodied Thumps out of the way, sat down at the desk, closed the website. "Sit down. You'll hear about it soon enough."

"You sure you don't want to talk to someone?"

"Like who?"

"Whom," said Thumps. "It's the object of the preposition."

Duke took his gun out, laid it on the desk. "You know the difference between a friend and a pedant?"

Thumps held up a Hollywood Indian hand. "Thumps friend."

"Cute." Duke took a deep breath, sagged in the chair. "I'm only going to do this once, so listen up."

Thumps waited. Duke let him wait.

"Macy was sick. You already know about the early-onset

Alzheimer's. It had gotten worse in the last while. She went to stay with her sister in Helena, while they did tests." Duke took another breath. "That's when they discovered the cancer."

Thumps watched as the sheriff's face began to melt.

"There were more tests, more specialists, but the cancer was too advanced. Was in most of her organs. Not much anyone could do. Joan told her the cancer was because Macy had turned her back on god, told her that prayer was the answer, said it could cure anything. Drove Macy nuts with Jesus this and Jesus that. You ever meet Joan?"

"Can't say I have."

"Woman's a pearl in the making." Duke put his hands on the desk, pushed down. Hard. "I was going to drive over, rescue her, bring her home. Figured we'd spend the time we had left together. Instead, she caught a cab to a motel. Locked herself in the room. That's where they found her."

Duke wiped at his face.

"Left me a note. Said she was tired of the pain. Said she didn't want me to see her die. Said she loved me."

The sheriff pushed out of the chair. "You want some coffee?"

"No."

Duke poured a cup, took a sip, winced, took another. "You sure? No one likes to drink alone."

Thumps sighed, closed his eyes. "Okay. Half a cup. No sediment."

Duke brought the cups back to the desk. "Joan called me after the memorial. Began blaming me for what happened to Macy. I told her she should blame her god, seeing as he's all powerful and such. That set her off. She began screaming, calling me names, damning me to the fires of hell."

Thumps tried the coffee. He could feel the undissolved solids on his tongue.

"You know what?" said Duke. "The screaming? Joan getting upset? I kinda enjoyed it."

THUMPS TOOK HIS time with the coffee. He wasn't going to drink it. From time to time, he'd lift the cup to his lips, make a face, set it back down. Duke settled in the chair, folded several Post-it notes into tiny missiles and began launching them across the room with a rubber band.

"Macy was a big reader." Duke bounced a Post-it missile off Thumps's chest. "That romance stuff. Said that writers killed off their female heroines in order to create pathos for the male hero. What do you think?"

"I think you should be banned from making coffee."

"You think I'm pathetic?"

"I don't think 'pathos' and 'pathetic' are quite the same thing," said Thumps. "'Pathos' is a noun. 'Pathetic' is an adjective."

Duke waved his cup around. "We could look it up on the internet."

"Or I could catch you up on our local happenings."

"Such as our valet-service car thief?" said Duke. "Our dead Mr. Greeley?"

"And our Nora Gage," said Thumps.

Duke wrinkled his forehead. "The woman Greeley was watching?"

"It seems she's disappeared."

"And you're thinking that your buddy Cisco Cruz is involved."

"He's not my buddy."

Duke stood, wandered over to the old percolator, banged the pot on the table. "Brings the nutty finish to the top."

Thumps checked his cup. There was a ring of black sludge where the coffee had been.

"What happened to the Jenga tower?"

"Stupid thing kept falling over," said Duke. "What kind of game is that?"

"You threw it out?"

"Bottom drawer." Duke started grinning. "Figure I'll gift-wrap it, send it to Macy's sister. The two of them can annoy each other."

"You should go home," said Thumps. "Get some sleep."

Duke came back to the desk, eased himself into the chair. "Or I could drink more coffee. Contemplate the infinite and our place in the universe."

Thumps hitched his pants, set his hat on his head. "There's a television in the holding cell. If you change your mind."

"Damn." Duke leaned back, stared at the ceiling. "I may never have to go home again."

13

Thumps got to Al's the next morning in good order. Just in time for the Wutty Youngbeaver rally. The place was crowded, and Thumps had to lean up against the plywood booths, wait for a stool to come free.

"Hey, Thumps. What size you wear?"

Jimmy held up a red T-shirt with "Wutty's Warriors" in gold lettering.

"Get the extra-large," said Russell. "They tend to shrink."

Al had a T-shirt. Chintak Rawat had a T-shirt. Stas Black Weasel had a T-shirt. Big Fish Patek and Lorraine Chubby had T-shirts. So did Fred and Della Blueford, who ran the local Salvation Army store, as well as Dolores Cardoza of Chinook Insurance.

Wutty slipped off his stool. "Okay, guys, let's give it a try."

Russell and Jimmy threw their hands over their heads, and the café exploded into a chant.

"Wutty, Wuuttyy, Wuuuttyyy, Wuuuuuttyyyy . . . Warriors!"

Thumps kept the smile at bay. There was no profit in trying to discourage the man and his fantasies. Then again, maybe he was just jealous. Wutty had the handicap to play in a qualifying round of the U.S. Open, something that Thumps had never done, had never dreamed of doing. It was, he had to admit, a notable accomplishment and worthy of support.

THUMPS LEARNED GOLF as a kid growing up in central California. He and his mother lived in a trailer park that butted up against the Sierra Springs Golf Course. It was a private club with a cyclone fence that ran the perimeter to keep the privileged safe from the undesirables and the curious.

Still, you could walk the outside of the wire and, from a distance, enjoy the panorama of the course, follow it, as it cut its way through the live oaks and the undulating landscape. Watch the men at play, as they roamed the fairways and the greens.

But exclusivity is a transient condition, and like all good fences, this one had a flaw. Several, in fact. There was an opening in the wire at the fourteenth hole, just below a large No Trespassing sign, and another where a steep gully cut into the course. Here the fence stopped at the edge of a rather treacherous drop and then resumed again on the far side, allowing the adventurous to swing out and around the last metal post and onto the club property.

Thumps preferred crawling through the fence. It was safer than risking the ravine, and here the woods were thicker, so there was little chance of being seen. From there, he could search the edges of the fairways for lost golf balls. Thumps didn't play golf, but he could sell balls at the farmers' market on Saturdays, make enough on a good day for a burger and a movie at the Tower theatre in town.

One summer Saturday, as Thumps was getting ready to take

his weekly haul of golf balls to the market, an old pickup pulled into the park, dragging an even older trailer, its sides painted to look like the Grand Canyon.

The man who got out of the truck was ancient, with scruffy grey hair, scruffy grey beard. Skin darkened and cured by the sun. Short and powerful with a limp that made him rock from side to side.

Gabriel Garcia.

"This a good place, kid?"

"You paint your trailer?"

"What's in the bag?"

"Golf balls," said Thumps. "There's a golf course on the other side of the fence."

"Private or public?"

"Private."

"These the balls you found?"

"Didn't steal them, if that's what you're asking."

"You play golf?"

"Nope."

"The balls for sale?"

"Sure."

Garcia stuck his hand in his pocket, came up with a wad of bills. "I'll take them all."

THE CHANTING WENT on longer than necessary. Jimmy and Russell shuffled back and forth through the café like a pair of cheerleaders, waving their arms and turning circles between the stools and the plywood booths.

"We are to go to the tournament," Rawat shouted. "Wait on the fifteenth tee for the conquering hero."

"Yes," said Stas. "And when Mr. Wutty steps to the tee, we are all to do the chant and wave our arms."

"And if he makes a hole-in-one, we are to rush onto the green and lift him high on our shoulders."

"I'm good with the T-shirt and the chanting," said Dolores, "but I'm passing on any heavy lifting."

"Come on," said Fred. "It'll be fun. Sort of like Woodstock."

"Got a reputation to uphold." Dolores pushed her plate to one side. "And now I have to get back to the office."

Dolores slid off her stool. Thumps waited a beat before he slid into place. Home at last. Safe and sound.

Al came by with the coffee pot. "You know how you can tell when the circus is in town?"

"All the monkeys?"

"I was thinking clowns," said Al. "The usual?"

"Please."

"You know, you're going to have to buy a T-shirt."

"I know."

"Longer you put it off," said Al, "the more painful it's going to be."

Out of the corner of his eye, Thumps could see Jimmy coming down the stools.

"Here you go."

"I don't wear T-shirts," said Thumps.

"You can't be on Team Wutty if you don't have a T-shirt."

Al filled Thumps's cup. "Remember what Thumper said to Bambi."

Thumps let his sigh roll out, long and gentle, reached into his pocket for his money clip. "All right."

"Twenty-five dollars."

"You're kidding."

"And Duke," said Jimmy. "You have to get one for Duke."

THE FOLLOWING SATURDAY, when Thumps stepped out of the trailer, Garcia was waiting for him, a bag of balls in one hand, a set of clubs slung over his shoulder.

"You want to show me what you got?"

"Sure."

Thumps had watched golfers. Sometimes, when he had nothing better to do, he would stand in the shadows of the trees and watch the men whack their way up the fairway. So he had a general sense of how to hit a ball.

Garcia pushed a tee all the way into the ground, set a ball on top of it, handed Thumps a club.

"This is 9-iron."

"Okay."

"Nice thing about golf is the ball doesn't move. Not like baseball or football, basketball or tennis. Ball just sits there waiting for you to hit it."

The first two swings found nothing but air. The third topped the ball, sent it skittering into the thick brush. The fourth slammed into the cyclone fence and stuck in the wire.

"Here's the thing," said Garcia. "You don't hit the ball. You make the swing. You make a good swing in rhythm, and the ball gets in the way. That make sense?"

"Okay."

For the rest of the morning, Thumps practised his swing. Every time a foursome would come up the fairway, Thumps and Garcia would step back into the trees and wait for them to clear the green.

Thumps was astounded at the variety of shots that were possible. Shots that snapped off to the right. Shots that hooked to the left. High shots, low shots. Until there were no more balls left in the bag.

Garcia picked up the tee, put the club back in the bag. "You see any balls on the green?"

"No."

"That's my fault," said Garcia. "I forgot to tell you to hit the balls on the green."

TEAM WUTTY EMPTIED the café en masse. Like bats fleeing a belfry. Al stood in her tracks at the grill, cocked her head.

"You hear that?" she called out.

Thumps listened for a moment. "Hear what?"

"Exactly," said Al.

Thumps guessed that living alone made you take silence for granted. He tried to imagine what it would be like to live in a normal household. Spouse, children, pets. The sounds of domesticity filling the home, rattling the walls, shaking the foundation.

Claire would tell him that, when it came to human interaction, there was no such thing as normal, but Thumps was pretty sure that there was a distinct line between living alone and living with someone, anyone, any number of someones.

Al came by with the coffee pot. "When does this little whoop-de-do come to pass?"

"This weekend."

"Unless Wutty wins."

"He wins," said Thumps, "he moves on."

"Out of town?"

"Out of sight and sound."

Al set the pot on the counter. "But if he loses, we're going to have to listen to a blow-by-blow recitation of what should have happened but didn't and all the reasons therein."

"Actually," said Thumps, "it'll be shot by shot."

"Along with the licking of the wounds to the male ego."

Thumps pushed his cup toward the pot. "So, we pray he wins."

"Almost as bad," said Al. "He wins, we'll never hear the end of it."

"Chances of Wutty getting to play in the Open itself are negligible. He has to win three qualifying rounds, and he'll be up against an army of professionals at each stage."

"The worst of both worlds," said Al. "He wins the local qualifying round and loses the next, we'll have to listen to victory and defeat in the same narrative."

"In the meantime," said Thumps, "how about we listen to the sizzle of my breakfast on the grill?"

"You going to wear the T-shirt?"

THUMPS SETTLED ON the stool, let his eyes droop and his shoulders sag. He was tired. For no good reason. Yes, the diabetes played havoc with his energies, especially if he allowed his blood sugars to drop too low.

But the exhaustion was more than that. Almost as if life itself had weight and the older you got, the more weight was piled on. Each year another ten pounds.

Ten pounds, ten pounds, ten pounds. Until you were squished flat.

It was a particularly cheerless metaphor for existence and probably inaccurate. Maybe it wasn't gradual and cumulative. Maybe it was sudden. A mouse in a spring trap. A bug on the windshield of a transport truck.

Maybe it was a little of both.

Al appeared with a plate of food. "You know, we're all going to have to go to this golf thingy."

Thumps peppered his eggs.

"If we don't show up, and he loses, he'll blame us for not supporting him." Al put her hands on her hips and waited. "But if we are there and he flubs up, he only has himself to blame."

"Can I get extra salsa?"

"And in spite of his dumpster load of annoying ideas, the man's our friend."

Thumps took a bite of the toast.

Al put the jar of salsa next to Thumps's plate. "And that's why you have to wear the shirt."

14

Thumps took his time walking to the office. The sun was out. Not too hot. Not too cold. No sign of rain. And best of all, no wind. A Goldilocks day. Everything just right. There was a moment, as he got to the door, when he entertained the idea of continuing to walk. Past the office. Down the block. Out of town.

Walk to someplace other than here.

DEANNA HEAVY RUNNER was at the desk, staring intently at the monitor.

Thumps came around, looked over her shoulder. "TikTok?"

"TikTok's got a lot of good information." Deanna made a face. "What happened to my Jenga game?"

"Bottom drawer," said Thumps. "Duke is thinking about sending it to Macy's sister."

"She the one didn't want Duke at the memorial service?"

"Does TikTok give us the name of our car thief?"

"Cooley's case." Deanna looked up from the monitor. "Big guy did a nice redecorating job on the holding cell. I could see spending a weekend there."

"Cooley in the holding cell?"

"Nope," said Deanna. "Sheriff's currently in residence."

"He's sleeping in the holding cell?"

"Not anymore." Duke came out of the back room, stretching and walking at the same time. "Could you two make more noise?"

"Morning, sheriff," said Deanna.

"You make fresh coffee?"

"You told me not to." Deanna stuck a finger down her throat. "Some bullshit about coffee needing to mature."

"I saw that." Duke went to the percolator, poured himself a cup. "You realize that the holding cell has cable?"

"I'm hoping to get a turn," said Thumps.

"As well as Amazon and Netflix." Duke shook his head. "I don't have Amazon at home. You know why?"

Deanna raised her hand. "Because Amazon froze your account, and since they don't have customer service, you can't talk to anyone to get the problem straightened out."

Duke nodded. "And?"

"Because the company is a corporate maggot feeding on the living body of humanity."

"Are you making fun of me, Deputy Heavy Runner?"

"No, sir." Deanna kept the same robotic tone in her voice. "Just quoting you."

Duke turned to Thumps. "Is she still probationary?"

"No," said Thumps. "Deputy Heavy Runner is a permanent employee."

"So, I can't fire her?"

"You can fire Deputy Small Elk," said Deanna. "He's still probationary."

"Damn."

Thumps took the T-shirt out of his bag and handed it to Duke. "PGA qualifying round. Wutty Youngbeaver is playing. We're supposed to show up wearing the shirts. For support."

"The hell you say?"

"And there's a chant."

Duke took his cup, headed back to the holding cell.

Deanna waited. Then she turned to Thumps. "You think he forgot his shirt on purpose?"

Thumps folded the shirt neatly, set it on the desk.

"He back on the job?"

"Not sure he knows," said Thumps. "So, we'll just stumble on regardless."

"I'm guessing the first order of business is locating this Nora Gage."

Thumps turned the puzzle over in his mind. "Why would a retired customs officer come to Chinook, rent a house on the river, and then disappear without a trace?"

"Don't forget Greeley and the dog."

"Greeley's in the morgue, and the dog, like Gage, is missing."

"The dog's easy," said Deanna. "Either Gage took it with her or she didn't."

It took a moment for Thumps to see what Deanna saw. "Deputy Heavy Runner, I think you've just won first prize in the detecting sweepstakes."

"If first prize is a free cup of that coffee . . ."

"If you're right," said Thumps, "I was thinking more along the lines of the holding cell for a weekend."

"If Duke ever moves out." Deanna settled herself behind the desk. "What about your buddy Cisco Cruz?"

"He's not my buddy."

"Appears to be part of our puzzle. We know where he is?"

That seemed to be the central question. Where was everyone? Nora Gage. Cisco Cruz. Howdy, the dog.

"Gage could have left town," said Deanna. "That would seem to be the obvious answer."

Thumps went to the table, lifted the percolator to his nose, set it back down. "You look for Gage. I'll look for the dog."

"You don't think Gage kept the dog?"

"Hard to move quickly with a dog. Hard to be invisible with a pet."

"Especially a large one," said Deanna. "Greeley thought the hound was a bear."

"There's that."

"And Cruz?"

Thumps set his hat on his head and made for the door. "If I know Cisco, he'll find me."

THE CHINOOK HUMANE SOCIETY was on the southeast edge of town, in what was supposed to be an industrial park, a section of land that the city council, in an optimistic moment, had set aside for various manufacturing and trade concerns that they hoped would come to town.

The building itself was a modest concrete-block rectangle with a red metal roof that looked as though it might have once been a drive-in theatre snack shack. There was a large sign at the entrance that said "You Can't Buy Love, But You Can Rescue It."

There was an animal print in the middle of the sign. Thumps couldn't tell if it was a dog print or some other animal. He had seen the muddy tracks on his floor that Freeway and Cookie had made, as they came in through the cat door after enjoying a fun afternoon in mud puddles.

Whatever had made the print on the sign, it wasn't a cat.

The young woman at the desk was probably still in high school. Thumps supposed that animal shelters had the same funding problems as daycare centres and homeless shelters.

"Hi, can I help you?"

"Sheriff DreadfulWater." Thumps flashed his badge. Showing off. One of the guilty pleasures of law enforcement.

"Ariella Hoy. Aren't you the photographer? Did Sheriff Hockney retire?"

There was a plate of cupcakes on the counter next to a homemade sign. Chocolate with chocolate frosting. Four dollars apiece.

"Acting sheriff," said Thumps. "You related to Dr. Hoy?"

"My grandmother," said Ariella. "And you didn't need to come. We've decided not to press charges. There was some breakage, but Rocky has expressed remorse and has promised to pay for the damage."

"Rocky being . . ."

"A raccoon."

"So, you're putting me on."

Ariella smiled. "Things can get really slow around here."

Somewhere at the back of the building, Thumps could hear barking.

"Let me guess," said Ariella. "You're here about a dog. You look like a dog person."

"Cats," said Thumps. "Two of them."

"No problem," said Ariella. "Contrary to popular myths, dogs and cats get along together just fine. Did you get your kitties from us?"

Thumps could feel the slope slipping under his feet. "I don't want a dog," he said quickly. "What I need to know is if an older woman brought a dog in. Probably yesterday. Large dog. Cross between a bear and a half-ton."

"Does a foster return count?"

"Foster return?"

"The shelter can't handle all the animals that people decide they don't want," said Ariella, "so we try to foster out as many as we can."

"So, you did get a dog yesterday?"

"Howdy," said Ariella. "More buffalo than bear."

"And the woman?"

"Bonnie. Barbara," said Ariella.

"Nora?"

Ariella worked the keyboard. "You're right. Nora. Nora Gage. She only had Howdy for a couple of weeks. You want to see him?"

THERE WERE SEVEN dogs in the holding area. None of them looked happy. All of them began barking frantically as soon as Ariella and Thumps came through the door.

Howdy was in a cage with a blanket and just enough room to

turn around. As soon as the dog saw Thumps, he leaped up and began barking, his tail whacking the bars. Not bars exactly. Wire mesh. But the same effect.

"He knows you," said Ariella. "He likes you."

"I think he likes everyone."

"He's such a good boy." Ariella squatted down. "Aren't you the good boy?"

"Kinda small cage for a large dog."

"We're fundraising to build an outdoor kennel."

"How's it going?"

"Remember what the new mayor said about the proposal for the new library?"

Barney Tingle, who owned Barney's Barbeque Bar and Grill in town, had ridden into office on a four-pronged platform. Throw the bastards out, no new taxes, cut all social programs, run the city like a business.

"'People who read don't work.'" Ariella put a hand up against the wire. "You believe anyone would say that? A fruit fly has a bigger brain."

Barney's Barbeque Bar and Grill was the fifth business Tingle had tried to start in Chinook. The first four had disappeared in a flurry of bankruptcies.

"There was a guy with the woman," said Ariella. "If that's important."

"You saw him?"

"No," said Ariella. "He stayed in the car."

"So, how do you know it was a guy?"

"The car. Tricked-out Mustang. Jet black with tinted windows. A guy car."

"You get a licence plate number?"

"Is Howdy a material witness to a crime?"

As soon as Howdy heard his name, he banged up against the sides of the cage, began turning circles, whining.

"More a person of interest," said Thumps.

"Then you better arrest him."

Thumps couldn't help the smile. "I'm not going to arrest a dog."

"Okay," said Ariella, "then take him into protective custody."

Howdy sat back, his tongue lolling out of his mouth, and waited.

"And don't forget to buy a cupcake," said Ariella. "Four bucks. Every little bit helps."

THUMPS WASN'T EXACTLY sure how it happened. What he did know was that when he pulled out of the parking lot, Howdy the dog was in the back, and there were two chocolate cupcakes on the passenger seat.

The dog hung his head out the rear window, let the wind blow ropes of dog slobber all along the flank of the car. Every so often, he would let loose a long yowl of glee.

As though he were a kid on a swing.

DEANNA HEAVY RUNNER looked up when Thumps and Howdy came into the office.

"You got a dog?"

Thumps set the cupcakes on the desk. Howdy padded over, put his head in Deanna's lap.

"No," said Thumps. "He's a material witness. Or something."

Deanna picked up one of the cupcakes, took a bite. "What? We got a dog-lending library that I don't know about?"

"I found him at the shelter. Gage dropped him off. Seems she was fostering the mutt."

Howdy moaned, came away from Deanna, leaned against Thumps's leg.

"You've hurt his feelings," said Deanna. "Calling him a mutt. Now you're going to have to apologize."

Howdy began licking Thumps's fingers.

"See that?" said Deanna. "Who's the bigger man?"

"Did you make any headway with finding Nora Gage?"

Deanna set the cupcake to one side. "Did a lot of eliminating. She's not staying at Shadow Ranch. Not at the Tucker. Not at Buffalo Mountain. Working my way through the lesser establishments, but no luck so far."

"She may be using a different name."

"Thought of that," said Deanna, "so I'm asking about older single women who arrived in the last couple of days."

Thumps's fingers were wet and dripping.

"And I told Cooley to be on the lookout for a late-model black Mustang. I figure if your buddy arrived with the woman, he might still be hanging with her."

"He's not my buddy."

"What you going to do with the dog?"

"Duke still here?"

"You're going to try to give the dog to Duke." Deanna snorted. "That I want to see."

"Is he here?"

"Nope," said Deanna. "You just missed him."

"Okay, maybe you could . . ."

Deanna held up her hands. "Don't even think about it."

"I can't take a dog home. The cats will go crazy."

"Take him over to Duke's." Deanna was enjoying the idea. "Open the door. Throw the pooch in. With any luck the two of them will bond. And if it doesn't work out, what's the worst the sheriff can do?"

Thumps thought about that for a moment.

"He could fire you," said Deanna. "And where's the harm in that?"

Thumps nodded. "Win, win."

"Jesus." Deanna waved a hand across her face. "Did the mutt just fart?"

15

Virgil "Dixie" Kane, Thumps's next-door neighbour, was mowing his front lawn. Pops the dog was on the porch, watching Dixie push the mower back and forth across the yard.

Thumps left Howdy in the car, not sure how the two dogs would get along. He was certain that Freeway and Cookie wouldn't appreciate Howdy running loose in what they considered to be their house. Better to leave the dog in the car for the time being, while he got changed for his dinner with Claire.

But that's not what happened.

As soon as Pops saw Howdy, he was off the porch and up on the side of the cruiser, pawing at the door, trying to get in, while Howdy pawed and licked at the window, trying to get out.

"You got a doggy." Dixie stopped mowing, wiped the sweat off his face. "That is so cool."

"Not my dog," said Thumps. "Just looking after it for a while."

"What's his name?"

"Howdy."

"What a great name for a dog," said Dixie. "Hey, you should let him out, so he and Pops can play."

"They won't kill each other?"

Dixie smiled. "Dogs aren't like humans. They want to get along."

Dixie was right. As soon as Thumps opened the door, Howdy burst out of the car, and the dogs began racing around the yard, knocking each other over, sniffing butts, barking, and leaping about, at joy with the world.

"I've thought about getting another dog," said Dixie. "So Pops wouldn't get so lonely. Especially when I'm gone."

The dogs came bounding back on the fly, tumbled into Dixie's legs. The big man bent over and gave them both a vigorous rub. And then they were off again.

"Cats are easier," said Dixie. "You can have a couple of kitties, and it's pretty much the same as having one, because cats don't really care. But you can break a dog's heart with a glance."

"Can you watch him while I get changed?"

"No problem," said Dixie. "Pops hasn't had this much fun in a long time."

Thumps looked down the street. All the usual cars were in their usual places.

"You know that guy who shows up from time to time? Drives a black Mustang."

"Your ninja assassin friend?"

Cruz was right. The nickname was getting old.

"Yeah. Has he been by?"

"Not that I've seen. Course, he generally breaks into your house when no one's looking." Dixie gave the mower a couple of pushes. "But I'll keep a lookout."

"Thanks."

"What are you going to do with your doggy?"

Pops had Howdy on his back in the flower bed. Howdy had his paws wrapped around Pops's neck. Thumps had no idea what the two of them were doing, but it felt slightly obscene.

"Not sure," said Thumps. "I'm hoping to find him a good home."

"What we all want," said Dixie.

Thumps started for the front door, when he realized that his grass had been cut.

"You cut my grass?"

Dixie shrugged. "It was getting a little long, and I needed the exercise."

"You didn't have to do that."

"Neighbours," said Dixie. "The bane of human society."

THUMPS TOOK A quick shower, shaved, found a clean shirt. Dark slacks, sports jacket, and presto chango, temporary deputy sheriff to man about town. His hair was still wet, but Thumps figured it would dry before he got to Buffalo Mountain.

Dixie had stopped mowing the grass, was playing with the dogs.

"You got a good dog here," he said. "Wouldn't be so quick in getting rid of him."

"Got two cats already," said Thumps.

"And look how well Freeway and Cookie and Pops get along," said Dixie.

Thumps had to pry Howdy off Pops, drag him back to the car.

"Good dog," said Dixie. "Make sure he goes to someone who will appreciate him."

DUKE CAME TO the door in a T-shirt and pyjama bottoms.

"What the hell is this?"

"Material witness."

Thumps released his grip on Howdy, and the dog bolted past Duke and into the house.

"Very funny," said Duke. "Now, go get your dog."

"Not my dog," said Thumps. "This is the dog Nora Gage had out at the house. I found him at the shelter."

"She left him there?"

"Evidently, she borrowed the dog."

"Borrowed?"

"She was fostering him. Brought him back the day after the incident with Greeley."

Duke turned to find the dog, but Howdy had disappeared into the interior.

"I'm eating dinner. I'm watching a game. I'm enjoying the profound silence of an empty house. If there's a point to be made, I'd appreciate it if you'd make it and then remove your hound."

Thumps kept his face flat. "I figure we could use the dog to find Gage."

Duke closed his eyes. "Like a bloodhound."

"Yeah," said Thumps. "Like a bloodhound."

"Do you know how stupid that sounds?"

Thumps took one step back, held out the leash, set the bag of dog food that Ariella had given him on the porch.

"I have a dinner date with Claire. Pretty important. I was hoping you could look after Howdy overnight."

Duke took his time with each word. "You. Are. Kidding."

"Just overnight."

Duke took a deep breath, blew it out. "Is this your feeble attempt to cheer me up?"

"Nope."

"'Cause it's not working."

Thumps took two more steps back, until he could feel his heel touch the edge of the porch.

"What's his name?"

"It's Howdy." Thumps walked down the steps backwards until he reached the grass. "But you can call him anything you like."

THE DRIVE TO Buffalo Mountain let him cycle through the last couple of days to see if there was anything he had missed.

Macy Hockney had committed suicide. It was a strange way to put it, as though it were a crime. Which, technically, it was. Not that anyone was ever arrested for it, even though it could devastate family and friends. It had laid Duke low, even if he didn't show it.

And there was always the inevitable question. Why? In Macy's case, the answer was easy or at least apparent. A brutal disease that had no happy ending. Nothing to look forward to with hope.

Suicide was, Thumps imagined, the only door that Macy could open in her own time, on her own terms. And had. Death comes for everyone. Macy had met it halfway.

Because I could not stop for Death . . .

Cisco Cruz had arrived back in town. Always a mixed blessing.

Thumps liked the man, just didn't trust him. And he had come with a friend. The mysterious Nora Gage. Retired customs agent, if Thumps were inclined to believe the woman.

Which he wasn't.

All complicated by Stan Greeley, private investigator, who had been hired to spy on Gage for reason or reasons unknown. And now Greeley was dead from the complications of a fall, so that part of the mystery was a dead end.

As it were.

Thumps didn't know what to make of Howdy. Where the dog fit into the puzzle. He just knew that he couldn't stand seeing him in that tiny cage with a blanket and a water dish.

Ever hopeful, ever waiting.

The car thief wasn't on the front burner. Thumps figured that that would get sorted out in good order. Cooley might have already managed to solve it.

Which left Claire. Thumps could count the times she had invited him to dinner. If the offer had been to her place on the reservation, he could hold out the hope that her reasons might have something to do with desire and summer rain.

But the dining room at Buffalo Mountain was more for commerce and colder storms.

THUMPS WAS WALKING across the lobby when an armoured personnel carrier pulled up beside him.

"DreadfulWater."

"Evening, Roxanne."

"About time you showed up."

Roxanne Heavy Runner was dressed in a gunmetal-grey,

shrapnel-patterned pantsuit. Her hair had been dragged backwards off her face, fastened in a tight bun, and held in place with a large metal clip that stuck up off the top of her head like the safety lever on a hand grenade.

"You need to be 110 percent supportive." Roxanne pushed forward. "You understand?"

Thumps retreated. "One hundred and ten percent."

"First of all, this isn't about you. It's about Claire and that little girl."

"Okay."

"Second." Roxanne's face softened. "How's that sister of mine doing?"

The question was simple and straightforward, but Roxanne made it sound like a cruise missile on its way to a target.

"Deanna?" Somehow Roxanne had trapped him in a corner. "She's terrific."

"You think she's too young for the job?"

"No."

"Some people might think a woman shouldn't be sheriff."

"Sheriff?"

"When Duke retires," said Roxanne. "Job's not that hard. Try running the tribal council."

Thumps considered pointing out that while Deanna *was* terrific, she had been on the job for less than two years.

"Don't know that Duke's going to retire just yet."

Roxanne took a step back. Thumps could feel the air rush in to fill the void.

"Was real sorry to hear about his wife. I liked Macy. Tough woman. You tell Duke I said that."

"Mean more coming from you."

"Probably not a good idea," said Roxanne. "Deanna tells me I can be abrupt. What do you think?"

Claire was sitting at a table by the floor-to-ceiling windows that looked out over the river and White Goat Canyon.

"Great view." Thumps pulled up a chair, sat down.

For as long as Thumps had known her, Claire had lived her life in jeans and blue work shirts. She kept her business attire—dark pantsuits, dark skirts with matching jackets for meetings with state and federal officials—locked up somewhere in her closet. Out of sight, out of mind.

Claire turned in her chair. "You look nice."

But there were other clothes in her closet as well, clothes for special occasions. Tonight, she was wearing a dark-green skirt and tailored jacket that made Thumps think of 1940 movies that featured rich people in nightclubs and on yachts.

"That new?"

"Old and new." Claire ran a hand over the lapels. "From Gabby Santucci's Daisy Buchanan collection. What do you think?"

"That would make me Jay Gatsby."

"You'd need an art deco tux." Claire shook her head. "Have you even read the book?"

"Better," said Thumps. "I saw the movie."

Claire's laugh was pleasant enough, never shrill or boisterous, always gentle and under control.

"Did we enjoy our chit-chat with Roxanne?"

"We did," said Thumps.

"And that's why you're sweating?"

"I'm not sweating."

"You know, she frightens everyone."

Thumps relaxed in the chair, took in the view, considered the menu. It had changed, and there were some intriguing choices. By the time the server came by to take their order, Thumps was still undecided.

"We have two specials," said the woman. "A slow-cooked buffalo stew. Onions, carrots, potatoes in a red-wine reduction. It comes with a sourdough baguette and a green salad."

"The buffalo," said Claire, "is from the tribe's new enterprise."

"And," said the server, "we also have a trout amandine served with wild rice and seasonal vegetables."

"I'll have the trout." Claire closed her menu, looked across the table, fixed Thumps with her eyes.

"And I should have the stew?"

"Yes," said Claire, "you should."

Thumps smiled at the server. "What's for dessert?"

By the time the food arrived, the mountains and the canyon had faded to purple. Thumps was always surprised how quickly it happened. Everything bright and golden one moment and not the next.

Claire split her fish with a knife especially designed for that purpose.

"I hear Cisco Cruz is in town."

Thumps broke the baguette into pieces, buttered each one in turn. "Apparently."

"And that you have a dead body."

"Accident," said Thumps. "Natural causes."

"Sustained while the deceased was surveilling a retired federal employee?"

"How's the fish?"

"Is it supposed to be a secret?"

"Nora Gage," said Thumps. "That why we're having dinner?"

Claire put her fork to one side. "No," she said. "It's not."

Thumps tried the stew. It was surprisingly good. He had expected the buffalo to be on the tough side, overcooked. But it wasn't.

"The other day at the picnic," said Claire. "With Lorraine and Big Fish? Did you notice anything?"

Thumps hated moments such as this, moments where he was supposed to remember a specific and important moment.

"Ivory," said Claire. "What little Hack said."

And he especially hated it when he got hints as to the moment in question and still came up empty.

"She's been having blackouts." Claire's shoulders slumped. "The doctor calls them 'absence seizures.' At first, it would only happen a couple times a week. But now, they've been getting more frequent."

"Blackouts?"

"She'll just stop. As though someone has thrown a switch. And then she's okay."

Thumps stopped eating. "You take her to a doctor?"

"Beth took a look. Sent us to a specialist in Helena."

Thumps didn't want to ask the obvious question, hoped that Claire would provide the answer for him.

"They did an MRI. There appears to be a shadow on her brain."

The first question would have been hard to ask. The second was impossible.

"A tumour?"

Claire took a deep breath. "They're not sure. It could be something called 'focal cortical dysplasia.'"

Thumps waited.

"It's an abnormal organization of layers of the brain. It can cause a kind of epilepsy."

"So, it's not a tumour?"

"Or it could be a low-grade glioma." Claire was fighting tears. And losing. "Which is basically cancer."

"Shit."

"I should have probably waited until we finished dinner." Claire wiped her eyes, forced a smile. "You want dessert?"

"Does Ivory know?"

"That there's something wrong with her brain?" Claire closed her eyes. "She knows something's not right. She knows I'm worried."

"What can I do?"

"You're doing it," said Claire. "You're having dinner with me. You're listening."

"Who else knows?"

"Beth knows," said Claire. "I've told Moses and Roxanne."

"And me."

"My insurance isn't going to cover treatment. It won't cover an operation, even if an operation is possible." Claire stared out the windows at the canyon in the dark. "She's not a U.S. citizen. The adoption isn't final yet. And when it is, they will claim that this was an existing condition and therefore not eligible."

"That's crazy."

"The American health care system isn't about health care. It's a wholly-owned, for-profit subsidiary of insurance corporations," said Claire. "And corporate profits must be protected."

"Profits, profits, *über alles*."

Claire frowned. "*Über* what?"

"Sorry," said Thumps. "Two semesters of German at university. Look, there has to be a way."

"How's your stew?"

"The stew's great." Thumps set his spoon down. "What about Ivory?"

"Ivory's mother and father were Canadian." Claire poked at her fish. "My father's from Siksika, so I have dual citizenship. The health care system there is actually about health care."

It took a moment for the pieces to work their way into place. "You're moving to Canada?"

"Calgary," said Claire. "There's strawberry trifle for dessert."

THE PLAN WAS simple enough. Claire and Ivory would move to Calgary. Ivory's uncle had found them a place to stay. There would be tests and specialists and more tests. Once they knew what they were dealing with, there would be more plans.

Thumps didn't finish the stew. And he passed on the coffee and strawberry trifle.

"When do you leave?"

"Soon."

"What about your place?"

"Roxanne is going to look after it."

Thumps folded his napkin, set it on the table. "This is where the hero is supposed to ride to the rescue."

"Right now, it's Duke who needs a hero," said Claire. "Ivory and I will be okay."

"Until you're not."

"If that time comes," said Claire, "I'm betting you'll find a horse."

16

Thumps didn't get back from Buffalo Mountain until late. The plan was to sleep in.

Which didn't happen.

"Hey, boss."

It took Thumps a moment to rub his eyes open, unstick his mouth.

"You there, boss?"

Thumps reluctantly rolled over, disturbing the cats.

"I'm here."

"Were you asleep?"

Thumps checked the time. Jesus.

"No."

"'Cause I always hate it when I'm trying to sleep in and someone wakes me."

Cookie crawled onto Thumps's chest, put his face next to the phone, began purring at decibels well above the legal limit.

"That a generator?"

Thumps pushed the cat away. "Cooley . . ."

"Right. You probably want to get down here."

"Because?"

"We found Greeley's rental."

"And?"

"And when you come in," said Cooley, "maybe you could pick up some doughnuts."

THE OPEN SIGN was lit at Dumbo's. Fancy Whelan was waiting for him.

"Your lads called, yeah?" Fancy set a large box on the counter. "Put in the order, so you wouldn't have to make any hard decisions."

The box was large enough to hold a couple dozen doughnuts.

"Don't suppose they paid for the order as well?"

"Be joking."

"Thought you were working at Pappous's."

"My night job. Uncle Morris don't pay shite." Fancy taped the box shut. "What's the law pay? You got to go to school?"

Thumps tried to picture Fancy in a deputy's uniform.

"Twelve-week course over in Helena."

Fancy wiped her hands. "Been working in this manky mansion for almost a year now. Twelve weeks in fresh air would be happy days for sure."

"Actually," said Thumps, "Duke's looking for a couple of deputies."

"Is he now?" Fancy handed Thumps the receipt. "And can you shoot folks?"

"It's frowned upon."

"Not what you see on the news." Fancy made her hands into

guns, complete with sound effects. "Might just give it a lash."

"You should do a ride-along," said Thumps. "See what the job is like."

"And where would I be getting a ticket for that?"

Thumps picked up the box. "Stop by the office."

"And would I be arriving for such an occasion with treats for the lads?"

"First impressions," said Thumps. "Always important."

THUMPS CARRIED THE box back to the car. The more he thought about Fancy as a deputy, the more he liked the idea. Selling doughnuts wasn't a gateway job to law enforcement, but working for Morris Dumbo had exposed her to bigots and difficult individuals, and you couldn't buy that kind of experience. And she was good with the general public, another skill that was difficult to teach.

Deputy Whelan.

When Thumps got to the office, Duke was in his chair, his feet on the desk. Cooley was standing by the file cabinet, watching the old percolator melt perfectly good coffee beans into volcanic magma. Howdy was lying on the floor, licking his genitals.

Duke shook his head. "Yeah, it's pretty disgusting."

"He does that a lot," said Cooley. "I think it makes him happy."

"And picking up his shit doesn't float my boat either."

"You brought the dog to work?"

"Not my dog," said Duke. "And not my idea. You know what happens every time I try to leave him behind?"

"He cries," said Cooley.

"He cries," said Duke. "Makes the most pitiful sounds you've ever heard."

"I figure he's got FOBLO," said Cooley. "It's not uncommon."

"Fear of being left out," said Duke. "Cooley looked it up on the internet."

"People get it too," said Cooley. "I think I may have a mild case."

"Dog won't let me out of his sight."

Thumps put the box on the filing cabinet. Looked at the coffee in Cooley's cup. Decided against it.

Duke took his feet off the desk. "Cooley cracked the case."

Cooley opened the box, considered the selection. "Wasn't exactly the case we thought it was."

"The case being . . ."

"The stolen cars," said Duke. "Appears our car thieves are two brothers."

Cooley took his cellphone out, made a couple of swipes, held it out for Thumps to see. "Elmer Little Horse, age eighty-six, and his younger brother, Elroy, age eighty-four."

Thumps stared at the image. "You're kidding."

"Nope," said Cooley. "A two-man team makes sense. The brothers drive around, find a car. Elroy boosts it. Elmer follows. And then back to their hideout they go."

"Which in this case is a garage over in Harlowton," said Duke. "Tell Thumps the good parts."

Cooley put the phone away, helped himself to a doughnut. "Well, to begin with, neither Elmer nor Elroy has a driver's licence, nor the required liability insurance that the state requires."

Duke smiled. "It gets better."

"Right," said Cooley. "And they don't see themselves as car thieves."

Thumps snorted. "What? They're misunderstood automotive detailers?"

Duke started chuckling. "Wait for it."

"No," said Cooley. "The brothers see themselves as horse thieves."

Duke waved a finger in a circle against the side of his head. "Seems the brothers Little Horse don't live in the current century."

"Horses." Thumps rubbed the back of his neck. "Right."

"At one point in our history," said Cooley, "we were great horse thieves."

"The brothers fix up the cars?"

"No," said Cooley. "That's Brian Little Horse. He's Elmer and Elroy's nephew. Runs the garage. Brian's mother is Elmer and Elroy's younger sister. She married Horace Fox, who is my dad's cousin—"

"Cooley . . ."

"So, when Brian realized what his uncles were doing, he was sort of in a . . ."

"Quandary?"

"Right," said Cooley. "He didn't want to turn them in, seeing as they're family. So, he figured if he fixed the cars, got them all nice and sparkling, and returned them, the owners wouldn't press charges."

"You can't buy stories like this," said Duke.

"Great work," said Thumps. "How'd you crack it?"

Cooley shrugged. "Brian called me."

Thumps waited for the punchline.

"It's no joke," said Duke. "Tell Deputy DreadfulWater why."

Cooley nodded. "Best I show you."

Cooley headed into the back. Duke reached out, scratched Howdy's head.

"I know you're hoping that I'm going to keep him," said Duke. "But that's not going to happen. Can hardly take care of myself."

"I take him back to the shelter, and they can't find him a home, they'll put him down."

"Nice try," said Duke. "Already talked to the shelter. They don't do that shit anymore."

Howdy moved closer, put his head in Duke's lap.

"Did you know that you can't give beer to a dog? I mean, what the hell. Nor can you feed the mutt ice cream, 'cause it causes diarrhea. Grapes will give him kidney failure. Chocolate will cause vomiting and death. And don't even think about coffee."

"I imagine that doughnuts aren't good for him either."

"But you know what he loves?" Duke waited a beat. "Peanut butter. You believe it? It's like pie or cake. And the crazy thing is, it's okay to feed him peanut butter. Go figure."

"Peanut butter?"

"But not too much," said Duke, "or he'll get fat. And not the ones with a sugar substitute."

"Here we go." Cooley came out of the back with a gun case. "Went over to the garage first thing this morning. Brian had returned all the cars his uncles rounded up, except for one."

Duke leaned forward. "You want to guess?"

"Stan Greeley's rental."

"That's the one," said Cooley. "Brian was detailing the car when he found this."

Cooley lay the case on Duke's desk. "Soon as he opened the case, he called me."

Cooley undid the latches, lifted the lid. Inside was a rifle broken down into pieces.

"Sniper rifle," said Cooley. "Remington CSR with 7.62 NATO rounds."

"This was in the car?"

"In the trunk," said Cooley. "Where the spare would normally go."

"That a suppressor?"

"Puts a whole new spin on our Mr. Greeley." Duke opened a drawer, took out a jar of peanut butter and a spoon. Howdy was on his feet in a flash.

Thumps lifted the receiver and the folding stock out of the case. "Three pieces. Easy transport. Fast assembly."

"Dead accurate out to five hundred yards," said Cooley. "Twelve hundred if you know what you're doing."

Duke scooped up a lump of peanut butter, held the spoon out. Howdy surged forward, began licking at it furiously.

"Not cheap," said Cooley. "Gun and case, suppressor, ammo, tax. Run you close to a thousand dollars."

"Except this one isn't new."

Cooley lifted the scope to his eye. "Even used isn't going to come cheap."

Duke wrestled Howdy for the spoon. "So, what's a low-end Sherlock like Stan Greeley doing with a high-end sniper rifle?"

Thumps put the parts back in the case. "Curiouser and curiouser."

"*Alice in Wonderland*," said Cooley. "All we need is a white rabbit."

"What are we going to do with Elmer and Elroy?"

"In the old days," said Cooley, "they used to hang horse thieves."

Duke put the peanut butter jar and the spoon back in the drawer. Howdy leaned against the side of the desk, a forlorn look on his face, sad noises in his throat.

"BLA," said Duke. "Unless you've got a better idea."

"The Black Liberation Army?"

"Best left alone," said Duke. "Do you have any idea of the aggravation and the paperwork that would be involved in prosecuting Elmer and Elroy? First, we'd have to get one of the car owners to press charges. Do we have any complaints at present?"

"Nope," said Cooley. "Nothing but happy customers."

"And," said Duke, "by the time the case made it to court . . ."

Thumps rubbed his ear. "So, the question is were the cars stolen or were they simply taken in for repairs and cleaning?"

"Chicken and the egg," said Cooley.

"Best thing to do," said Duke, "is eat a doughnut, drink a cup of coffee."

Cooley tapped his forehead. "Almost forgot. Beth called. Wants you to stop in."

"She means you," said Duke. "I'm still on leave."

"Then why'd you come in?"

"For the doughnuts," said the sheriff. "And to drop off the dog."

"No can do," said Thumps. "Can't take a dog to a morgue. It's a sterile environment. Beth would have my hide."

"DreadfulWater . . ."

"And before I forget, Fancy Whelan is thinking she might want to be a deputy."

Duke grunted. "Dumbo's niece? The one who runs the shop?"

"I figure if she can deal with Morris," said Thumps, "she can deal with hardened criminals."

"Not a bad idea," said Cooley. "She sort of scares me in the same way my aunt scares me."

"Roxanne scares everyone," said Duke.

"I suggested that she do a ride-along," said Thumps. "See what the work is like."

"You're in charge."

"What does that mean?"

"It means you're in charge." Duke stood, hitched his belt, grabbed the leash. "Me and Howdy have to go find a grassy knoll."

"What do you want me to do with the sniper rifle?" said Cooley.

Duke turned. "Just before you see me bend over to pick up his shit in a little bag," said the sheriff, "shoot me."

17

The old Land Titles office was a two-storey brick building. Beth Mooney lived in an apartment on the second floor. Her doctor's office was on the first floor. The basement was reserved for the county morgue. There was a panel with three buzzers near the front door. Each time Thumps came to call, he would start with the buzzer for the apartment and hope for the best.

Then he'd try the doctor's office buzzer.

He did his best to avoid the buzzer for the basement.

When he was a cop, he had seen his fair share of bodies. But he had never gotten used to the idea of death. Especially violent death, where a life was ripped away, an existential snatch and grab. Accidents, manslaughters, murders, none of it made sense.

In each instance, someone's child lost.

So, the button for the apartment first. If Beth was there, they could sit in her living room, and she could tell him, in an airy and civilized space, over a cup of coffee, what it was she had discovered.

Silence.

Okay. Thumps moved his finger to his second choice. Beth's doctor's office wasn't as nice as the apartment, and it didn't have a coffee machine, but it was preferable to the basement.

Again, silence.

Reluctantly, Thumps pressed the third button. There was a momentary twinkling of hope, and then the door clicked open.

THERE WERE TWO ways to get into Beth's basement. There were the bay doors at the back of the building that opened onto the alley through which Beth could offload supplies and bring in bodies. And there was a set of metal stairs that ran down from just inside the front door.

There was no quiet way to come down the stairs. The steel treads echoed with each footfall, sounding for the world as though you were walking to an execution.

"About time."

Beth was standing next to the stainless-steel table. Stan Greeley was lying on the table. Thumps had read any number of novels in which dead bodies looked as though they were asleep. Or at peace.

Greeley didn't look at peace. He looked dead, his chest spread open, the top of his head cut away.

Thumps leaned against the pillar.

"You okay?"

"Fine."

"If you pass out again," said Beth, "I'm not picking you up."

Thumps took several deep breaths. Which was the wrong thing to do. Morgues and hospitals had much the same smells. A cornucopia of cloying decay with a bright antiseptic aftertaste.

Thumps steadied himself. “Okay, what did you find?”

Beth wiped her hands on her apron, went to her desk, came back with several swatches.

“I’m going to paint the place, but I can’t decide on a colour.”

“You dragged me down here to help you choose a paint colour?”

“Gabby’s lobbying for the seafoam green.”

“It’s a morgue,” said Thumps. “Paint it black.”

Beth set the swatches down next to Greeley. “Just for that, you don’t get a vote.”

Thumps turned toward the stairs. “I’ll see myself out.”

Beth smiled. “There is one other thing.”

Thumps turned back. “Greeley was murdered?”

“Murdered?” Beth rolled her eyes. “No, the man wasn’t murdered. He died of a traumatic brain injury. Like I thought.”

“Okay.”

“And he also had serious cataracts.”

“Cataracts?”

“Not to mention severe myopia and macular degeneration.”

“He couldn’t see?”

Beth shrugged. “Not all that well. With the cataracts, he was, I imagine, seeing double most of the time.”

Thumps shifted from one foot to the other. “So, he’d have difficulty looking through a pair of binoculars.”

“Absolutely.”

“What about a rifle scope?”

Beth put her hands on her hips. “You going to tell me what’s going on?”

“Greeley had a sniper rifle,” said Thumps. “In the trunk of his rental.”

“And you want to know if he could see well enough to use it.”

"I do."

"Well," said Beth. "If someone was shooting at me with a sniper rifle, I'd want it to be our Mr. Greeley."

WHEN THUMPS CAME out the door of the old Land Titles building, he paused to bask in the fresh air and bright sunshine. Such things, he reminded himself, should not be taken for granted. Beth could paint her basement any colour she liked. It would still be a creepy crypt awash in mouldering body fluids.

Thumps wondered if smells were toxic, if he was putting his health at risk each time he ventured into the morgue. Then again, it was probably no more hazardous than spending time with Cisco Cruz. The man from Pie Town had put him in any number of dicey situations, almost got him shot on at least two occasions.

Were there more than two?

Probably.

And now Cruz was back in town. This time with one Nora Gage in tow. A retired customs agent, if Thumps was willing to believe the story. Nora Gage, who rents a house, borrows a dog, and promptly disappears after Stan Greeley stumbles off a short cliff in the dark.

Stan of the bad eyesight. Stan for whom looking through a pair of binoculars would have been a chore. Stan of the sniper rifle, who wouldn't have been able to hit the sky on a cloudless day.

Of course, there was nothing to say that the rifle was Greeley's. Sure, it was in the trunk of his car, but the car was a rental. Maybe the renter before him had been a hit man who had completed his task, left the weapon behind. Jason Bourne? Agent 47? The Bride?

Get a grip.

Thumps took out his phone. Cooley answered on the second ring.

"Sheriff's office. Deputy Peacekeeper Small Elk."

"Deputy what?"

"Deputy Peacekeeper," said Cooley. "Deanna figured that we're probably the only sheriff's department outside some of the reservations that has three Indigenous deputies."

Thumps waited.

"So she thought we might want to get creative," said Cooley. "I wanted to go with 'Warrior.' You know, Warrior Small Elk at your service. But Deanna said it sounded aggressive and blindingly male."

"Okay."

"She said 'Peacekeeper' sounded intelligent and considered. What do you think?"

"You run it by Duke?"

"Not yet," said Cooley. "Thought I'd try it out on you."

Thumps lay the phone against his forehead for a moment. "Greeley's car rented from the airport?"

"It was," said Cooley.

"Can you check with them, find out who rented that car before Greeley?"

"Before? Wait. You thinking it wasn't Greeley's rifle?"

"Just crossing the t's."

"Hey," said Cooley. "Maybe it was John Wick."

Nora Gage. Cisco Cruz. Nothing about the case made much sense. If it was even a case. Greeley's death had been an unfortunate accident. A lot of forest and no trees.

Time to find a tree and shake it.

"Tell Deanna to keep on Nora Gage."

"You want me to call you Sheriff Peacekeeper?"

"I do not."

"Amazing," said Cooley. "That's exactly what Deanna said you'd say."

18

The problem with shaking a tree to see what might fall out was that Thumps didn't have a tree. Greeley was dead. Nora Gage was in the wind, and Cruz was his normal obstinate and irritating self. Trying to make sense of the flustercluck made his head hurt.

What was it that Ora Mae had said? That he'd be surprised who had bought houses in Ironstone River Estates? Was the woman bragging or was she offering him a clue?

Okay, maybe he'd start with a shrubbery.

At one point, all public records were kept at the old Land Titles building, the building that Beth had bought and converted into an apartment, her medical office, and the county morgue.

Now, the county recorder's office was on the second floor of the new city hall, in a nondescript room that smelled of flowers on the turn. There was a long counter that cut the room in half, a barricade of sorts to keep the public on one side and the keepers of titles on the other.

The man sitting at the desk reminded Thumps of a chubby owl. Glasses, large eyes, a beak of a mouth. Bow tie that hung under a double chin like a dead mouse.

"Yes."

Thumps held up his badge. "I need some information on house sales."

The man didn't look up, stayed hunched over his keyboard. "Go to property.mt.gov, find the proper form, fill it out."

The name plate on the desk said "Raymond Hooper."

There was a name that rang alarm bells. "You related to Andy Hooper?"

Hooper looked up. Saw Thumps for the first time. "My cousin. Wait. You the guy cost him his job?"

Andy Hooper had been Duke's deputy when Thumps arrived in town. Andy had been all blue skies and empty spaces. Local sports hero with the brains of a football. Thought the badge and the gun made him special.

"Police work wasn't his calling," said Thumps. "He still selling cars?"

Hooper stood, came to the counter. "He got canned from that too. Asshole has been mooching off me and my wife, living in our basement, eating our food."

"Ah," said Thumps.

"All he does is watch TV and complain," said Hooper. "World's against him. Nothing is his fault. Could I lend him a hundred."

"So, he's still in town."

Hooper's face broke into a grin. "Nope. I was saved by reality TV."

Thumps put his hands on the counter and pushed. The thing was sturdier than it looked.

"Raggedy Andy started watching those reality shows on gold mining. Figured it looked easy enough, so he jumped in his car and headed up to Alaska." Hooper began bobbing his head. "And you know what? I gave him the money for the gas."

Thumps gave the counter another shove, felt it move.

"You want to stop that."

"What happens when he returns?"

Hooper pushed the counter back into position. "You burn enough bridges, you don't get to come back."

Thumps suspected that these sorts of pronouncements were wishful thinking. Burn enough bridges, and the Andys of the world would just wade into the water and float home.

"Let me guess," said Hooper. "You don't want to fill out forms."

"1492 River View Road," said Thumps. "Save me a lot of time if I could take a quick look at the records."

"Ironstone River Estates? Now there's a can of worms."

"Flood plain."

Hooper shook his head. "That's not going to stop the fat cats. They got too much money sunk into that hole. Flips will be worth millions."

"Flips?"

"Some of the houses out at Ironstone were bought by individuals, retirees for the most part. Made a little money while they were working. Want their piece of heaven. But most of the properties were snatched up by corporations."

"Corporations?"

"It should be illegal," said Hooper, "but it's not."

"Okay."

"So, one corporation buys a fancy house, and it sells it to another corporation for a nice profit, and that corporation turns around and sells it back to the first corporation for an even bigger profit. You keeping up?"

"The corporations sell back and forth between themselves."

"Price keeps going up," said Hooper. "Suddenly, that house in Ironstone that was selling for half a million is now going for over a million."

Thumps took a long breath. "And along comes a buyer other than the corporation, who winds up paying the inflated price?"

"Bingo," said Hooper. "Really screws up the economy for the rest of us. House prices go up in Ironstone, they begin to go up in town as well. Bubble swells, people mortgage their lives to buy a place, and then, bang, the bubble bursts, and the foreclosures begin."

Hooper shook his head.

"And guess who buys up all the bankruptcies? Just in time for the cycle to begin again."

Thumps thought about giving the counter a really good shove, but resisted. "How many houses in the development are owned by corporations?"

"You got two types. You got the big corporations. Insurance, hedge funds, private equity. They're the real problem, the ones that manipulate the market."

Hooper hit a couple of keys, pointed to the screen.

"Then you got the small corporations."

"Cardoza Enterprises?"

"Dolores Cardoza," said Hooper. "The insurance lady. These corporations are fairly easy to figure out. Bunch of sole proprietorships. For instance, Aegean AK is the bookstore guy."

"Archimedes Kousoulas?"

"Owns that restaurant as well," said Hooper. "And this one? BT Group? That's our idiot mayor, Barney Tingle. Uses his own initials."

"And the address I gave you?"

"That place is owned by VR Inc."

Thumps stared at the screen. "We know who owns VR Inc.?"

Hooper pushed his glasses up his nose. "Imagine you can figure that out for yourself."

"Shit."

"Shit, indeed," said Hooper.

Thumps set his hat on his head. "Thanks for the help."

Hooper nodded. "Andy said when he strikes it rich, he's going to buy me a new pickup. You think I should start looking?"

Thumps tried a smile, but his heart wasn't in it. "You might want to wait for the new model year."

"Yeah," said Hooper. "That's what I figured."

SHADOW RANCH WAS a sprawling complex banked against the western slope of the foothills. No matter how many times Thumps had been to the resort, he was always surprised to come up over the rise and see it all alone on the prairies, looking for the world like the set for an epic western.

Or the long-lost city of an alien civilization.

The resort included a four-star hotel, a Las Vegas–style nightclub, a family water park, tennis courts, riding stables, a skeet-shooting range, along with a championship eighteen-hole golf course.

The only thing the place didn't have was a casino. Vernon

Rockland, lord and master of the manor, had been trying to get a gambling licence ever since Shadow Ranch opened its doors, but to no avail.

The tribe had the only casino in the area. Buffalo Mountain was on tribal land and technically not subject to the state regulations or oversight, and Rockland had argued long and loud that this was unfair, his favourite mantra being "a level playing field."

Not that the playing field had ever been level.

But now that it had tipped slightly in favour of Native people, the Vernon Rocklands of the world, who had always enjoyed doing business on a slant, were irate to find themselves labouring across flat ground.

So, if you wanted to throw your money away on bad odds and fast dice, you had to drive up to Buffalo Mountain.

But if your idea of fun was chasing a little white ball over hill and dale, chunking it in and out of sand traps, losing it in water hazards and deep rough, then Shadow Ranch and the South Forty was for you.

THE U.S. OPEN qualifying tournament had drawn golfers and fans alike, and the parking lot at Shadow Ranch was filled beyond capacity. Thumps did one circuit, in case there was a space that had been missed, and then pulled the cruiser into the loading zone near the front door to the resort.

Official business had its privileges.

He walked straight through the lobby, past the hotel reception desk, down a long hallway with "Corporate Offices" stencilled on the glass.

"Welcome to Shadow Ranch." The woman was all smiles. "How may I help you?"

There were offices off to the side, all with glass walls. Thumps could see people at their desks, people walking around, people on telephones. It was like standing in an aquarium.

Thumps nodded. "This all new?"

"It is," said the woman. "We're in a contemporary business world, and that world is a world of glass."

"You can see everyone."

"Transparency," said the woman. "I am told the goal is transparency."

Thumps took a moment to check the enclosures. "Don't see Vernon."

"Do you have an appointment with Mr. Rockland?"

"Official business." Thumps showed his badge.

"The nature of the business?"

"Official."

The smile faded. "So," said the woman, "no transparency?"

"None whatsoever," said Thumps.

VERNON ROCKLAND'S NEW office was behind panelled walls and heavy wood doors. The only glass in the room was the long window that looked out onto the eighteenth green.

"Just had a call from security." Rockland held out a hand. "Said there was a police vehicle in the loading zone."

"That would be me."

"Wanted to know if they should tow it." Rockland smiled. "I told them to leave it be."

"Appreciate that."

"How's Duke doing?"

"Resting," said Thumps. "Healing."

"So, can we count on the sheriff's office to help with tournament security?"

"Don't have the manpower," said Thumps.

"So, serve and protect doesn't extend to successful businesses and major sporting events?"

Rockland's desk was perched on a low riser, giving the man the impression that he was larger than life.

"Ah," said Rockland, "you want tickets to the tournament."

"Nope."

"Good, because we're sold out." Rockland leaned back in the chair. "But I'm glad you're here. Wanted to talk to you about the fall program."

Thumps waited.

"Long and the short of it is, I may not be able to offer you a show this year. I mean your last show did fine, but architectural photography isn't what it used to be."

"I do landscape."

"You know what's hot right now?" Rockland made a sour mouth. "Cellphone photographs. Good friend of mine manages the Brown Palace in Denver. He's been after me to give his niece a show here at the Ranch. She does cellphone photos of people walking down the street. Big blow-ups of their feet."

"Feet?"

"And in colour." Rockland held his arms out to show how helpless he was in the matter. "Who is going to buy a colour mural of feet?"

Thumps nodded. In some ways not having to put a show together was something of a relief. He hadn't really done any new photography for a while, and the time it took to select and print and mat and frame each photograph for a show was daunting.

He wasn't even sure that he still had the enthusiasm and drive. He suspected that he was a dinosaur. Landscape photography? Black and white? With a large-format field camera? Sheet film?

And while he was sure that cellphone photos of feet weren't the answer, he was intrigued to see what another imagination might do with such a subject.

"I know that's disappointing," said Rockland. "But maybe we can put something together next spring."

"Didn't come about golf or photography." Thumps waited a beat. "Came about Ironstone River Estates."

"Ironstone?"

"You own property there, don't you?" Thumps watched Rockland's face. "VR Inc.? That's you, isn't it. Vernon Rockland Incorporated?"

Thumps waited another beat, and then kept going.

"A house. Nice place on the river. 1492 River View Road. But you're not living there right now. I figure it's an investment. Or maybe a retirement place."

Rockland seemed to shrink just a little. "There a problem?"

"And in the meantime, while you wait for the powers that be to solve the flood plain issue, you rent the place out."

"Sounds like there's a problem."

"Nora Gage. Cisco Cruz."

Rockland opened his mouth. Thumps held up a hand.

"You're probably going to say that you don't know a Nora

Gage or a Cisco Cruz. And you're going to tell me this because Cruz told you that Gage was a matter of national security. Or something along those lines."

"DreadfulWater—"

"But you see, I've got a dead body on my hands, and while it appears that my corpse died of somewhat natural causes, as an officer of the law, I have to do a complete and thorough investigation."

"Look, if I could help you, I—"

"And as part of that investigation, I need to talk to Ms. Gage. But I can't find her. She seems to have disappeared. Where could she have gone?"

Rockland sunk a little further into his chair.

"But then I realize that the guy who rented the house to Gage also owns a large luxury resort with many rooms. And I say to myself, maybe my person of interest has been moved to the resort."

Thumps sat back, waited to see who was going to blink first.

"And since I only have two deputies, searching the place room by room could take a while. We'd do the search professionally, of course."

Rockland came forward in the chair. "You wouldn't do that."

"Yes," said Thumps. "I would."

"What if I gave you my word that your person of interest isn't here?"

"We'd probably start with the condos and work our way to the main building."

Rockland turned, looked out the window at the eighteenth green with its little flag and the prairie beyond. Then he turned back, picked up a pen. "You know," he said, "I liked you a hell of a lot better when you were just a photographer."

19

The newest addition to Shadow Ranch was the Venezia, a cluster of upscale villas set on an irrigation ditch that snaked its way through the complex. If he squinted and suspended his disbelief, Thumps could imagine a resemblance to Venice.

Not the one in Italy. The one in California.

Palazzo Veneziano was at the far end of the Venezia, just before everything ran off onto the prairies. Stucco exterior in earth colours, with brightly painted shutters and flower boxes under the windows.

The doorbell was in the shape of a small pineapple. Or a tiny meatball.

"Knock, knock."

Thumps glanced at the ditch-cum-canal. There was artificial grass along the bank, plastic water lilies in plastic pots sunk into the water, and three rusty metal herons at the ready, in case a school of ceramic fish came swimming by.

"Don't make me huff and puff."

The door stayed shut. "Go away."

"Not happening." Thumps pressed the doorbell again. A tinkling rendition of "Santa Lucia."

"I could shoot you."

"Open the door, Cisco."

More "Santa Lucia." Followed by the sound of the deadbolt being retracted. Thumps pushed the door open the rest of the way and stepped inside. Cruz was standing in the shadows of the hall, a gun at his side.

"Is that the new Glock?"

"Sig Sauer," said Cruz. "If you stop stepping on your dick, I'll get you one."

"Stop lying to me," said Thumps. "And leave my dick out of this."

"*Cabrón*, you're taking this acting sheriff thing much too seriously."

"I've got a dead guy in the morgue and a whole bunch of questions."

"Hello, Mr. DreadfulWater." Nora Gage appeared in the kitchen, a cup in her hand. "You're quite the persistent fellow."

Cruz quickly shut the door. "Anyone follow you?"

"And who would be following me?"

"There's coffee," said Gage. "Beer in the fridge."

Palazzo Veneziano was a one-bedroom suite. Italian villa facade with a Holiday Inn interior. Particle-board sofa with matching chairs, tables with glass tops and pot-metal legs, flat-screen television, prints of famous paintings in plastic frames on the walls.

All the ambience of a fast-food drive-through.

Cruz kept his pistol at his side. "What the hell are you doing here?"

Thumps walked past Cruz into the kitchen, stopped in front of Gage. "You and I need to have a conversation."

Gage looked at Cruz.

"Don't look at Cisco," said Thumps. "Look at me."

"*Pendejo.* You need to leave this thing alone."

"Sure," said Thumps, "just as soon as you tell me what this *thing* is."

"I'm not sure I see your concern," said Gage. "Have I committed a crime?"

"I've got a dead body," said Thumps. "Which means I can hold the two of you without charges for seventy-two hours."

Cruz tried a hard stare. "You don't want to do that."

"Yes, I do."

Gage took her coffee to the sofa, sat down.

"All right, Mr. DreadfulWater," she said. "I'll answer your questions."

"Truthfully?"

Gage smiled. "You'll have to be the judge of that."

Cruz put his pistol back in its holster. "You don't have to do this."

Gage put her cup on the end table. "We don't want Mr. DreadfulWater banging about. There's no telling what he might run into in the dark."

"Your call." Cruz turned, headed for the door. "I'm going to mingle. See what I can see."

Gage waited until she heard the door shut. Then she waited some more.

"Mind me asking what Mr. Cruz has told you?"

"That's not how this works." Thumps waited for a moment. "Let's start with Stan Greeley."

Gage didn't flinch. "Who?"

"The man we found behind the house you were renting."

"Ah," said Gage. "Our Mr. Brown."

"Turns out he was a private investigator," said Thumps. "But I imagine that Cruz has told you this already."

Gage waited.

"Greeley is dead," said Thumps. "Traumatic brain injury."

"From the fall?"

"Probably," said Thumps. "Question is, why was he there in the first place? Why would someone hire a gumshoe from Great Falls to watch you?"

"Too bad we can't ask Mr. Greeley," said Gage.

Thumps waited.

"I suppose," said Gage, "that Mr. Cruz told you about Black Ice."

Thumps kept the surprise to himself. He knew that name. Couldn't remember where. He went through the alphabet, hoping one of the letters would trigger a memory.

"Are you all right?"

"Peachy." Thumps helped himself to one of the wingback chairs. "Yes, let's start there."

"Are you a student of history, Mr. DreadfulWater?"

"Can't say that I am."

"What do you know about chaos?"

"Don't suppose we're talking about Eris, the Greek goddess of chaos, strife, and discord, daughter of Zeus and Hera?"

"I was thinking more along the lines of a tornado. Or a hurricane. Amazing the destruction there is in wind. Can't do much about it, but sometimes you can see it coming."

"Gives you time to hunker down."

"That's one response," said Gage. "You can hunker down,

ride it out. You can get out of the way. Or, you can get flattened."

Thumps looked out the sliding glass doors at the prairie sky. There was a hawk off in the distance, circling. Or maybe it was a vulture.

"Our tornado was 9/11. We didn't see it coming, and we got flattened. Our immediate response was to create the Department of Homeland Security, whose main activity was to absorb existing departments and to create new ones to try to deal with the new world reality.

"I was in customs at the time. We were one of the agencies that got absorbed. I wound up getting seconded."

"Black Ice."

Thumps expected that saying the name out loud would do the trick. He even tried to picture it in his mind. The answer was there. He could see it lurking in the shadows, at the edge of his vision.

"We didn't call ourselves that," said Gage. "Not in the beginning."

"Guessing Black Ice wasn't involved in winter road maintenance."

"As it turned out, that's where the name came from. One of our number was involved in a fender bender on the beltway. Area was hit by an ice storm. All day long, the weather people talked about black ice this and black ice that, how it was dangerous, because you couldn't see it. And our forensic accountant said, 'Hey, that's us, dangerous and invisible,' and the name stuck."

"A bit melodramatic."

"Indeed." Gage smiled. "Especially since all we did was gather information, pass the information on, go back and gather some more. Worker bees bringing pollen back to the hive."

"Ever wonder what happened to the information?"

"You mean how it was used?"

"Must have been curious."

"Wasn't paid to be curious."

Gage went to the refrigerator, brought out a plate of fruit, set it on the coffee table between them, along with a bottle of sparkling wine.

"Compliments of the management." Gage set the bottle off to one side. "Who drinks this crap?"

Thumps helped himself to a handful of grapes. Gage picked out a chocolate-coated strawberry.

"There were eight of us in the beginning. Five men, three women. Names aren't important. Everybody had more than one skill set. International finance, forensic accounting, cryptography, hard sciences, computers, psychology. Most of us spoke one or two other languages. Arabic, Russian, Korean, Japanese, Chinese, Spanish, French. One of the guys was a Go master. One of the women was a world-class hacker."

"Sounds like a bad movie."

"But then all that changes. In 2005, Tom Ridge steps down, and Michael Chertoff takes over. Shuffle, shuffle, shuffle, and suddenly, our little room in the basement gets a new team leader and a new mandate."

"So, you guys analyzed tornadoes."

"Yes, Mr. DreadfulWater," said Gage. "And then we began to create them."

There were individually wrapped wedges of cheese in with the fruit. Thumps picked one up and squeezed it. Nothing on the wrapper to tell him what kind of cheese it was. It could be a soft havarti or a brie. Then again it could be something smelly and runny.

"Sorin Dalca," said Gage. "Romanian expat. Ph.D. in mathematics and game theory. When he arrived in late 2006, our mission changed. We continued to gather the raw data, but under Sorin, we began to generate our own vortexes."

"Prospero conjuring up a storm."

Gage took another strawberry. "You might suppose that most of our attention was focused on terrorist groups and drug cartels, the poster boys for American paranoia. And you'd be right. We certainly had a good time throwing sand into their gearboxes. But along the way, we discovered that an equally potent threat to national security was coming from our own corporations."

"The military-industrial complex."

"Such a liar, Mr. DreadfulWater," said Gage. "You *are* a student of history."

Thumps unwrapped the cheese. It wasn't havarti, and it wasn't one of those French abominations. It was a rubbery lump of off-white plasticine, which reminded him of C-4.

"There has always been a problem with restricted technology making its way to bad actors. Weapon systems, artificial intelligence, biological agents, nuclear materials. Anything that has a military application. Some of this is straight theft. Spies, criminal organizations, individuals with an agenda."

Black Ice, Black Ice, Black Ice. Thumps could almost see it, as it ran across his memory.

"But the bulk of the restricted goodies are simply sold on the international black market." Gage took two grapes off the plate. "Let's say a large, well-known U.S. of A. corporation designs a new generation of drones with stealth technology, drones that have a greater range, drones that can carry a more lethal payload."

Gage set one grape in the middle of the table. "And the folks at Grape One are only too happy to sell our government as many drones as they like. But they can make more drones than the folks in Washington need."

"Hard to imagine."

Gage set the second grape next to the first.

"Grape One and Grape Two are the same corporation, but they have different customers and different revenue streams. Grape One reports profits, pays taxes. Grape Two hides profits in off-shore accounts and pays no taxes."

"Capitalism in action," said Thumps.

"It's illegal, of course. What Grape Two does. We make weapons of mass destruction to protect ourselves and friends. We don't make them to sell to our enemies, so they can be used against us."

"National security being more important than profits?"

"Your cynicism aside, the majority of corporations are both honest and ethical. More or less. But there are a select few who see the sale of contraband as a grey area. Or they simply ignore the rules and regulations altogether. What to do, what to do?"

"I'm guessing prosecuting them isn't an option?"

"God, no," said Gage. "Lawyers? Depositions? Courtrooms? Forensic accounting? Televised congressional hearings? It would take years. Besides, you don't want these industries crippled, you *want* them up and running."

Thumps felt his patriotism slipping away. "Where else would we get our bombs for peace?"

"Like it or not," said Gage, "in this country, national defence and corporate profits are an old married couple."

"And this . . . Sorin . . ."

"There was little to be gained in disturbing a perfectly good military-industrial complex and throwing workers out of jobs, just to punish a handful of greedy shits."

Gage picked up a strawberry, weighed it for a moment, put it back.

"What do you know about civil forfeiture laws?"

When he was a cop on the Northern California coast, Thumps had been involved in several cases that involved forfeiture. A fishing boat suspected of bringing in illegal aliens. A truck and trailer transporting marijuana. A warehouse filled with stolen electronics.

Gage rearranged herself on the sofa.

"Before 2000, forfeiture was pretty easy. You didn't have to charge someone with a crime. You didn't have to get a conviction. You just had to demonstrate, by the preponderance of evidence, that the property in question was legally forfeitable."

Gage began chuckling to herself, as though she remembered something humorous.

"The good old days. But in 2000, Congress enacted the Civil Asset Forfeiture Reform Act, the main feature of which was a series of protections. It didn't stop civil forfeiture by law enforcement, but it did provide some legal recourse for innocent individuals and companies who had lost property to the process."

Thumps leaned forward. "So, Black Ice began confiscating corporation property?"

"No," said Gage. "That would have taken too long, and it would have been visible and raised too many gnarly questions. But we applied the same principles. We went after the money. And the naughty boys made it easy for us. The legitimate money was in one set of accounts, while the money derived from illegal activities was in another set. The first was visible and known. The second was secret and out of sight."

"So, you hacked into these accounts and what, took the money?"

"You're probably thinking of the concept of due process," said Gage, "which doesn't apply in most forfeiture cases. Besides, who was going to complain? Exactly how would you explain to the authorities that someone had taken the money you made through an illegal activity?"

"What happened to the money?"

"Sorin Dalca." Gage paused, let the name hang. "Dalca created something he liked to call the Vault. It was a bank for all intents and purposes, a place to hold the money that was confiscated. Until such time as we could get a legal decision on what should be done with it."

"And you were in no hurry to do that."

Thumps had to admit that the idea had its appeal. Powerful people were well protected. Going to court, even with a strong case, would have been an uphill battle. In all but the most egregious cases, a deal would be made that involved a fine and a firm lecture on the importance of ethical business practices.

"The government has used forfeiture to cripple terrorist groups and drug cartels for years. Can't tell you the number of bank accounts we froze, the real estate we confiscated, the cars and boats and planes we seized. Sorin had us apply the same principles and methodology to target corporations."

"How much money are we talking about?"

Gage gestured to the plate. "Please," she said. "I'll never finish it on my own."

"Stan Greeley rented a car." Thumps waited for Gage to catch up with the non sequitur. "In the trunk, we found a sniper rifle."

Gage sat back, put her hands in her lap. "My, but you do have a gift for burying the lede."

Thumps picked out a large strawberry, bit it in half.

"You're telling me you think someone wants me dead."

"And just why would someone want you dead?"

Gage yawned, rubbed her eyes. "You know what? I'm old. I'm tired. I need to lie down. Can we continue this later? Does that work for you?"

Thumps stiffened.

"Don't worry," said Gage. "I promise not to disappear again. Besides, I suspect that even if I did, you would find me."

"Doesn't sound like you're giving me a choice."

Gage smiled. "No," she said, "I'm not."

20

Thumps was glad to be outside. The sky was high and blue, and the fresh air made him feel clean again. Sitting in the villa, listening to Gage explain covert government agencies and their rationales had been like sitting in a grubby theatre, watching a World War II propaganda film on civics and patriotism.

Thumps wasn't a pedant. He knew that the law had spongy edges, places where it would bend, areas that were in shadows. Lines in the sand that were drawn, erased, redrawn, and then erased again.

Gage had been candid about Black Ice and guarded at the same time. She had told him just enough to stimulate his imagination, and then left him hanging.

Oneirataxia.

Thumps had come across the word in a novel, had had to look it up. The inability to tell fantasy from reality. The next time he talked with Gage, he'd watch for an opening, drop it into a sentence, watch for ripples.

Secret government agencies. Covert activities. Bad guys, good guys, money, money, money. Thumps suspected that much of what Gage had told him was true, and much of it was false. The truth and the lies so tightly wrapped around each other that you couldn't find where the twisty thing began or ended.

A Gordian knot.

Maybe he could play the part of Alexander. Maybe Cruz could be the sharp sword.

But first he had to find the man from Pie Town.

A few years back, Vernon Rockland had torn down the old pro shop and built a combination pro shop and restaurant with windows that overlooked a new practice facility, complete with a putting green, bunkers, and a driving range.

The practice area was crowded. Golfing enthusiasts were milling about, watching the tournament players chip, putt, and hit golf balls into the late morning. There was a full house on the restaurant patio, more people drinking beer, eating french fries, telling golf stories about the time they were this close to Tiger Woods at the British Open or how they were greenside at the 2012 Masters when Bubba Watson hooked a wedge shot out of the pines and onto the green in his sudden death playoff with Louis Oosthuizen.

THAT SUMMER INTO the fall, Gabriel Garcia took the time to teach Thumps the game of golf.

"It's dead easy," Garcia told him. "Get the ball from the tee to the hole. Doesn't much matter how you do it. Hit it straight, hook it, slice it, top it. Hit a tree, bounce it off a cart path, skip it across a pond, run it through a sand trap. Drive it, chip it, putt it. Keep track of each stroke. Person with the lowest number of strokes wins."

Thumps enjoyed the driver best of all, the thrill of hitting the ball flush and watching it sail off into the sky.

"Driving's a lot of fun," Garcia told him. "But it's the putter that's money."

Garcia had caddied for some of the big names in the game. He had photos of himself with Arnold Palmer, Lee Trevino, Payne Stewart, Raymond Floyd.

"I wasn't their every-tournament caddy. I was the go-to guy when their regular caddy wasn't available."

"Like a substitute teacher."

"Yeah," said Garcia, "like that."

Each evening, after the golf course cleared, Thumps would practise hitting balls over the cyclone fence onto the green. Then he'd crawl through the hole in the wire, retrieve the balls, and do it again.

"Mr. Thumps."

Chintak Rawat and Stas Black Weasel materialized from the crowd. Wearing their Team Wutty T-shirts.

"You are not wearing your T-shirt."

Thumps tried to remember where he had put the T-shirt. In a drawer? In the laundry? "I'm on duty."

"Of course," said Rawat. "To wear the T-shirt while on duty would be inappropriate."

"Wutty is on driving range," said Stas. "We are to help him with game."

"The two of you?"

"I am bodyguard," said Stas.

"Wutty needs a bodyguard?"

"He is celebrity," said Stas. "Rawat is caddy."

Thumps looked at Rawat. The pharmacist was a slight man with dark hair and an easy smile.

"Rawat is champion golfer when he is in India," said the big Russian.

"Junior champion," said Rawat. "But when my father died, I had to give the game up and find a career."

"Which wasn't golf."

Rawat shook his head. "Sadly, I wasn't good enough to compete at the highest level. But I will be a most excellent caddy."

"We must go," said Stas. "Watch Wutty hit balls, offer advice, do the cheer, encourage confidence."

Thumps hitched his pants. "You think he has a chance?"

"In golf," said Rawat, as he and Stas started off for the driving range, "anything is possible."

ONE EVENING, IN the early fall, Garcia came out to where Thumps was hitting balls over the fence.

"Let's go."

"Where?"

Garcia dragged his set of clubs through the hole in the cyclone fence and down the fourteenth fairway. Thumps followed behind.

"We're not supposed to be here."

"No one's on the course," said Garcia. "They're all at the clubhouse, drinking and watching the Ryder Cup."

Garcia set a ball on a tee and stepped back.

"Okay," he said, "show me what you got."

The fourteenth hole was a par four, 395-yard, dogleg left with a small creek that crossed the fairway 225 yards off the tee.

"Golf is about decisions," said Garcia. "Which club to hit off the tee is the first one you have to make. If you think you can hit it straight and clear the creek, use the driver. If you're worried you can't carry the creek, then lay up with the three-wood or a long iron."

"I'll hit driver."

"Just because it's in your bag doesn't mean you have to use it."

Thumps didn't catch the ball cleanly. It landed short of the creek, rolled down the bank and into the water.

"Risk and reward," said Garcia. "Try again."

Thumps hit the driver again, this time clearing the hazard and landing in the middle of the fairway.

"Okay," said Garcia. "Just one shot too late."

The lie was good. From here, the course ran uphill to the green. Thumps could see the top of the flag.

"It's 145 yards," said Garcia. "It's an elevated green, so you're going to have to carry the ball all the way."

Thumps's second shot landed in a greenside bunker.

"Didn't plug," said Garcia, "but you don't have much green to work with."

The third shot was a blast out of the sand that sailed over the green and disappeared into the thick rough near the fence. The fourth shot dribbled onto the green, and Thumps two-putted from there for a six.

"Double bogey," said Garcia. "See how much fun golf is? Let's try it again."

• • •

CRUZ WASN'T ON the patio drinking beer, and he wasn't hanging around the driving range watching the golfers practise. There was a large merchandise tent that had been set up behind the pro shop. If he couldn't find the ninja assassin, he could at least look at the latest equipment that manufacturers had to offer.

Cruz was at the Callaway display, a driver in hand.

"Took you long enough."

"You play?"

Cruz gave the club a couple of waggles. "You must be kidding. Five hours of your life wasted chasing a ball around a field? Only thing more boring is cricket."

"And where did you play cricket?"

Cruz put the club back, stepped over to the TaylorMade display, helped himself to an iron.

"And the equipment." Cruz gripped the club, lined up an imaginary shot. "Every year, the manufacturers bring out a new line of drivers and irons guaranteed to have you hitting the ball farther and straighter."

Thumps took a three-wood off the display. It was lighter than he remembered.

"So how come in the last twenty years, the average score of the average golfer hasn't gone down a single stroke?"

"Equipment's better," said Thumps, "the golfers are the same."

Cruz put the club back. "All this shit is like cellphones and cars. Each new model is supposed to be light years ahead of the last, but in reality, they're just the same old, same old, but in higher heels and a shorter skirt."

There was a price list. Thumps read it a second time. Someone had to have made a mistake.

Cruz strolled over to an Astroturf green, selected a putter from the rack, rounded up four balls.

"With putters," said Cruz, "you're mostly paying for the brand. This Scotty Cameron is six hundred dollars. That Odyssey over there is three hundred."

Cruz stroked a putt that rolled out across the carpet, broke a little left, and curled into the hole.

"To hear golfers talk about putters, you'd think they were Harry Potter wands that you can wave over your game."

"We need to talk."

"Don't you want to hear my treatise on golf balls?"

THE SECOND TIME, Thumps hit a three-wood off the tee. The ball landed well short of the creek.

"Longer shot into the green," said Gabriel, "but it's uphill. Hit a long iron into the slope and let it run out."

"What about the sand traps?"

"Hit it straight," said Gabriel.

His second shot was well struck, and as the ball rocketed toward the hole, Thumps was sure it was going to carry over the putting surface and wind up in the woods.

But it didn't.

As soon as the ball hit the false front, it lost all power, took one hop, and rolled out onto the green.

"Putting for birdie," said Gabriel. "All you have to do is make the putt."

Thumps didn't make the putt. The ball stopped well short of the hole. The next putt rolled past on the low side. The third putt found the bottom of the cup.

"Bogey," said Gabriel. "Don't let it go to your head."

THE RESTAURANT IN the main building at Shadow Ranch was surprisingly empty. Cruz grabbed a table for four by a window.

"Okay, so what did Gage tell you?"

"Sorry," said Thumps. "It's classified."

"Very funny." Cruz searched Thumps's face.

"She might have mentioned something called Black Ice."

"But you don't believe her."

"Secret agency. Secret agents. Secret projects." Thumps paused for effect. "Not a recipe for truth."

"No such thing in our business."

"And exactly what business is that?"

"You had lunch?" Cruz waved at a server. "I'm hungry."

Thumps waited while Cruz ordered coffee and a piece of pumpkin pie.

"Coffee and pumpkin pie isn't lunch."

Cruz spread a napkin on his lap. "You're just jealous 'cause you're diabetic."

WHEN THEY GOT back, Gabriel grabbed two soft drinks from his trailer, handed one to Thumps, eased himself into a folding chair under the sun awning.

"Careful with that one," said Gabriel. "It's got a wonky leg."

The chair tilted to one side, and Thumps had to lean to the right to keep it level.

"The top golfers make a good living." Gabriel took a sip. "The rest manage month to month."

"Not sure I want to be a golfer."

"Problem is," said Gabriel, "if you're born poor and raised poor, your choices are limited. All the talk about equal opportunities in America is bullshit."

"We're not that poor."

"You and your mom are living in a trailer park," said Gabriel. "Only thing below that is living in a car or living on the street."

"We do okay," said Thumps. "I'm going to get a job."

Gabriel took a long pull on his bottle. "You want half a chance in this life? Get an education. Get a decent job. You won't get rich, but you'll eat regular."

"What about you?"

Gabriel smiled. "I got a beat-to-shit pickup and a busted-up trailer, a bunch of framed photographs, and a set of golf clubs that I couldn't sell for a tank of gas. I'm a big success."

"You knew all the big names."

"Good stories," said Gabriel. "But they don't pay the bills."

THE FOOD ARRIVED. Cruz turned his attention to the pie. Thumps hadn't been hungry before, wasn't hungry now.

"This is great." Cruz took another bite. "There's nothing like good pumpkin pie."

But now he was. Not hungry. Just curious. Thumps picked up a fork, reached across the table.

"Hey." Cruz pulled the plate out of harm's way. "Get your own piece."

"It *is* good." Thumps licked the fork. "So, if you're not here to help with the real estate, you must be here for the money."

Cruz made Thumps wait while he drank his coffee, finished the pie. "All right," he said. "I'll read you in, but it doesn't go any further."

"Have to tell Duke," said Thumps. "And my team."

"Then I have nothing to say."

Thumps took a moment to get the server's attention. "How about I make some educated guesses."

"You're going to order a piece of pie, aren't you?"

Thumps settled in his chair, cleaned his fork with the napkin. "The answer to most of life's questions is pie."

"You know," said Cruz, "you are one annoying gringo."

21

Thumps was sure that pie was not the answer to much of anything. Still, Cruz was incredulous.

"Whipped cream *and* ice cream?"

"It's pumpkin pie," said Thumps.

"I didn't have any of that crap on mine."

Thumps twirled his fork in the cream. "Your loss."

"Diabetes?"

"That's what insulin is for."

Cruz made a face. "No. It's. Not."

Thumps could have had the chocolate cream pie. Now there was a mistake waiting to happen. Chocolate and cream. A sugar load if there ever was one. So, he had shown restraint. Pumpkin, after all, was a vegetable, and according to the experts, vegetables were supposed to make up half your plate.

And there it was. Half the plate, vegetable. The other half, dairy. End of discussion.

"How about we compare notes." Thumps took another bite of pie and whipped cream, loaded a bit of ice cream onto the end of the fork. "How about we start with Black Ice?"

"You first."

"Government program originally tasked with gathering information on any group that posed a threat to national security. Terrorists, drug cartels, right-wing militias, cyber criminals."

"Don't forget reality television."

"And in the course of their information gathering, Black Ice discovered that one of the greatest threats was coming from our own military-industrial complex, specifically large corporations who were selling restricted technologies to the Boris Badenovs and Natasha Fatales of the world."

Thumps helped himself to another bite of pie.

"Change of administration, change of mission. The technology leaks can't be allowed to continue, but no one wants to spark a public spectacle, so Black Ice is tasked with the job of quietly hacking into the secret slush funds of the naughty corporations and making off with their ill-gotten gains. A slap on the hands, if you will."

Cruz stayed stone-faced. "Gage *has* been chatty."

"Your turn," said Thumps.

Cruz shrugged. "It appears you know everything."

"And I'm guessing the reason that Gage told me as much as she did is because Black Ice has been . . . what . . . disbanded?"

"'Decommissioned' is the word you're looking for."

Thumps tapped his fork against the plate. "What happened to the rest of the team?"

"Classified."

"As in retired? Reassigned? Dead?"

"As in."

"And Sorin Dalca?"

"Jesus. She told you about Dalca?"

"She did."

"No comment."

"How much money are we talking about?"

"No comment."

"Wow," said Thumps. "That much."

The server came by with a fresh pot of coffee. Thumps thought Cruz might order a second piece of pie. With whipped cream and ice cream this time. But he didn't.

"Okay," said Thumps, "so what happened to the money that Black Ice confiscated?"

"Under civil forfeiture practices, monies from a forfeiture would normally go to the agency that initiated the action," said Cruz. "Or they might go into a general fund."

"Thank you for the textbook answer. Now, tell me about the Vault."

"You going to eat all that pie?"

"Sorin Dalca? The Vault? A shitload of money just sitting there?"

"If you don't eat it soon," said Cruz, "the ice cream is going to melt, and the crust is going to get soggy."

"Dalca would have access to that money." Thumps waited to see if Cruz wanted to jump in. "Who else?"

Cruz put down his fork, picked up a spoon. "See? Soggy."

"You're not going to help me, are you?"

"Hey, *jefe*," said Cruz. "Helping you is not my job."

"What I can't figure out is why Gage is here. Why you're here." Thumps watched Cruz's face for clues. "Hope you don't expect me to believe that you're assisting her with the vagaries of real estate."

Cruz shrugged. "Why can't that be a possibility?"

"Gage isn't in witness protection," said Thumps. "If she were, the Secret Service would be doing the heavy lifting."

"Why is everything with you so cloak and dagger?"

"How about this? After Black Ice was decommissioned, what did Gage do?"

"Retired."

"What? She sat around. Knitted socks for her nephews?"

"Don't think she has any nephews."

"You know, I'm happy to arrest you."

"Okay," said Cruz. "It's no secret. When Black Ice was decommissioned, Gage retired, started a small consulting business."

"Doing?"

"Cybersecurity. Company called Data Sentry Associates. Nothing big, but pleasantly lucrative."

Thumps rolled the name around in his head. "Data Sentry Associates? DSA? Like CIA or NSA?"

"Hadn't thought of it like that." Cruz helped himself to a forkful of Thumps's pie.

"Hey!"

Cruz nodded. "You're right. The whipped cream and ice cream really set the pumpkin off."

The pie, as it turned out, was a mistake. Thumps could feel the sugar begin to bloom in his body. Maybe letting Cruz poach his plate wasn't such a bad idea. He could disguise self-interest as generosity.

"So, Gage retires, starts a business." Thumps slid his plate over to Cruz. "Settles into a regular routine. Life is good. Life is stable."

"This for me?"

"It is," said Thumps. "And while you're eating that delicious pie, why don't you tell me what happened."

"So, this is a bribe?"

"Cruz . . ."

"Nothing happened," said Cruz. "D.C. is a shithole. Noise, traffic, poverty. Politicians, lawyers, lobbyists all screwing over the planet at the same time. Decided that she needed a change in geography."

"And her business? Data something?"

"Data Sentry Associates," said Cruz. "Sold it."

"Just like that."

"Packed her bags, jumped on a plane, and here she is. Woman always wanted to see the West. I told her to try Chinook. Home on the range. Buffalo roam. Land under starry skies above."

Thumps thought about taking the pie back. Just on general principles. He didn't want to eat it, but it made no sense to reward Cruz for sarcasm and bad behaviour.

"Something happened."

"Such as?"

"A woman like Nora Gage doesn't just cut and run." Thumps pointed his fork at Cruz. "You want to tell me what spooked her?"

Cruz held his hands out, palms up, to show he had nothing to hide, nothing up his sleeves.

"Not me you have to worry about," said Thumps. "It's Duke. Chinook's his town. He finds a rope lying around loose, he's likely to start pulling on it."

Cruz was grinning. "Is this going to be one of those western homilies I've heard so much about?"

"Best he doesn't find you on the other end."

"Christ," said Cruz, "you even sound like John Wayne."

Thumps was working on a clever retort when he felt his phone vibrate.

"DreadfulWater."

"Hey, boss, where are you?"

"Shadow Ranch. What's up?"

"You might think about meeting me at the airport," said Cooley. "Been following up on the car rental question."

"And I need to be there because?"

"Not exactly sure what I've got," said Cooley. "Thought you'd want to see it in person."

"But not a dead body."

"Nope," said Cooley. "Definitely not a dead body."

Thumps put the phone back in his pocket. Cruz was relaxing in the chair, his fork at the ready.

"Okay, here's what's going to happen. I'm going to go off, do some sheriff work, give you and Gage time to chat about how obstructing an investigation is a crime. Come tomorrow, I'll be back with the same questions. And I'll keep coming back until I get answers. That seem fair?"

"This a variation on your big bad wolf routine?"

"The story of police work. Huff and puff, huff and puff." Thumps set his hat on his head. "You enjoy the pie. We don't serve dessert in jail."

22

The airport parking lot was mostly empty. Cooley was waiting for him by a bright blue kiosk with a sheltered overhang.

"Hey, boss."

Thumps hadn't been to the airport in a while.

"This new?"

"It is," said Cooley. "According to the guy at the rental desk, this is the latest innovation in car rentals."

Under the kiosk was a stand of metal lockers. Each locker was numbered. Off to one side was a central keypad.

"It's really neat," said Cooley. "You make a reservation, and they send you a code. So when you arrive, you just come here, punch the code into the keypad, and the appropriate locker opens. Inside is the rental agreement and the keys to the car."

"You don't have to go to the main desk?"

"Nope," said Cooley. "Skip the line. And when you return the car, you just drop the keys in the drop box, and Bob's your uncle."

"Show me."

Cooley punched in a number and locker number twelve on the far end snapped open.

"This Greeley's locker?"

"It is," said Cooley. "The great thing is that the locker is yours for as long as you have the car."

"So you can store things in the locker."

"Yep. Let's say you have stuff you don't want to carry around with you, you can leave it here until you return."

"And Greeley stored some stuff?"

Cooley nodded. "He did. Take a look."

Inside the locker was a cellphone, a folder, and an automatic pistol with a suppressor screwed onto the barrel.

"Phone's cheap but new," said Cooley. "I think it's a burner. Only has one number programmed into the memory."

"You try the number?"

"It's long distance," said Cooley. "Texas area code. Figured I'd give you the honours."

"And the folder?"

"Photographs," said Cooley. "Bunch of people."

There were eleven photographs in all. Thumps recognized a younger Nora Gage and a younger Cisco Cruz.

"Isn't that your buddy?" asked Cooley. "Looks different in a suit and tie."

Thumps would never have imagined Cruz in anything but black leather, yet here he was, suited and tied, buzz cut, ramrod straight, apple pie and the dawn's early light. A model for a military recruitment poster.

"That the Gage woman?"

"It is."

"How about the rest of them?"

"No idea."

Cooley turned Cruz's photo over. "Call PK" was written in

tight, precise letters on the back. "Guessing we don't know who PK is either."

"Which leaves the pistol."

"Staccato 2011," said Cooley. "Cute little compact."

"Nine millimetre?"

"It is," said Cooley. "And not cheap."

"So, we got a sniper rifle in the trunk and a pistol with a suppressor in the locker."

"All we need," said Cooley, "is Colonel Mustard in the library with a candlestick."

Thumps double-checked the locker, in case Cooley had missed anything. "So, you rent the car online or by phone, pay for it with a credit card, come here, open the locker, get the key. Everything completely anonymous."

"That's about it."

Thumps shielded his eyes. "That a camera?"

"A dummy," said Cooley. "The guy at the rental desk called it a deterrent. You know, like those Beware of Dog signs when you don't have a dog."

"You check the credit card information?"

"I did," said Cooley. "Car was rented by a Sarah Croce."

Thumps walked out to where he could see the rental cars. And then he walked back to the kiosk. "Any of this make sense to you?"

"Nope," said Cooley, "but then I'm only a probationary deputy."

Thumps slipped the burner phone into his pocket. "Scoop staying over tonight?"

"Deanna has graveyard," said Cooley. "Think she plans to use the holding cell."

Thumps shut the locker. "You know, it's not a hotel room."

"Maybe we could rent it out," said Cooley, "when we're not arresting people, that is. Might help with the budget shortfall."

The lights in the parking lot came on. Somehow the late afternoon had slipped into evening.

Cooley zipped up his jacket. "I hear Claire and Ivory are moving to Calgary."

Thumps shoved his hands in his pockets. "Tomorrow morning, drive up to Shadow Ranch and arrest Cruz. I'll meet you at the jail."

"What's the charge?"

"Being annoying."

"We can arrest someone for being annoying?" Cooley gave a low whistle. "He's not going to like that."

"Yeah," said Thumps. "I know."

THUMPS WASN'T SURE why he was driving to the reservation or what he was going to do or say when he got to Claire's place. He slowed as he came onto high ground. And stopped.

Below, the house was dark, the barn silent, the driveway empty, the Russian olive in the moonlight a ghost in a graveyard.

So, she and Ivory were really gone.

Thumps got out of the car, leaned against the hood, and started counting stars. By the time he got to twenty, he realized that he had lost track of where he was in the sky and had to start again. After the third attempt, he gave up.

He thought about going down to the house, checking the rooms and closets. The bathroom. How much stuff had Claire taken with them? What might that tell him about how long she planned to stay? Did she expect to return?

And then again, maybe it was better not to know, better to leave hope alone. And alive.

What was the bog in *The Pilgrim's Progress* called? The Slough of Despond? The nasty bit of swamp where the protagonist sinks under the weight of his sins? The perfect place to spend an evening such as this. Under a sky such as this.

The phone in his jacket began ringing and vibrating at the same time. Thumps wasn't sure which he hated more.

"DreadfulWater. Where are you?"

Duke didn't sound happy, and he didn't sound depressed.

"At home in bed."

"No, you're not," said Duke. "You're on the reservation. At Claire's place."

Thumps looked at the phone. "Are you tracking me?"

"If I wasn't tracking you," said Duke, "how would I know you were on the reservation?"

"Jesus."

"Grow up. Everybody tracks everybody. Hell, Amazon knows what you had for dinner."

"I haven't had dinner."

"Well, when you do, they'll know."

In the background, Thumps could hear a dog. Not barking. Not whining. Low moans and grumbles that sounded more like conversation.

"You staying with Claire tonight?"

"No."

"In that case," said Duke, "you need to stop by the house on your way home."

"Your house?"

"Yes, my house."

Thumps took one last look at the dark house, the barn, the tree in the driveway. "You want to give me a hint?"

"Why spoil the surprise."

"I don't like surprises."

"How about that," said Duke. "Neither do I."

DUKE'S BUNGALOW WAS a house on fire. House lights, porch lights, security floods. Party central. All that was missing was loud music, a keg set up on the porch, and people dancing on the front lawn.

Thumps was halfway up the walk when the front door opened.

"Get in here."

Duke was dressed in a pair of dark pyjama bottoms with little yellow ducks. And a Marshall Tucker Band T-shirt.

"What took you so long?"

Thumps was humming the chorus of "Fire on the Mountain" as he came up the walk. "Just how old is that T-shirt?"

"Never mind the smart questions," said Duke.

Thumps didn't remember Duke's living room all that well, but he was reasonably sure that the last time he was here, the sofa had not been ripped apart. There was a lamp smashed on the floor as well, and it looked as though the baseboards along one wall had been attacked by a beaver.

"What happened?"

Duke put his hands on his hips. "Howdy."

"Your dog did this?"

"He's not my dog," Duke snarled. "I go out to get groceries, and when I come back . . ."

In terms of damage, the dog had played no favourites. In addition to the sofa and the lamp and the baseboards, Howdy had chewed through a chair leg, knocked a vase off the dining room table, and ripped a corner off the rug.

"Wait until you see what he did to the bedroom."

"He was probably lonely. He missed you."

"And the kitchen." Duke wrinkled his nose. "He peed all over the kitchen floor."

Thumps looked around. "Where is he?"

"Hiding," said Duke. "He knows I'm not happy."

"He just wants your attention. So he does stuff he shouldn't."

"And now you can help me find him."

Thumps held up his hands. "I have to get home."

"You take a step toward the door," said Duke, "and I'll shoot you before you make it to the porch."

"If you talk to him gently, tell him he's a good boy, he'll probably come out of hiding."

"He's not a good boy," said Duke. "He's a bad boy."

"Where is he?"

"You might have noticed the hole in the screen door," said Duke.

"So, he's outside?"

Duke handed Thumps a flashlight. "He could be in Budapest for all I care."

IT TOOK THE two of them the better part of an hour to find the dog. Howdy had wedged himself in the crawl space beneath the back deck.

"He's scared. You need to reassure him."

"Me?"

"He knows you're angry with him."

Duke got down on his knees next to Thumps. "Come on out, you little shit." Duke pitched his voice high in a singsong rhythm that was all sunshine and unicorns. "So I can wring your neck."

Howdy pulled back further into the shadows.

"He knows you're not sincere."

"You got any ideas?"

"We could try food," said Thumps. "My cats are suckers for food."

"You want me to give that mutt a treat for tearing my house apart?"

"You never liked that sofa anyway."

Duke found a package of hot dogs in the freezer, heated them up in the microwave.

"Probably not good for dogs," said Duke. "Probably give him diarrhea."

It took more coaxing and soft words, but Howdy finally wiggled out from under the deck, his eyes filled with remorse. As he crawled close to Duke, he began beating his tail against the ground and moaning.

"See," said Thumps. "He's sorry."

Howdy crawled onto Duke's lap and began licking his face.

"And he lovey, lovey, loves you."

Duke reared back, tried to get out of the way of the dog's tongue.

"Sorry, sorry, sorry."

"Jesus, DreadfulWater." Duke gathered Howdy up in his arms, carried the dog back to the house. "Would you shut up."

Thumps helped Duke pick up the pieces of the sofa, put them into a garbage bag.

"Can't believe he chewed through a table leg." Duke pulled back the ruined baseboards. "Real wood. Not that plastic shit they put down in new homes. Why couldn't he have wrecked something I didn't like."

Thumps swept up the remains of the lamp. "Such as?"

"Might as well leave everything as is." Duke grabbed Howdy by the ears and swung the big dog's head back and forth. Howdy started moaning and shaking all over. "Until we come to an understanding."

"He just wants your attention."

Duke rolled Howdy over on his back, began whacking the dog's tummy. From a distance, the affection might have been mistaken for a beating.

"Well," said Duke, "now he's got it."

23

Thumps got to Al's early the next morning to find the café virtually deserted. Al was wiping down the napkin dispensers.

"Glad to see someone remembers me."

Wutty and Russell and Jimmy weren't in their usual places across from the grill. Nor were the other regulars. The only people in the café were three men at the end of the counter.

Thumps stood in the doorway for a moment. "Where is everyone?"

"Shadow Ranch." Al made each word sound like a complaint. "Evidently, they're having a Team Wutty breakfast in anticipation of this weekend's tournament."

"Why didn't they have it here?"

"Not upscale enough for the golfing crowd would be my bet," said Al.

"Maybe not enough space."

"Maybe that too."

"Well, I'm here," said Thumps. "And I'm hungry."

Al tossed the dishcloth over her shoulder. "Do you want breakfast before or after you finish your business?"

Thumps moved down the counter to his favourite stool. Al followed him with the coffee pot at the ready.

"What business?"

"With those three gentlemen," said Al. "They've been waiting for you."

The younger of the three men got off his stool.

"You Sheriff DreadfulWater?"

"Deputy sheriff," said Thumps. "Temporary."

"I'm Brian Little Horse," said the man. "Cooley said I might find you here."

It took Thumps a moment to place the name.

"From Harlowton? The two old guys are my uncles, Elmer and Elroy."

"Think horse thieves," whispered Al.

"Not really," said Brian. "That's what I wanted to talk to you about."

"Your uncles are the ones who have been stea . . . taking cars?"

"Yeah," said Brian. "About that . . . Do you have uncles?"

Eugene DreadfulWater had had a brother and two sisters. But when his father walked out of his life, all of his relations on that side of the family disappeared as well.

"Elmer and Elroy more or less raised me and my sisters after our parents died. It's their garage."

"So, they know cars."

"Inside and out," said Brian. "Now I run it."

Thumps sipped his coffee. Black and hot.

"They were raised on horse-stealing stories," said Brian. "Their grandfather, my great-grandfather, actually did some of that stuff, and I think they figured that stealing horses was part of a family tradition. You know the story of White Quiver?"

There were clouds of steam rising off the grill. Thumps could smell potatoes on the fry.

"Old people get stuff in their heads, and it's hard to get it out."

"How many horses did they get?"

"Twenty or so," said Brian. "They had me working overtime. Fixing the cars they took, cleaning them up, dropping them off so their owners could find them."

"Chinook is a ways from Harlowton."

"Not so much," said Brian. "Evidently, some of the stories that Naas told, we'd go all the way to Minnesota for a good horse."

"So, they're still stea—"

"No," said Brian quickly. "We had a long talk about jail and the time I was spending on the cars and the cost of the parts. I would have had that rental car back, but then there was the you-know-what in the you-know-where."

"So, you called Cooley."

"Yeah," said Brian, "I called Cooley."

Al came down the counter with breakfast.

"You boys having a good time?"

"You make a really good breakfast, Mrs. Al," said Brian. "Uncle Elroy wanted me to ask you if you were married."

"Now that's sweet," said Al.

"He has a wife," said Brian. "But Auntie can't cook as well as you."

Al headed back to the grill. "Well, you tell your uncle he can come by any time, have breakfast, admire me from afar."

Brian turned to Thumps. "Let me tell you, that rental was a mess. Oil hadn't been changed since it came off the assembly line. And filthy? You should have seen the front seat. Burger wrappers, coffee cups, box of stale doughnuts. And the side windows? Looked like someone squeegeed them with lard. Really disgusting."

"So, no more horse stealing."

"Hand to god," said Brian. "There's a video game called Rustler. It's sort of medieval, but you get to steal horses. I'm going to try to get them hooked on that."

Thumps smiled.

"They're all I got left of the old people," said Brian. "Figure I should try to keep them safe."

"I got a deputy who wishes your uncles had gotten hold of her car."

Brian motioned to his uncles. "Tell her to bring the car over to the garage. On the house."

Elroy and Elmer got off their stools, filed past Thumps, smiling and patting him on the shoulder as they went.

Al swung back around with the coffee pot. "Couple of sweeties."

"For horse thieves."

"Wouldn't mind having uncles like that in my life." Al put the pot on the counter. "Hear Duke has a dog."

"No comment."

"You take any photographs of the blessed event?"

Thumps cut his sausage into pieces.

"Hear the sofa was a work of art," said Al. "School of Deconstruction."

"They've come to an understanding."

"Claire off to Canada?"

"I guess."

"That's it?" Al pursed her lips. "You know, conversations are supposed to be two-sided. I tell you things. You tell me things."

"How about you cook, I eat."

"That's not a conversation," said Al. "That's just a division of effort."

Thumps lowered his head, leaned over his food.

"In the end," said Al, "the critical question is, who does the dishes?"

Thumps parked behind the sheriff's office, sat there and watched clouds form, listened to the wind whistle in off the eastern face of the mountains in the distance.

He wasn't sure why he hadn't realized it sooner. Claire had not left a contact number. She and Ivory were gone, and he had no way to reach them. Surely, she would have left a number with someone. Roxanne, Moses, Scoop.

Just not him.

Duke was behind the desk. Howdy was sprawled out on a blanket.

"That the quilt from the holding cell? The one that Cooley bought?"

"It was," said Duke. "Now it's the mutt's porta-potty."

Thumps looked at the dog. "I don't think you mean porta-potty."

Duke leaned forward, smiled. "Give it a sniff."

Thumps turned toward the back room and the holding cell. "Cooley come in yet?"

"Haven't seen him. Deanna is doing the career-day thing at the community college. It's just you and Howdy."

As soon as the dog heard his name, he was on his feet, turning slow circles on the blanket.

"'Cause I'm not taking him home with me," said Duke. "I've already lost a sofa, two chairs, a run of baseboards, and part of a table."

"Duke . . ."

"You got two cats, so you won't even notice another animal."

Thumps took off his badge, slipped his pistol out of the holster, put everything on the desk. "Then I quit."

"You can't quit."

"Sure I can."

Howdy had worked his way to Duke, started licking the sheriff's fingers.

"Besides," said Thumps, "he loves you."

Duke pulled his hand away. "You know how many times I have to wash my hands? When he's not chewing my shoes or destroying the house, he slobbers on everything."

Howdy stopped licking, put his head on Duke's lap, just as the phone rang. It rang again, and then a third time.

"You going to answer that?"

"I quit, remember."

"Oh, for the love of . . ." Duke grabbed the phone. "Sheriff's office."

Howdy left Duke, wandered over to Thumps, sat down beside him, looked up at him, his eyes filled with love and longing.

"Don't worry. We're not going to take you to the shelter."

Duke made a clicking sound with his mouth, held the phone out. "It's for you," he said. "Appears our Mr. Cruz has been shot."

"Shot?"

Duke stood up. "You see this?" The front of the sheriff's uniform pants was wet and sticky with slobber. "The mutt's a biohazard."

"What about Cruz?"

"He's at the hospital," said Duke. "I'd send you, but you just quit."

Thumps scooped the badge and gun off the desk. "I'd better see Howdy on his blanket when I get back."

When he was a cop on the Northern California coast, he constantly found himself in and out of hospitals. He had never come to terms with them, and the years and distance had not softened his attitude. Overdoses, accidents, altercations, domestic abuse. Anything that bled or cried out in pain wound up in a hospital.

Thumps understood that hospitals weren't a reflection of humanity, but neither were they a recommendation.

Cooley was waiting for him when Thumps got to the emergency room. "Hey boss, we got a problem."

"How is he?"

"Well," said Cooley, "he got shot."

"How serious?"

"In the leg," said Cooley. "Doctor says it's a flesh wound."

"What happened?"

"I went to the Ranch, just like you told me," said Cooley. "Had a speech all worked up. You know, 'You're under arrest. Anything you say may—'"

Thumps held up a hand. "You found him?"

"Nope," said Cooley. "When I got to the Ranch, he wasn't there."

Thumps waited. "Because . . . ?"

"He was here at the hospital. You know Gina Tucci?"

"Yes, I know Gina Tucci."

"Gina recognized Cruz from the night that Greeley did his runner. She put two and two together, figured his getting shot had something to do with police business and called me."

"She called you?"

"Gina's married to my cousin," said Cooley. "So, we're family."

Thumps knew there was solid logic somewhere in the explanation. "You talk to him yet?"

"Nope."

"Okay, where is he?"

Cooley rocked on his heels. "That's the problem."

Thumps and Cooley caught up with Dr. Caitlin Taran in the cafeteria. She was a large-boned woman, a natural blonde with glacial eyes, who looked as though she could be an Olympic athlete in a sport that favoured brute strength over speed and agility.

Thumps showed her his badge. "Deputy Sheriff Thumps DreadfulWater and Deputy Cooley Small Elk."

"Do you gentlemen like coffee?"

"You bet," said Cooley.

"Then don't drink it here."

Thumps considered getting a cup, just to compare it with the coffee that Duke made. But there seemed little value in knowing which was worse.

"You treated a gunshot victim. Cisco Cruz."

Dr. Taran poked at her salad with a fork. "And don't order the soup."

"Cisco Cruz?"

"Interesting gentleman," said Taran. "Gunshot to the thigh. Didn't hit bone. Not all that serious."

"I'll need the bullet."

Taran shrugged. "Don't have it."

"It's still in him?"

"No," said Taran. "I removed the bullet, cleaned the wound, dressed it. Went back to the desk to get the forms we have to fill out for a gunshot, and when I got back, Mr. Cruz was gone."

Thumps knew the answer to the question before he asked it. "And the bullet?"

"It was in a pan next to the bed," said Dr. Taran. "It appears Mr. Cruz took it with him."

COOLEY WALKED THUMPS back to his car. "What do we do now, boss?"

"You go back to the office. Tell Duke what's happened."

"You know where Cruz is going?"

"And if Duke tries to take the dog to the pound, lock him up in the holding cell until I get back."

"The dog or Duke?"

Thumps thought about that for a moment, smiled. "Use your best judgment."

24

Thumps drove the cruiser back to Shadow Ranch with lights and siren, only turning off the overheads when he hit the turnoff for the resort. Cruz's car was parked behind Palazzo Veneziano. Thumps touched the hood as he went past.

Hot.

The door was open. Thumps quickly stepped into the villa, his gun at his side. Cruz was in the living room, on the sofa, his leg up on the ottoman.

"What took you so long?"

"Where the hell did you get those pants?"

"Pro shop," said Cruz. "Hospital wrecked my good pants."

"You couldn't find another colour?"

"Choices were neon fuchsia and electric yellow," said Cruz. "I could have gone with a pair of tan walking shorts, but I didn't want anyone to see the bandage."

Thumps put his gun back in the holster, took in the villa for the first time. The place had been trashed. Chairs knocked over, the glass table smashed, pictures on the walls askew.

"Okay. Maybe you should tell me what happened."

Cruz rubbed his leg gently. "I went back to that fancy house on the river."

"Ironstone River Estates."

"Thought I'd start from the beginning. I was sitting in my car when someone started shooting. First couple of rounds hit the front fender. One came through the door panel and nicked me."

"You got the slug."

Cruz pulled a baggie out of his pocket. Inside was a deformed lump of lead.

"Didn't see anyone. Shooter must have been on the high ground above the house."

"How bad?"

"Could have been worse. Having to wear these godawful pants hurts more."

"Any idea who?"

"Soon as I left the hospital, I came here." Cruz grimaced. "But I was too late."

"Gage?"

"Gone."

"So, either kidnapped or she did a runner."

"How about we get something to eat," said Cruz. "I'm wounded and my blood sugars are dropping."

"Not sure I can take you anywhere in those pants."

"Someplace quiet where we can talk." Cruz swung his leg off the ottoman. "How about we take your car. I had a hell of a time getting here, working the clutch."

• • •

The Mustang parking lot was empty.

"Place even open?"

"Just too early for the motorcycle boys," said Thumps. "They're just getting up."

Lorraine was behind the bar.

"Sit wherever."

"Yo-Yo in the kitchen?" Thumps took a booth, so Cruz could put his leg up.

"Like the pants," said Lorraine. "Wish I could get Big Fish into a pair like that."

"If you got a black garbage bag with a belt," said Cruz, "I'll trade you."

"What's wrong with your leg?"

"He got shot," said Thumps.

"Probably not the first time," said Lorraine.

"Most assuredly not," said Cruz. "Cheeseburger, extra tomato, fries, and a vanilla milkshake."

"Sheriff?"

"Same," said Thumps. "Where's Big Fish?"

"Up at Shadow Ranch," said Lorraine. "He's part of Team Wutty."

"Which part?"

"The part that sits around and drinks beer." Lorraine wiped down the table. "I'll have Yo-Yo bring everything out when it's ready."

Thumps waited until Lorraine disappeared.

"Well, here's another nice mess you've gotten me into."

"You know," said Cruz, "most people think that comes from

Laurel and Hardy, but W. S. Gilbert used it in *The Mikado* and in *The Grand Duke.*"

"You kidnap a dead man. You lose your principle. You get yourself shot."

"Gage isn't my principle, and Greeley wasn't dead when I brought him by your office," said Cruz. "That happened later. On your watch."

"Principle or not, you lost Gage."

"Didn't lose her," said Cruz. "Just don't know where she is."

"And all because you wouldn't accept expert help when it was offered."

"I'm injured." Cruz settled himself in the booth. "I may have to rest and wait for refreshments to come."

FIFTEEN MINUTES LATER, the door to the kitchen opened, and Yo-Yo appeared with a large tray.

"Deputy Dog and friend." Yo-Yo set the tray on the edge of the table and began unloading the food.

Yo-Yo's real name was Doug Jacobs. He was a string bean of a man with large ears and a frog butt. A couple of the Mustang regulars had gone on a rally to Burning Man, had watched a young woman do a trick with a yo-yo called "walking the dog," which reminded them of Doug's peculiar way of bobbing and gliding as he walked. All at the same time.

And the rest was history.

"Hey, you're that ninja assassin guy." Yo-Yo blinked several times. "Big Fish said if you showed up again, I was to get your autograph."

Cruz looked at Thumps.

"He was hoping you might do it in blood." Yo-Yo could sense the danger, started bobbing back to the kitchen. "But I'm betting ketchup would do."

CRUZ ATE HIS food in silence. Thumps was patient. At some point, the man from Pie Town would have to come out from behind the burgers and fries.

"Okay." Cruz finished his shake. "You first."

Thumps leaned forward, lowered his voice. "We found Greeley's rental."

"Did you?"

"Hidden in the trunk was a sniper rifle."

Cruz's face darkened.

"Which is somewhat peculiar," said Thumps, "seeing as how the man suffered from cataracts and macular degeneration. Beth figures he'd have trouble shooting himself in the foot."

"Sounds like there's more."

Thumps took the envelope out of his bag. Laid the photographs out on the table.

"These were in Greeley's car-rental locker at the airport."

"Car-rental locker?"

"Pilot project. Allows you to rent a car anonymously. You rent a car, they give you a code. When your flight gets in, you go to the locker and get the key. Drop the car off the same way. Locker doubles as storage."

Cruz picked up the photo of himself. "This is at least ten years old."

"You recognize the rest?"

"Nora Gage." Cruz touched another photo. "If I had to guess, I'd put my money on the Black Ice team."

Thumps did the math in his head. "Gage said that there were eight members of Black Ice. Dalca would make nine. You make ten." Thumps waited for Cruz to catch up. "But here we have eleven images."

Cruz stared at the pictures. "I can get the names of the team, confirm the faces."

"There was also a burner phone," said Thumps. "One number programmed into the memory. A number in Texas."

"You saving the best for last?"

Thumps took a breath, let the air out slowly. "We also found a Staccato 2011. With suppressor."

"That's a sweet ride." Cruz pushed his plate to one side. "Okay, you want in, I'll read you in."

"The whole truth and nothing but the truth?"

"You already know about Gage and Black Ice and what they did."

"Shit."

"What?"

"Black Ice," said Thumps. "I remember now. Boris Lukin."

Cruz did his grumbly face. "Took you long enough."

"What the hell does a dead Miami gangster have to do with any of this?"

Boris Lukin was a major coin dealer, who had come to Buffalo Mountain for a regional coin show to acquire a 1933 double eagle, one of the rarest coins in the world, a coin that was not supposed to exist.

"Mobster," said Cruz. "Not gangster."

"The difference being?"

"Gangsters are individuals," said Cruz. "Much easier to take down. Mobsters are part of an organization. Takes more effort to kick them to the curb."

"Like a corporation."

Lukin was killed by a taser. Accidently, as it turned out. Black Ice had nothing to do with his death.

"Yes," said Cruz, "there was a moment when we thought Black Ice was a rival mob. Imagine our surprise when we discovered that Black Ice was one of the good guys."

"Right hand, left hand."

"There's that," said Cruz.

"Let's rewind to the beginning," said Thumps. "Black Ice is what? Homeland Security? CIA? NSA? FBI?"

Cruz shrugged. "More or less."

"None of those agencies is going to second someone from customs. That means Gage was CIA or NSA. A field agent? An analyst?"

"Okay," said Cruz. "She was an analyst."

"And I'm guessing she was lead at Black Ice."

"More or less," said Cruz.

"Is there a straight bone in your body?"

"My leg is killing me."

"Doctor said it's a flesh wound."

"It's not your leg."

"Black Ice. Nora Gage."

Cruz yawned, sighed a long sigh. "Black Ice was a collective. Originally, their mandate was to gather information, ammunition for the hunter/killer agencies."

"An activity without teeth."

"Oh, there were the drug busts and the mass arrests, the occasional congressional hearing, calls for action. The War on Drugs. The War on Poverty. The War on War."

"The War on Stupidity?"

"That all changed in 2005."

"Yeah, Gage told me. Tom Ridge retires, Michael Chertoff steps in."

"Then she told you about Sorin Dalca, and the change in Black Ice's mission."

"According to Gage," said Thumps, "Black Ice began going after the industrial-military boys, the ones who were selling restricted technology to the opposition and making obscene profits."

"Black Ice already knew who was selling what and to whom and how financial transactions were being made. Now, they had the green light to do something about it."

"Goodbye congressional hearings," said Thumps. "Hello state-sanctioned muggings."

"Civil forfeiture," said Cruz. "We call it civil forfeiture."

"And the guilty corporations can't complain because those accounts and monies aren't supposed to exist."

Cruz sat back. "And there you have it."

Thumps held up a hand, took out his phone. "Cooley? Need you to do something . . . The house in Ironstone River Estates . . . Yeah, that one . . . Get out there with a crime scene kit and take the place apart . . . Right . . . And do a search of the high ground above the house. You're looking for shell casings or anything else to suggest a shooting . . . No, I'm okay . . . Right, right . . . Oh, did Duke try to take the dog to the pound? . . . The shelter, yes, I know it's called the shelter . . . Okay, just keep an eye on him."

Thumps put the phone back in his pocket. "Okay," he said. "Continue."

"There's no continue," said Cruz. "That's it."

"Didn't we have a chat about lying?"

"I'm not lying."

"Omissions then," said Thumps. "Omissions are the same as lying."

Cruz grimaced. He moaned, then moaned again to make sure the honest world could hear him, twisted his face in pain. Thumps had seen killdeers do the same thing. Feign an injury, drag a wing, make pathetic chirps, to lure a predator away from their nest.

"Dalca takes over at Black Ice. He creates a holding company called the Vault. All the confiscated money goes into it. How much are we talking about?"

"Did you ask Gage?"

"I did."

"What did she tell you?"

Thumps took a moment to come up with a number. "Said it was around forty million."

"Did you just make that up?"

"I did."

"So far as we can tell, the figure was quite a ways north of that." Cruz moved his leg to a more comfortable position. "You see the problem yet?"

Thumps took a moment. "You're telling me that Dalca was the only person who had access to the Vault?"

Cruz pushed the plate toward him. "Give that man a french fry."

"That's crazy. Somebody above Dalca and Black Ice should have had access. Where did they think all the money was going?"

Cruz was smiling, but it wasn't a happy smile. "You ever work in D.C.? If you had, you wouldn't bother to ask that question. Black Ice took the money. Dalca set up the Vault. Dalca had the access codes. Homeland didn't even know the Vault existed. It's the very definition of bureaucracy."

"Unbelievable."

Cruz continued to smile. "And did Gage happen to mention that he's dead?"

"Dalca?"

"Sailing accident in French Polynesia," said Cruz. "Ran into a storm near Huahine."

No, Thumps thought to himself, she had neglected that detail as well.

"You see the problem?"

"A team of government thieves who rob corporations, a shit pile of money squirrelled away, and a dead man who knows how to get at it?"

"Yes," said Cruz. "That's the first part. And you're going to love the second."

25

Cruz shifted his leg. He was looking tired, even a bit gaunt.

"You don't look so good."

"I was shot."

"A flesh wound."

"They call it a flesh wound?" said Cruz. "Because it doesn't kill you."

"You want to call it a day?"

"No," said Cruz. "There are a few other things you need to know."

Yo-Yo came out of the kitchen with the coffee pot. "Thought you might like coffee. I can get you a beer if you like, but seeing you're on duty and all . . ."

"Coffee's fine," said Cruz.

"You mind me asking a question?" Yo-Yo bobbed in place. "There any job openings?"

"For?"

"You know. Ninja stuff."

Cruz closed his eyes.

"Cooks are pretty invisible," said Yo-Yo. "Nobody much notices us. We slip in and out of kitchens. Sneak up on you from behind before you even know I'm there."

Cruz opened his eyes. "You don't want to be a ninja assassin."

Yo-Yo stopped bobbing. "I don't?"

"For starters," said Cruz, "we don't get paid."

"Really."

"And we're not allowed to have sex."

Yo-Yo swayed from side to side. "You're shitting me."

"Hand to god," said Cruz. "You have to take a vow of celibacy."

"Jesus," said Yo-Yo. "No pay, cel . . . cel . . ."

"Celibacy."

"That's a shitty job," said Yo-Yo.

"You have no idea," said Cruz.

Yo-Yo CLEARED THE table, took the dirty dishes back to the kitchen.

"That wasn't very nice."

"I got shot," said Cruz. "My leg hurts."

"You know where you find 'sympathy' in the dictionary, don't you?"

"Yeah," said Cruz, "between 'shit' and 'syphilis.' It's a really old joke, and it's not very funny."

"Yes, it is."

"You want to know about Black Ice or you want to keep doing stand-up?"

"What I want to know is how a gangster such as Boris Lukin is tied to a covert government program such as Black Ice."

"Show me those photos again."

Thumps took the envelope out. "You recognize someone, don't you?"

"Maybe."

"And you're going to share with the rest of the class."

"Don't be a baby." Cruz arranged the photos in three rows. "The first two photos are easy."

"You and Gage."

"These seven are probably the Black Ice team minus Gage."

That left two photos. Both men.

"I'm guessing that the swarthy fellow with the beard and glasses is Sorin Dalca." Cruz touched each photo in turn. "The one-percenter in the bespoke suit and Christian Lacroix tie is Porter Kincaide."

"Wow," said Thumps. "Porter Kincaide."

"You don't know who he is, do you?"

"No clue."

"That's because you don't read *The Economist*."

"I must have let my subscription lapse."

Cruz held up the photo. "You know, you're not that funny."

"Porter Kincaide," said Thumps. "Para Bellum Global. World leader in all things that go boom. Company is a regular guest at congressional hearings on corporate malfeasance."

Cruz smiled. "Thought you said your subscription lapsed."

"CNN. Fox News." Thumps took a moment to put the new pieces in place. "The cellphone we found in Greeley's locker?"

"Best guess," said Cruz. "Kincaide's private number at Para Bellum."

"Para Bellum being one of the companies that Black Ice hit."

"Hard," said Cruz. "Word on the street is that Kincaide lost tens of millions."

"You know," said Thumps, "this is beginning to sound like *Mission: Impossible*, but without the cool masks and the clever dialogue."

"I'm glad you find this amusing."

"And Boris Lukin?"

"Lukin's organization controls all the cargo traffic in and out of the Port of Miami. He and Kincaide had an understanding."

"As in Kincaide would pay Lukin to move restricted technologies around the globe."

"We think that Kincaide somehow found out about Black Ice, passed that information on to Lukin."

"So, Black Ice had a leak."

"Maybe," said Cruz. "We never were able to pinpoint the source."

Thumps rolled his shoulders, stretched his neck. "So, back to Sorin Dalca. He sets up the Vault, dies in a sailing accident, and the access codes die with him."

"Which brings us," said Cruz, "to the second part of the problem. About a month back, Gage came home from work to find an old friend waiting for her."

"Sorin Dalca?"

"Back from the dead."

Thumps brushed some crumbs off the table. "Sailing accidents in French Polynesia not being as fatal as first reported."

Cruz shifted his leg again. "You're probably wondering why Dalca would reappear. I mean, he's dead. He has the access code to millions. He can reach out and help himself, and no one would know."

"Okay," said Thumps. "I'll bite. After all the effort to disappear, why does he break cover?"

"Did I mention that Dalca is paranoid?" Cruz beat a quick rhythm on the table. "According to Gage, something spooked him. Dalca thought that the Vault had been compromised, and that if he tried to access the money, he would be exposed."

"Is it safe?" Thumps tried to capture Laurence Olivier's voice and intonation.

"What?"

"*Marathon Man*," said Thumps, "but without the evil dentist."

"Dalca is desperate," said Cruz. "There's all that money within his reach. But he's afraid to touch it. What does he do?"

Thumps thought about it for a moment. "Do a test run on the Vault? See what happens? Take a chance?"

"Nope," said Cruz. "Dalca wants Gage to help him hit Para Bellum again. New nest egg, new secure account."

"You're kidding."

"If she doesn't help him, Dalca threatens to sell her name and her involvement with Black Ice to Kincaide, along with the hint that Gage knows where the money that Black Ice originally took from Para Bellum might be found."

"I'm guessing that she said no."

"She did," said Cruz. "And contacted us."

"Us being?"

"You know," said Cruz. "Us."

Thumps started smiling. Then he started chuckling.

"What's funny?"

"Here I thought you were protecting Gage," said Thumps.

"But she's just bait, isn't she? You're hoping to find Dalca and the money. You don't give a shit what happens to her."

Cruz tried to look concerned. "Not true."

"So, who grabbed her?"

"Could be Kincaide's men," said Cruz. "But my money is on Dalca. Kincaide's too smart to stick his neck out. He'll sit back and let Dalca bring Gage to him. Good news is Dalca's not going to hurt her. If he wants to be paid, he needs her healthy and chatty."

"Then who shot you?"

"Don't think they wanted to kill me," said Cruz. "Could have been Dalca. Could have been Para Bellum. I think they were hoping to scare me off."

Thumps sat back in the chair. He could feel the beginnings of exhaustion coming on. Always after a meal. Most unpleasant. Most unwelcome.

"You shouldn't have had that milkshake," said Cruz.

"You going to stay at the villa?"

"No," said Cruz. "That place is blown. I'll find somewhere else to hole up."

Thumps got to his feet. "Come on," he said. "I know the perfect spot."

26

Deanna and Cooley were huddled around the desk, hard at work on the Jenga tower. Cooley looked up when Thumps and Cruz came into the office. Deanna kept her attention on the game.

"Hey, boss, you found him. You want me to slap the cuffs on?"

"Quiet," said Deanna. "Need to concentrate."

"What the hell is that?" said Cruz.

"Jenga," said Cooley. "You never played Jenga?"

"Wood blocks? Sure, when I was four."

"You guys are going to make me lose." Deanna took a step to one side, stared at the tower from a different angle.

"Okay, so how's it work?"

"You stack the wood pieces into a tower," said Cooley, "and then you pull pieces out until the tower falls over."

"That's it?"

"You want bright lights and bells and people getting all excited over seeing three cherries pop up," said Deanna, "go to Buffalo Mountain. This is a game of skill."

Deanna gently pulled a block out of the centre. The tower wobbled and slowly toppled over.

"Shit."

"That's two games to two," said Cooley. "Next one decides the champion."

Cruz shook his head. "What's the winner get?"

"Winner doesn't have to drink any of Duke's coffee," said Deanna.

Thumps patted Cruz on the shoulder. "Why don't I tell you about your new accommodations."

"Don't even think of sticking me in the Wagon Wheel," said Cruz. "That woman scares the hell out of me."

Thumps guided Cruz to the back room. "Got you something cozy with a central location."

Thumps had to admit that the holding cell did look inviting. Easy chair, flat-screen, poster of an Indian on a bicycle on the wall.

"Only thing it hasn't got is a vibrating bed."

"This is a cell."

"Think of it as a short-term rental."

"With bars." Cruz stopped at the door. "I'm not sleeping here."

"If I arrest you, you will."

"You arrest me and you won't be able to find Gage."

"You *lost* Gage," said Thumps. "Let's compromise. I don't arrest you, and you stay here, where I can keep an eye on you."

Deanna had restacked the Jenga tower. Cruz stopped and watched as Cooley slid a block out of the centre of the structure.

Cruz turned to Thumps. "This is your idea of tax dollars in action?"

Deanna pursed her lips. "I thought you were going to arrest him."

"If I arrest him," said Thumps, "city has to feed him."

"And we need the holding cell," said Cooley. "I got graveyard, so Scoop is going to be staying over."

"Used to have a nice quilt on the bed," said Deanna. "Until poochy seconded it for an ass wipe."

"Going to have to put it through one of those commercial washers a couple of times," said Cooley. "Get the smell out."

Cruz held up a hand. "How about someone gives me a ride back to my car?"

"Where's your car?"

"Shadow Ranch."

"I can run you up," said Cooley. "Give me a chance to check on Team Wutty."

Cruz rubbed the back of his head. "I'd ask what a Team Wutty was, but I don't think I want to know."

THUMPS SPENT THE REST of the day dealing with the management of the office. He had forgotten just how boring police work could be. Thumps went through the messages once more.

"No message from Moses?"

Deanna was packing the basket with coffee. "Moses Blood?"

"Yeah," said Thumps. "Sometimes there's a problem with someone breaking into one of the trailers."

"You just want to get out of the office."

"Should check in on the old man."

"Scoop's doing that," said Deanna. "Remember, her and Cooley are living out there now."

"Maybe I'll catch some speeders," said Thumps. "Could use the practice."

Deanna banged the percolator on the table. "Sure," she said, "run off, have a good time, leave me with the grunt work."

"Or you could see it as a chance to practise being in charge, being the big chief."

Deanna smiled. "Chief Heavy Runner. It does have a nice ring. Maybe I'll run out to the reservation and arrest Roxanne. For practice. Tell her it was your idea."

Thumps blanched. "Please don't do that."

Deanna came back to the Jenga tower. "You see Scoop, tell her if she expects to use the holding cell tonight that she better bring an extra helping of that stew with her."

AS SOON AS Thumps hit the city limits and was on the open road, he felt his body begin to relax. Dead private investigators, kidnapped mystery women, ninja assassins, back-from-the-grave Romanian mathematicians, nefarious corporate executives, Jenga towers, and large slobbery dogs all disappeared in the rear-view mirror.

There was a moment, as he got to the turnoff for Moses Blood's place, when he thought about keeping to the main road and heading to Canada. Nothing to stop him from calling Duke and giving the sheriff notice.

He could put the badge and the office cellphone in the mail.

All things considered, he could probably be more help in Calgary, looking after Claire and Ivory.

But Claire had been clear. She wanted to do whatever needed to be done on her own, and she hadn't left any room for interpretation. If Thumps was being honest with himself, he'd have to admit that she had hurt his feelings.

And not for the first time.

There was a certain bluntness to Claire. Bright skies and mountain meadows one minute. And then the avalanche.

Moses Blood lived on fifty acres of bottomland that fronted the river. There was a small house, a barn, a chicken coop, and half a dozen trailers that had been left in Moses's hands for safekeeping. At one point, there had been over forty on the property, but the trailers had come and gone, like children, until the only ones that remained were the ones too tired or broken to move.

The afternoon sun lit the western face of the house and made the windows glow. Thumps pulled the car into the yard, turned the engine off, waited. Times past, Moses would come out to greet guests, but the years had slowed the old man. Thumps wondered, not for the first time, just how old Moses was.

Not that it mattered. You were either alive or you were dead. The only thing in between was the waiting.

Thumps took his time walking to the house, tried the door, found it open, stuck his head inside.

"Moses, it's Thumps DreadfulWater."

Moses's house was one large room. More or less. Kitchen at one end, living room with a big-screen television at the other. Table, chairs, purple hide-a-bed, and a white Naugahyde recliner.

"Moses, you here?"

Moses didn't drive. Scoop could have taken him somewhere. Shopping, to the doctor, maybe to see relatives and friends. Otherwise, the old man was always home.

Thumps stepped out of the house and into the yard, stood in place, tried to think of what to do next.

"Mr. DreadfulWater."

Thumps turned to see Scoop Macleod come out from behind a large single-wide.

"Thumps," said Thumps. "Please."

"Doesn't seem right," said Scoop. "You being the sheriff and all."

"Temporary," said Thumps.

"You here to see Moses?"

"I am."

"Good," said Scoop. "Maybe you can talk some sense into him."

Thumps did a full 360. "He's here?"

"Fishing." Scoop made a face. "The old man almost died of COVID. He's weak as hell, and what does he do?"

"He goes fishing?"

"He goes fishing. What is it with you guys?"

"I don't fish."

"No more sense than a horseshoe." Scoop turned her face to the river. "He's over there by the cottonwoods."

"Okay."

"You can't miss him," said Scoop. "He's the old fool with the pole."

"Deanna was hoping you'd bring her some stew when you come in?"

Scoop nodded. "Cooley is proud of that holding cell."

"He did a lot of work on it."

"The quilt and the flat-screen are nice," said Scoop, "but it's the bars that make the difference."

"Pardon?"

"You know." Scoop fiddled with her hair. "Being locked up in a cell with the big guy is kinda sexy."

Thumps was reasonably sure he didn't need to know that.

"Pretty sad Claire and Ivory having to leave the country to get decent health care. When are you going to join her?"

Thumps could see the line of cottonwoods from here. The tall trees stood along the bank, leaning out over the river, wondering if the grass might be greener on the other side.

"You're not going to join her?"

"It's complicated."

"Claire wants to do it on her own?"

"She does."

Scoop nodded. "I do that too sometimes. Push people away."

If Moses was in amongst the cottonwoods, Thumps couldn't see him.

"Good thing Cooley doesn't listen to me." Scoop shaded her eyes. "Going to head into town. When you see Moses, tell the old fool that if he catches a fish, he can clean it himself."

27

Thumps took his time walking the bank. The day had softened. The ripples on the river still held sharp edges of light, but in the deeper pools, the water ran dark and haunting. He stopped several times, listened to a world at peace.

Not that the world was exactly silent. There was the crackle of the breeze in the grass, the song of birds he couldn't see, the bark of an animal at play somewhere beyond the ridge.

Moses was in the shelter of a large cottonwood that had been undercut by the spring floods. The tree was still upright but leaning out into the current. He had a heavy blanket over his shoulders, and from a distance, Thumps could see where the old man might be mistaken for a bear at rest.

"Moses."

Moses turned slowly, gave his pole a jiggle. "Ho, it's the law."

"Good to see you."

"If you're here to arrest me, I'll have to call my lawyer."

"I'm not here to arrest you."

"That's a relief," said Moses. "I don't have a lawyer."

Thumps sat down across from Moses. "How's the fishing?"

Moses lifted the pole. The lure at the end of the line flashed in the light.

"Is that a . . ."

"Roxanne gave it to me," said Moses. "Said clip-ons were inconvenient."

"You're fishing with an earring?"

"She gave me a yellow one as well," said Moses, "but the fish prefer the red."

"There's no hook."

"Clip-ons don't have hooks." Moses's voice was slow and patient. "The hooks are on the other ones."

Thumps chuckled. "So, you're not trying to catch the fish."

"There's good stew back at the house," said Moses. "If I caught a fish, Scoop would want me to clean it."

The clouds had slipped out of the sky, had piled up along the horizon. They didn't look as though they were organizing for a storm, but Thumps knew that with clouds, you could never be sure.

"You want to give it a try?" Moses handed Thumps the pole. "Jiggle it every so often."

"If you're not trying to catch fish," said Thumps, "what's the point?"

"When Claire's little girl fishes with me," said Moses, "she sings to the fish. The trout and the bass and the little sticklebacks find it entertaining."

"I'm not singing to the fish."

"I used to sing to the fish," said Moses, "but my voice isn't what it used to be."

"So, we're entertaining the fish?" Thumps looked down into

the water. "What happens when the small fry come up to look at the earring, and then the big fish come along and eat them?"

Moses pulled the blanket up around his shoulders. "Yes," he said, "I haven't quite worked that out yet."

Thumps leaned back against the tree, let the day settle in around him. He could imagine a world in which you spent your days by a river, sitting with friends. But it was not the world in which he lived.

"Did you come out here to visit," said Moses, "or do you need some of my sage advice?"

"A bit of both," said Thumps.

"Ah," said Moses. "Claire Merchant."

Thumps didn't think of Claire as Claire Merchant, and just hearing Moses say the name made Thumps think of two separate people. Claire Merchant, the former tribal chair, and Claire Merchant, Thumps's on-again, off-again lover.

As though you could tear the woman into two distinct pieces.

Moses rolled over on his side, used the tree to pull himself up to a standing position.

"This is why there are trees in the world." Moses stood, caught his breath. "To help old people get off the ground."

Thumps pushed off a large root, congratulated himself on standing in one motion.

"That was impressive." Moses brushed off his pants. "Did it hurt?"

Thumps rubbed his leg. "Just a little."

"Claire Merchant will be a long conversation," said Moses, "so we should probably go back to the house and have something to eat."

"Sounds like a fine idea."

"Maybe you can carry the blanket," said Moses. "It gets heavy at the end of the day."

"I could carry you as well." Thumps smiled. "If you like."

Moses waved him off. "I call that bold talk for a man with a sore leg."

"John Wayne," said Thumps. "*True Grit*."

Moses moved slowly and he moved stiffly. "Actually," he said, "it was Robert Duvall."

THE SUN DROPPED below the horizon. The air cooled. In the distance, the mountains softened to an evening purple. As soon as they got back to the house, Moses limped over to the recliner, eased himself into the chair.

"You said there was stew?"

"In the refrigerator," said Moses. "Pots are on the shelf, dishes in the cupboard, knives and forks are in the drawer."

"We got any bread?"

"In the freezer." Moses pulled the blanket across his lap. "You know that *Camelot*?"

"The musical?"

"They got a song about leaving in winter or summer," said Moses. "At first, I thought it was a song about dying."

"But it wasn't."

"No," said Moses, "it wasn't. But it got me thinking."

Thumps put the stew in the pot. Put the pot on the stove. "You're not going to die. You're going to live forever."

"The trick is making sure that you die at the right time," said Moses. "For instance, I wouldn't want to die in summer."

Thumps found the bread, set it to one side.

"Summertime is for enjoying the land. Nobody wants to go to a funeral in the summer. It's too hot to be standing around, listening to songs and stories about the dead."

The butter was in the refrigerator. Thumps put it out on the counter, hoped that it might soften by the time the stew was ready.

"And you wouldn't want to die in winter," said Moses, "'cause the snow and the ice would keep people away. Too cold. Hard to dig a hole. Nobody wants to come to a funeral in the winter."

"That just leaves spring and fall," said Thumps.

"Spring is the season for everything coming to life, for being born." Moses shook his head. "Spring would be a bad time to die. Spring is a time for enthusiasm. A funeral would send the wrong message."

"Autumn?"

"Autumn would be okay," said Moses. "I could fall down with the leaves."

"Then it's settled," said Thumps. "Let's eat."

THUMPS COULDN'T IMAGINE anything much better than hot stew and fresh bread. Even if the butter was a bit on the hard side.

"In the old days," said Moses, "we would never discuss important matters until we had had a good meal."

"No objections from me."

"Empty stomachs are responsible for almost as many bad decisions as religion and politics." Moses helped himself to another piece of bread. "And we have fresh berries for dessert."

Thumps had a second bowl of the stew. "Is this buffalo?"

"No," said Moses. "This is elk. From last season. Leroy Little Bear brought by a haunch for the freezer."

"It's delicious."

"And better for you," said Moses. "It's lower in saturated fats. But sometimes wild game can give you diarrhea, if your stomach's not used to it."

"I'll put water on for tea."

"Berries and tea," said Moses. "That will put us in the mood to solve your problems."

THUMPS WASN'T SURE why he bothered to tell Moses about Nora Gage and her disappearance. He was more concerned about Claire and Ivory.

"Ho," said Moses, "this sounds like a three-meal problem. You may have to stay over."

"Going to have to do with stew and berries," said Thumps.

"Okay," said Moses, "so, you've misplaced two women? That's impressive."

"I didn't misplace anyone. I know where Claire went. I offered to go with her."

"And the other woman has vanished."

"We think she was kidnapped."

"This is beginning to feel like a *Castle* rerun," said Moses. "There's this one channel that has all the old stuff."

"Maybe we should stick with Claire?"

"Sure," said Moses. "But I don't think I can tell you anything you don't already know."

"I have two options," said Thumps. "I can go to Calgary or I can stay here."

Moses held the cup in both hands, let the steam swirl over his face. “Claire could be angry with you if you showed up in Calgary, and she could be angry with you for not coming.”

“That’s about it.”

“Too bad you don’t have a third option. A third option would probably be the right one.”

“Except I don’t have a third option.”

“All in all,” said Moses, “the lost woman might be easier to find, and probably won’t mind being rescued.”

“What would you do?”

Moses put his cup to one side. “I think I’d have another bowl of those berries.”

THE DIRT TRACK that ran down to the river bottom and Moses’s house was generally a nightmare of deep ruts and bone-rattling washboards. But one of Cooley’s many cousins had come down with a small dozer, scraped the tract smooth, and Thumps made it up to the main road with his undercarriage intact.

The way back to Chinook was a dark drive under a moonless sky. Thumps lowered his window and leaned into the night. Moses hadn’t offered much in the way of wisdom. But talking to the old man, being able to describe the two situations had helped to clarify a couple of things.

First, Claire would do what Claire would do. He didn’t have much say in that matter. So, it stood to reason that Thumps should do what he wanted to do. Maybe it was time to be more forceful and decisive. Not bend in the wind. That was it. Be the wind.

Nor had Moses much to offer on the matter of Nora Gage. At least Gage’s situation was straightforward. Claire’s going to Calgary was personal. Gage’s kidnapping was criminal.

If it was a kidnapping.

As he had explained Nora Gage to Moses, Thumps realized that he didn't know for sure that her disappearance was a kidnapping. There were at least two other explanations.

One, she had been spooked and decided to disappear. How she expected to do this was unclear. She didn't have a car. Didn't know the area. Where would she go on her own? She could have staged the signs of the struggle at the villa, but why bother?

Two, Cruz felt the villa was compromised. If Thumps could find them there, so could others. That meant Cruz was lying to him about the abduction and wasting his time. Cruz could easily have moved her from Shadow Ranch to a more secure location. He had the means. He was familiar with the landscape. It wouldn't be the first time the man from Pie Town had been less than forthcoming.

The second scenario made the most sense. But then there was the shooting. Cruz hadn't shot himself. The only reason for the shooting was to take Cruz off the board. The shooting brought everything back to a kidnapping.

The road cleared the last rise. The lights of Chinook in the distance. And none too soon. Thumps was exhausted. He'd check his blood sugars when he got home, might have to eat something sweet, just to get them back up to level. He'd need to be awake and sharp for what was to come.

Claire Merchant and Nora Gage.

Two conundrums at large in his world. Much like the Jenga tower back at the office. Which blocks to take away, which blocks to leave in place. Pull out one, and nothing happens. Pull out another, and the whole thing falls down.

Not exactly a metaphor for life. But in lieu of something better, it would have to do.

28

Thumps was up early the next morning. The cats were waiting for him in the bathroom. Cookie was draped over the side of the bowl, his head in harm's way. Freeway was stretched out on the floor in front of the sink.

"I have to use the toilet."

Cookie didn't move.

"You won't like it if I pee on your head."

Actually, Thumps wouldn't like it. If he did pee on the cat, he would then have to clean him up, and wrestling the big dummy with a washcloth was not appealing.

Nor was picking up the enormous cat and carrying him to the bedroom. Cookie was an armload of wet laundry. Thumps set the cat on the bed, went back to the bathroom.

He had just started to shave when Freeway began to lick his toes.

"Knock it off."

For a reason known only to cats, both Freeway and Cookie liked feet. They liked to smell feet, sit on feet, lick feet. In particular, they liked to play mole-in-the-hole, a bedtime game that consisted of pouncing on Thumps's toes and trying to bite them. During the winter months, this wasn't a problem. The duvet was thick enough to repel the attacks.

But during the summer, on hot nights, when there was just a sheet between the cats and the mole, things would quickly get out of hand.

"Leave the toes alone."

Thumps took a shuffle step to one side. Freeway shuffled along with him.

Thumps had no idea why dogs' tongues were smooth and silky and cats' tongues were sandpaper rasps.

An irony of nature.

A large, snarling, wild-eyed dog, his teeth bared, ears laid back, hair on his neck erect, but with a great floppy tongue, soft as warm butter. As opposed to a sweet-faced cat who cuddles up on your lap, purrs loudly enough to push nails out of a wall, sticks out her little pink tongue and strips the skin off body parts.

Thumps sat on the edge of the bed, his toes a-tingle. He slipped on his socks and contemplated, not for the first time, the simplicity of a life lived alone, being responsible for yourself and nothing else.

And perhaps that's what Claire sensed in him. A reluctance to participate in the tumble of life. If he couldn't manage something as simple as a dog or a cat, how could he be expected to cope with another human being? Two human beings? A community?

Or did Claire think that Thumps saw her and Ivory as replacements for Anna and Callie? He could see where it would be an easy assumption to make. Replace the dead with the living. Relive a past. Get it right this time.

• • •

Thumps had got out of bed that morning with two plans in place. The first was to have breakfast at Al's. The second was to find Cruz and squeeze the truth out of him.

And then, every so often, plans came together.

When Thumps walked into the café, Cruz was at a middle stool, sitting between Chintak Rawat and Stas Black Weasel.

"You see," said Rawat. "As I predicted."

"A late prediction." Stas checked his watch. "Thirty-two minutes late."

"Time is fluid," said Rawat. "Time is a river."

"This is not Russian time," said Stas. "Russian time is a countdown."

Cruz turned on the stool. "They've been going on like this since they arrived."

"Ten, nine, eight, seven, five . . ."

"Six," said Rawat.

"Yes," said Stas, "six, five, four, three, two, one . . . boom!"

"This is, of course," said Rawat, "not the kind of counting we need."

The big Russian patted Thumps's arm. It was meant as a friendly gesture, and Thumps was fairly sure that the bruising would be minimal.

"Your friend has been telling us about his derring-do," said Rawat. "Did you know Mr. Cisco lived in the Kashmir? He speaks Kashmiri and Hindi. Very impressive."

"And he has lived in Ukraine," said Stas. "Kyiv. His Russian is *ne tak uzh khorosho.*"

"It's better than that," said Cruz.

"And he has seen Hard Man," said Stas. "Who is really Soft Bully. Ukraine, so stupid. No one learns from war. No one learns."

"Mr. Cisco does not tell us this," said Rawat, "but we believe he has killed people."

"Gossip," said Cruz. "And fake news."

"So, I shall say no more about it."

"Yes," said Stas. "I say no more as well."

Thumps was trying to figure out how to extract Cruz from the communal embrace of the pharmacist from India and the master mechanic from Russia when Al came along with the coffee pot.

"Maybe a little less talking," she said, "and more ordering."

"I must get back to the store." Rawat pushed off the stool. "And then I shall go to the course for last-minute preparations with Mr. Wutty."

Stas followed suit. "And I must fix Mr. Cisco's car."

Thumps stopped what he was doing. "You only work on European cars."

"Yes," said Stas, "this is true. But Mr. Cisco has been shot, so he is honourable Russian."

"Honorary," said Rawat.

"So, I am duty bound to fix car. Repair bullet holes. In this, I have much practice."

"Tournament is tomorrow," said Rawat. "Don't forget."

Stas followed Rawat out the door. "Must wash team shirt, practise cheer."

Cruz waited for the café to return to quiet. "Nice guys."

"That they are," said Thumps. "Can't believe you talked him into fixing your car."

"Showed him my bullet wounds," said Cruz. "Man appreciates gratuitous violence."

Al leaned against the counter, set the pot down on the Formica. Hard. "I'm hoping to hear the sound of an order about now."

"Breakfast," said Thumps. "The usual."

"And your bullet-riddled buddy?"

"I'll have what the sheriff is having," said Cruz.

"He's temporary," said Al. "You know that, right?"

Cruz pushed his cup forward, smiled. "Aren't we all."

For the next little while, Al fiddled with a mound of potatoes on the grill. Cruz fiddled with his cellphone. Thumps fiddled with his coffee cup. Until he was tired of fiddling.

"So, where'd you stay last night?"

Cruz held up a finger, fiddled some more with the phone, slipped it back in his pocket. "What was the question?"

"Shadow Ranch?"

"Compromised."

"The Tucker?"

Cruz sneered. "You know how much they want for a room?"

"Okay. So where?"

"What does it matter," said Cruz. "I'm here now. New day. New start."

Al arrived with breakfast. "I gave the ninja whatever some of your potatoes so you don't go all diabetic-high on me."

"Potatoes are a vegetable," said Thumps.

"Don't make me call Beth." Al filled both cups, went back to the grill.

Thumps waited while Cruz lavished pepper on his eggs.

"New day, new start. So how about a new Cruz? The Cruz who shares with the rest of the children. The Cruz who tells the truth, in spite of himself."

Cruz tried to look hurt. "You know everything I know."

"For instance, are you really from Pie Town, New Mexico? Do you have a mother?"

"*Cabrón*, everyone has a mother."

"Nora Gage, Sorin Dalca, Porter Kincaide, Stan Greeley, yourself, of course. Who am I missing?"

"If Kincaide is involved," said Cruz, "he won't get anywhere near the action himself. He'd send in a team."

"Great," said Thumps. "Now I'm looking for a snatch-and-grab team as well?"

"Going to be hard to spot," said Cruz. "If I were Kincaide, I'd use the golf tournament as cover."

"So, you want to go to Shadow Ranch? Look around?" Thumps loaded egg onto his toast, took a bite. "If there *is* a crew in play, they're not going to be wearing T-shirts that say 'Para Bellum Snatch Team.'"

Cruz took a forkful of potatoes. "You think Al uses Yukon Golds for her hash browns?"

"How many?"

"Minimum of two," said Cruz. "Maximum of four. If I were planning a grab, I'd go for four. Two to make the actual snatch, two to act as backup in case something goes wrong."

"So, the options are one, Gage is kidnapped by Sorin Dalca and is being held at a secure location until he can sell her to Para Bellum. Two, she's grabbed by Kincaide's men, who take her to a secure location and interrogate her. Or three, Gage sees the danger ahead of time and disappears before either Dalca or Para Bellum can find her."

Cruz held up a forkful of hash browns. "Russets aren't as firm and full-bodied as Yukon Gold."

"And whether it's option one, two, or three, here you sit having breakfast."

"Most important meal of the day," said Cruz. "Dalca's not going to kill her. No upside. And Para Bellum isn't going to kill her, at least not until they get the information they want."

"And when Kincaide discovers that she doesn't know anything?"

"Probably let her go."

"Because they're really good guys at heart?" Thumps waggled his hand. "Or because killing her would create an unwanted and unnecessary stink."

"Course they *could* kill her," said Cruz, "dispose of the body where it would never be found."

"Charming." Thumps mopped up the last of the eggs. "Do you really speak Hindi and Russian?"

"Only when I have to." Cruz pushed his plate to the edge of the counter. "Can we use your car? The leg is still killing me."

29

They were halfway to Shadow Ranch before Thumps asked the obvious question.

"Why are we going back to Shadow Ranch?"

"You did lock down the villa?"

"Yes," said Thumps. "I locked down the villa. And we processed the place. Came up empty."

"What about the house out at Ironstone Estates?"

"Locked down as well," said Thumps. "All of which puts me in the mood for locking you down."

"We're going back to Shadow Ranch because *I* want to look at the villa."

"You already looked at the villa."

"I was shot at the time," said Cruz. "Pain and trauma can make you less observant."

"I wasn't shot. I didn't miss anything."

"You're a hick sheriff in a hick town," said Cruz. "Of course you missed something."

Thumps pulled the cruiser into the No Loading zone in front of the main entrance.

"Why don't you pull in behind the villa," said Cruz. "Hell of a lot closer."

Thumps started off across the property. "Walk will do you good."

"I got a bad leg."

"You want to talk about hick towns," said Thumps, "let's talk about Pie Town."

Cruz limped along behind him. "You're just being a shit."

"A hick shit," said Thumps.

THE VILLA HAD a crime-scene sticker pasted across the door and the jamb. Thumps took out his knife and slit the sticker.

"If we were going to start from the beginning," said Thumps, "we should start with the house out at the river."

"Did that already." Cruz tapped the sensor with his card key. "Got shot for my trouble. Remember?"

Cruz pushed through the door, limped his way to the living room. Thumps followed along behind.

"Tell me again what happened?"

Cruz turned the lights on. "After Greeley blew our cover, we packed up and came here."

"And the dog?"

"Don't know why Gage wanted the dog in the first place," said Cruz. "Mutt did nothing but slobber all over the place. Should have seen my rear window."

"So, you dropped Howdy off at the shelter."

"Howdy?"

"The dog."

"Right," said Cruz. "Gage took him in. I waited in the car."

"Yeah," said Thumps, "the woman at the shelter remembered your car."

"Too many loose ends," said Cruz. "After I got Gage settled, I went back to the house to make sure we hadn't left anything behind."

"Or you went back to see if anyone else might show up."

"Okay," said Cruz. "Little bit of both."

"How long were you there?"

Cruz walked the room, careful not to step on the broken pieces of ceramic and glass. "About an hour."

"And then?"

"Got in the car and started to drive away."

Thumps opened a drawer, shut it. Opened a cupboard. "And that's when you were shot?"

"Bang, bang. And bang."

"How far away?"

"No idea," said Cruz. "Probably a hundred yards. Maybe less."

"You see anything?"

"Didn't even see the flash," said Cruz.

Thumps walked to the far end of the living room. "What do you think happened?"

"I left Gage here," said Cruz. "So, she didn't come in and find someone waiting for her."

"No damage to the door."

"Kidnapper could have had a key card," said Cruz. "Resort security might have a record of any entries."

"And if they didn't use a key card, Gage would have had to open the door herself. Does Gage know anyone out here besides you?"

"You think Sorin Dalca came knocking?"

"If he did, would Gage have let him in?"

"Did you find any blood?" Cruz pushed a couple of pieces of broken ceramics around with his foot.

"Nothing," said Thumps. "If it was a forceable abduction, you'd expect to see blood."

Cruz walked to the door. "Knock, knock."

Thumps sweetened his voice, a little singsong. "Who is it?"

"Your good buddy Sorin," said Cruz. "We need to talk."

"Not by the hair of my chinny chin chin," sang Thumps.

"Huff puff," said Cruz. "Huff puff. Come on. We're friends. Look, I didn't mean what I said back in D.C. Open the door."

Thumps took his hat off, wiped the sweatband. "So, Gage opens the door, and what? Dalca pulls a gun? Come quietly or I'll shoot you?"

"Answers the blood question."

"It does," said Thumps. "But then why bother to trash the place?"

"Jesus," said Cruz, "enough with the breakage. A better scenario is Kincaide."

"Para Bellum."

"They would come with numbers," said Cruz. "Get in the villa, no problem. Grab Gage, easy peasy. A little breakage on the way. Van out back, and off we go to an undisclosed location to have a friendly chat about cabbages and kings."

"And why the sea is boiling hot," said Thumps. "And whether pigs have wings."

"And they say a public education is a waste."

"Let's say it's Kincaide and Para Bellum," said Thumps. "And let's say it's a team of four. You have any good ideas on how to identify them, and even better yet, find them?"

"They'd come in as golf enthusiasts," said Cruz. "Here to watch the tournament. They wouldn't hang together. But they'd be of a type."

"Military. Four guys in good shape. Late twenties to mid-thirties."

"We can eliminate the golfers," said Cruz. "No way Kincaide could arrange that."

"Good," said Thumps. "That brings the number of possibles down to under a thousand."

"And they won't be here now," said Cruz. "They'll be where they're holding Gage."

"If Para Bellum is involved."

"It feels as though we're chasing our tails."

"We are chasing our tails." Thumps put his hat back on, headed for the door. "And I have other things to do."

"You're not going to help me?" Cruz followed Thumps out the door. "Losing Gage is not going to look good on my resumé."

There was no wind to speak of, but Thumps could see a chinook arch forming on the western horizon. If the wind did make an appearance, the golfers would be in for an interesting tournament tomorrow.

Thumps squinted at the high prairie light. "I can understand why Para Bellum might have grabbed Gage. Kincaide thinks that she knows where the money is buried."

"But she doesn't."

"Something's wrong." Thumps turned away from the sun.

"Something material to our discussion?"

"Gut feeling."

"Ah," said Cruz, "indigestion."

"According to Gage, Dalca was worried that the Vault had been compromised, that if he tried to access the money, he would be arrested."

"Which is why he wanted Gage to help him hit Para Bellum again," said Cruz. "A kind of encore that would give him enough money to disappear."

"Why would he think that?"

"Think what?"

"That the Vault was compromised. That's where it all starts." Thumps tilted his head to the side. "How about you get on your spy cellphone, make some calls to the dark side of the moon, and see what else you can find out about Sorin Dalca and the Black Ice operation."

"You think we're missing something."

"We are missing something," said Thumps. "We just don't know what it is."

30

Thumps took his time driving back to town. Cruz leaned up against the door, tried to get comfortable.

"So, what are we missing?"

Thumps stared out at the road. "No idea."

"You ever read any Agatha Christie novels?"

"Sure."

"Annoying, aren't they." Cruz rubbed his leg. "She throws up this vomit of suspects and possibilities, but she always withholds the critical clue until the very end, so you can't figure out who done it until the last ten pages."

"I figured out *Ten Little Indians*."

Cruz made a face. "Seeing the movie doesn't count."

"I'm just saying that this feels like a Christie novel." Thumps rolled his shoulders, tried to relax his neck. "We know too much, and we know too little."

"Profound," said Cruz. "Worthy of a fortune cookie."

"We know that Gage was part of Black Ice. We know what Black Ice did. We know about Sorin Dalca and the Vault. We know that Dalca faked his death. We know he wants to access the millions that Black Ice accumulated, but he's worried that the money has been compromised. So, he goes to Plan B, tries to sell Gage to Porter Kincaide and Para Bellum for a pile of cash to make up for the money he doesn't dare touch."

"And what we don't know," said Cruz, "is who grabbed Gage, and where she is."

"Smart money is on Dalca," said Thumps. "Gage is his golden goose. With the Black Ice money radioactive, she's the only thing of value he has left. Para Bellum isn't going to pay him for a name. They'll want the woman herself before Dalca sees a cent."

Cruz nodded. "Dalca forces Gage to come with him."

"He's not going to risk a long car trip with a woman in his trunk," said Thumps. "He'd need a safe place, until he can make the exchange with Para Bellum."

"Which means, he hasn't left the area."

"Be my bet."

Cruz leaned back, closed his eyes. "Dalca doesn't know our little piece of heaven. Where would he find a safe house?"

Thumps didn't know where the idea came from. One minute it wasn't there, and the next, it was.

"How about a bunch of vacant McMansions in the middle of a flood plain?"

ORA MAE FOREMAN was standing in front of her wall of listings, humming a song Thumps thought he recognized.

"'Kiss an Angel Good Mornin'?"

Ora Mae didn't turn around. "You know Charley Pride was married to the same woman for over sixty years. Had twenty-nine number one hits. Most of his fans didn't even know the man was Black, until they saw his picture on his first album."

"Can't say I'm partial to country and western," said Cruz.

"Of course you're not." Ora Mae slowly turned away from the board. "Goodness gracious. Deputy Dawg *and* the ninja assassin."

"Afternoon, Ora Mae."

"I'm guessing you two didn't drag your raggedy selves in here to buy a house."

"However," said Cruz, "I do like Willie Nelson's rendition of 'Help Me Make It through the Night.'"

"Got a couple of questions," said Thumps.

"You see a Tourist Information sign hanging over my door?"

"And I really like Kate & Anna McGarrigle's 'Talk to Me of Mendocino,'" said Cruz. "And Dido singing 'White Flag.' But they're not really country."

"It's about Nora Gage," said Thumps. "She's missing."

"Missing?"

"She may have been kidnapped."

Ora Mae crossed her arms, buried her feet in the floor. "Last time I looked, kidnappings didn't have squat to do with real estate."

"Just pulling on all the loose threads," said Thumps. "Wanted to know how many of the houses out at Ironstone River Estates are vacant."

"That mean your kidnappee is no longer in her rental?"

"Ora Mae . . ."

"And next month's rent due in six days?" Ora Mae squeezed

her eyes down into gun slots. "So, which one of you two buckeroos is going to pick up the slack?"

"The vacant places?"

Ora Mae went to her desk, sat down on the chair with a thud. "We talking vacant 'cause the building part's not done yet or we talking vacant 'cause folks aren't supposed to be living there until the flood plain issue is settled?"

"Houses like the one you rented to Nora Gage."

"Sounds like an accusation."

"So, you rented more than one."

"Maybe I did," said Ora Mae, "and maybe I didn't."

"And if maybe you did," said Thumps, "who might you have maybe rented it to?"

"This official sheriff business?"

Thumps touched the brim of his hat. "It is."

Cruz took his cellphone, held it out. "These names, you recognize any of them?"

Ora Mae took her time looking at the list.

"Nora Gage."

"We know about her."

"And José Martinez." Ora Mae sucked on her lower lip. "Rented a place."

"Ironstone Estates?"

"Nice property overlooking the river."

"This Martinez," said Cruz, "what did he look like?"

"Never met the man," said Ora Mae. "Business was conducted through emails and wire transfers. Said he was an artist, needed a rental with peace and solitude."

"An artist?"

"We ain't got a lot of things out here," said Ora Mae, "but we sure as hell got a shitload of peace and solitude."

"We're going to need an address," said Thumps.

"Hope you're not planning to go out there and kick down doors."

"Depends."

"On?"

"Whether or not you're going to give me a key."

Ora Mae shook her head, opened her desk drawer, huffed. "I'm not going to get next month's rent out of either place, am I?"

1812 RIVER VIEW ROAD was at the far end of the development. Thumps stopped the cruiser well back from the two-storey.

Cruz undid his seat belt. "Why do these clowns want their houses to look like something out of a horror movie."

Thumps opened the glovebox, took out the binoculars.

"Are those things supposed to be turrets?" Cruz shook his head. "And where are the windows?"

Thumps adjusted the binoculars, pulled the house into focus. Cruz was right. There were no windows facing the road or the rest of the development.

"Windows will be on the river side."

Cruz tapped his fingers on the dash. "And I'm guessing there's no way to get around to the river side to see if anyone is home."

"Not without being seen."

"So, what? We sit here and wait."

"Could."

"I don't do stakeouts," said Cruz. "They lead to doughnuts."

Thumps handed the binoculars to Cruz. "The name Ora Mae recognized. He's Black Ice?"

"Was," said Cruz. "Martinez died of a heart attack a couple of years back."

"Show me the list."

"It's classified."

"You showed it to Ora Mae."

"Christ, but you're a pain in the ass." Cruz unlocked the phone, handed it to Thumps. "You got something?"

Thumps ran down the names. "George Banks rented the motel room where Greeley was staying. Sarah Croce rented the car he was using."

"And José Martinez rented a house."

"Black Ice."

"Except Banks and Croce and Martinez are dead." Cruz put the phone back in his pocket. "Croce died of breast cancer. Banks was killed in a traffic accident."

"Any of the deaths suspicious?"

"Heart attack and the cancer were natural. Traffic accident was bad luck."

"We're thinking that Dalca has a bunch of Black Ice IDs in his back pocket?"

"Don't leave home without them," said Cruz. "Hey, what are you doing?"

"Sending the names to Deanna." Thumps worked Cruz's phone. "Going to have her run a check on everyone."

"What? You don't believe me?"

Thumps settled in the seat. "So, what does Dalca want?"

Cruz leaned against the door. "This going to be twenty questions?"

"He wants money. He wants the money Black Ice confiscated from Para Bellum and others. But the money is in the Vault, an account that he can't touch while he's alive."

"So, he fakes his death."

"Now he can help himself to the money at his leisure."

"But he doesn't."

"Why not?"

Cruz whistled a couple of bars of "Every Breath You Take."

"Dalca is worried that the authorities have found the Vault," said Thumps, "and that they're watching it."

Cruz pulled the visor down to block out the afternoon sun. "Tell me about Claire. How did you screw that pooch?"

"Can we focus on the task at hand?"

"How long have you two been together? Weren't you going to buy a house?"

Thumps closed his eyes. "Sorin Dalca? Nora Gage? Black Ice?"

"Did she really move to Canada?"

Thumps held up a hand. "How would you do it?"

"What?"

"If you were Dalca, and you were selling Gage to Para Bellum, how would you do it?"

Cruz sighed. "I'd grab her, stash her someplace safe, get in contact with Para Bellum, arrange for the trade. Gage for a wire transfer."

"How much time would you need?"

"Not much," said Cruz. "I'd set everything up ahead of time."

"Before you grabbed Gage?"

"Sure. I'd already have the safe house in place. Soon as the money hit my account, I'd be gone."

"Two days? Three?"

Cruz nodded. "If I was doing the deed, no more than a day."

"So, Dalca has had more than enough time to make the trade and disappear?"

"If he's as good as me," said Cruz. "Few are."

Thumps pulled the car into gear. "Only one way to find out."

"We going to go knock-knock?"

"We are."

Cruz sat up straight, raised the visor. "I love knock-knock."

THUMPS PARKED THE cruiser across the driveway. Mostly for show. And the movies. Anyone bursting out of the triple garage could easily manoeuvre around the patrol car.

As they walked to the front door, Cruz gave Thumps a refresher on kicking in doors. "Lock and hinge placement. That's the important detail."

Thumps pulled a key out of his pocket, held it up. "But we're not going to kick in the door, are we."

"You know, you take all the fun out of knock-knock."

The door was a tall, massive double-entry affair, heavy timbers with bronze fixtures. Thumps pressed the doorbell. Somewhere in the bowels of the house, he could hear the plaintive opening of Tchaikovsky's *1812 Overture*.

"Rich people." Cruz made a disparaging noise. "What's wrong with ding-dong?"

Thumps waited, listened for footsteps that never came, put the key in the lock, pushed the door open.

"So, this is where they keep the elephants."

The foyer was enormous, two storeys high with a double staircase. Cruz limped up the staircase to the right, turned halfway up, struck a pose.

"Imagine me descending from on high in a designer gown all ready for my cotillion."

"You don't even know what a cotillion is."

"Oh, my." Cruz threw his hand to his forehead. "I do feel a swoon coming on."

"Take the upstairs," said Thumps. "I'll check down here."

Cruz turned. "I do so love a forceful man."

Thumps had to admit that the place was over the top. Too much space. Ornate to the point of gaudy. And he had been right about the windows. Floor to ceiling with a view of the canyon and the river and the mountains.

Spectacular all the way down. The living room stretched out across the view, ending in a dining area with a table that could seat twenty with ease. Thumps wasn't awed so much as he was overwhelmed. How many minutes would it take to walk from the sink to the refrigerator?

If you could find it.

The kitchen was all built-ins. Everything hidden behind white oak panels, so you couldn't tell the refrigerator from the dishwasher from the wall ovens, of which there appeared to be three. Thumps reckoned that one of them was a warming oven.

Thumps could hear Cruz moving around above him.

"Find anything?"

"You got a kitchen down there," Cruz shouted.

"I do."

"I've got one up here as well." There was a long pause. "And something else."

Thumps cupped his hands. "You found the elephants?"

"You better come up."

THUMPS WAS PANTING by the time he got to the top of the stairs. Cruz was waiting for him.

"You didn't take the elevator?"

"There's no elevator."

"Yes, there is. And there's a safe room."

"A safe room?"

"And guess what's in the safe room."

Thumps could feel his patience slipping away. "An elephant."

"Would you stop with the elephant jokes?" Cruz headed down a long corridor with rooms on either side. "Six bedrooms, six baths, not counting the two bedrooms and three baths downstairs."

"What's in the safe room?"

"It's more a hotel than a house. You need to stop to rest?"

THE BEDROOM WAS enormous with windows that looked out onto the river. Thumps might not appreciate the conspicuous consumption of the house itself, but the views were priceless.

The room had a huge ensuite with a separate shower and tub, a double sink, two toilets and two bidets. Everything in soft green glass and white tile.

The safe room was through the ensuite at the back. Small and compact with a refrigerator, a microwave, a sofa, and a flat-screen attached to the wall. There were empty water bottles scattered on the floor, a plate with the remains of a micro-wave pizza.

"Kind of cramped compared to the rest of the palace," said Cruz, "but it has its own half-bath."

Someone had looped a long chain around the base of the toilet, locked it off. On the other end was a pair of handcuffs.

"This is cute." Cruz touched the chain with the toe of his boot. "You ever see *Black Snake Moan*?"

Thumps squatted down, ran a hand along the base of the toilet, gave the chain a yank.

"In that movie," said Cruz, "a guy chains a woman up in a room, gives her enough slack to move around."

"Charming."

"Turns out he's doing her a favour, trying to help her get her life straight."

Thumps gave the chain another yank. "Don't think that's what Dalca had in mind for Gage."

"You thinking we're a day late and a dollar short?"

Thumps stood, walked to the door of the safe room. "This open when you found it?"

"It was."

"Why leave it open?" Thumps looked at the keypad. "Why not shut and lock the door? Rest of the house is pristine. We would never have known that Gage was being kept here if the safe room door was shut."

"Maybe Dalca didn't care. Deal was done. He was home free."

Thumps nodded. "Would you have closed the door?"

"Probably."

"Me too." Thumps did a last, slow inspection of the room. "It's the smart play. The longer it took to find this place, the more time Dalca would have to disappear."

"Not looking good, Pancho." Cruz pointed his lips at the left-over pizza. "In the meantime, you happen to be hungry?"

31

Thumps locked the house, pocketed the key. Cruz followed him back to the cruiser.

"You know, there's a chance Gage is still alive." Cruz raised a hand to keep the sun out of his eyes. "They won't believe she doesn't know anything, so they'll spend some time trying to convince her of the error of her ways."

"As in torture."

"As in."

"Odds?"

"I'd keep my money in my pocket," said Cruz, "but I've seen stranger things happen. There was this one time in Kabul . . ."

"Or they could just kill her."

"Lot of heat for nothing," said Cruz. "Something that multinationals with fat government contracts would prefer to avoid."

Thumps leaned against the car. "I'm Para Bellum, and I'm pissed off that Black Ice helped themselves to my money."

"Your illegally acquired money."

"Tomayto, Tomahto. So, they pay Dalca for giving them Gage. They grill her for the information they want, but they don't get it. It's decision time. They can kill her, lose the body, and get on with business as usual or . . ."

". . . they can let her go with all sorts of dire warnings about saying anything."

"Killing her is clean, but it may come back to bite them on the ass."

"And letting her go runs the risk of her talking to the authorities."

Thumps shifted his weight. "But Gage isn't going to do that."

"Sorin Dalca." Cruz nodded.

"Gage knows that Dalca is alive. If she's going to shine a light on anyone, she'll start with him."

"Which means Dalca has a vested interest in making sure that Gage is not left alive to talk."

Thumps turned back to the house. "So, he covers his bases. He gives Gage to Para Bellum and gets paid. Either they kill her or they don't. If they do, Dalca is free and clear. And if they don't, Dalca is going to have to finish the job."

"Tricky," said Cruz. "Dalca would have to know in advance that Para Bellum was going to turn her loose. And he would have to know where and when, because as soon as Gage is free, she's going to run for cover."

"How would you do it?"

"You asking for trade secrets?"

"Tracker," said Thumps. "When she was in the safe room. Probably more than one."

Cruz shrugged. "Wristwatch. If she has one. Shoes are a good place. Hell, they have trackers you can swallow and sprays that can be followed via satellite."

"But?"

"But the good stuff is high tech. Expensive. Not easy to come by. And in addition to the tracker, you need a shitload of gear and a team to be able to follow the signal."

"Something a guy just back from the dead wouldn't have?"

"Para Bellum could have the gear."

"Sure, but why would they bother?"

"How about we take a break from all the thinking," said Cruz, "and get something to eat."

"As in, I take you out to dinner?"

Cruz opened the door, slid in. "And don't even think about the giant squirrel."

Miracle of miracles, Thumps was able to find a parking space almost in front of Pappous's.

"You're kidding."

"Best food in town," said Thumps.

"The guy hates me," said Cruz. "He'll probably put something in my food. Give me diarrhea."

"Just don't order the octopus."

Cruz followed Thumps in through the door. "What I said about the giant squirrel? I may have been hasty."

Pappous's was empty. Fancy Whelan was moving from table to table, arranging place settings, tenting napkins.

"Sheriff DreadfulWater. And mysterious friend."

"Evening, Fancy."

"Try late afternoon," said Fancy. "We're not open yet."

"Archie here?"

"He is. And the lad is in a foul mood."

Thumps waited.

Fancy rolled her eyes. "The octopus he ordered didn't arrive."

"Sonic Drive-in," said Cruz. "You must have a Sonic in town."

Thumps frowned. "Aren't you supposed to be at Dumbo's?"

"You mean, why am I here during doughnut business hours?"

"Doughnuts," said Cruz. "Nothing wrong with doughnuts for dinner."

"Uncle Morris is thinking of closing the shop."

Thumps felt the ground move under his feet. "What?"

"Says he's retiring," said Fancy. "To Puerto Rico."

"His girlfriend?"

"Found his *anamchara*, he has," said Fancy. "And about time. Another year or so and Uncle Morris'll be nothing but gristle and noise."

"But Dumbo's doughnuts . . ."

"Your guess is as good as mine," said Fancy. "But I expect we'll know soon enough. Uncle Morris isn't one for acting the maggot."

Thumps heard the kitchen door open behind him.

"This can't be good news."

"Evening, Archie."

"It's not evening," said Archie. "It's late afternoon."

"Hoping we could get an early dinner."

Archie eyed Cruz. "He kill anyone yet?"

"Not yet."

"I've got some lamb pilaf made up. You like lamb pilaf?"

"If it's got lamb in it," said Cruz, "I'll like it."

Thumps and Cruz settled into a table, took a collective deep breath. Thumps moved the flatware around. Cruz moved the candle to one side.

"So," Cruz said, after he had rearranged the salt and pepper shakers for a third time, "you got any more ideas?"

"Lots."

"Intelligent ideas."

"Logic says that Gage is dead or about to be dead. Because Dalca can't afford to leave her alive."

Cruz nodded. "Can't fault the logic."

"And if she's dead, then Dalca is long gone or about to be long gone."

"Again, the logic is good."

"Can you leave the salt and pepper shakers alone?"

"The folks back east aren't going to be happy."

Thumps sat back. "And they would be . . . ?"

"You know," said Cruz. "The folks back east."

"How about you answer a couple of questions."

Cruz turned his hands palm up. "Sure."

"I'm serious," said Thumps. "First off, the . . . folks back east . . . had to know what Black Ice was doing, had to know about the money."

"They did."

"Which means they knew about the Vault."

"Sure," said Cruz. "Dalca told them. It wasn't a secret."

"He just neglected to tell them how to access the money."

"All right." Archie and Fancy came banging out of the kitchen, carrying plates. "Dinner."

Fancy set a plate in front of Cruz. "This is the good stuff."

"It's all good stuff." Archie helped himself to a chair. "About time we all got caught up."

Catching up for Archie was a sacred ritual. Knowing what was going on in Chinook at any moment, a religion. Thumps tried to fill him in between mouthfuls of food.

"I hear you caught the car thieves."

"Mmmmm."

"Two old guys."

"Mmmmm."

"But you're not going to prosecute."

"No harm," said Thumps, "no foul. We couldn't find anyone who wanted to make a complaint."

Archie looked at Cruz. "And the missing woman?"

"No comment."

"You don't like the food?"

"The food is great," said Cruz. "Are there seconds?"

"The woman is still missing," said Thumps.

Archie crossed his arms, leaned forward. "You two are going to have to do a lot better than that if you want dessert."

ARCHIE BROUGHT OUT seconds of the pilaf, reminisced about working on his uncle's fishing boat in Greece. Cruz countered with anecdotes of growing up in Pie Town, New Mexico, and by the time dessert arrived, the two men were deep into a bonding ritual of storytelling.

Thumps thought about joining the fray, but in the end, he was content to sit back and listen. And think. Always a problematic activity. Thinking, Thumps found, generally led to the complications and tribulations of life.

Claire and Ivory. For example.

He hadn't heard from Claire since she set sail for Canada. It was too soon for Ivory to have had the tests to determine if the absence seizures were something she might grow out of or if they were a harbinger of something more serious.

Claire had disappeared. Like Gage. Thumps knew the comparison was specious. Gage had been kidnapped, was very likely dead, while Claire had simply gone into seclusion, as she often did when she needed time and space. She would reappear. Eventually. He could stay and wait. Or he could not. His choice.

And for now, he would wait.

"Did you know this *treló átomo* has been to Machu Picchu?" Archie shook his head in disbelief. "He hiked the Inca Trail."

Thumps had seen a half-hour special on the site. The views had been spectacular.

"Tell Thumps how many days it took."

"Four days," said Cruz. "It's not the distance or the slope that gets to you. It's the altitude."

"And they give you coca leaves to chew?"

"Helps to prevent altitude sickness."

Archie sat back. "I've always wanted to go."

"Never too late," said Cruz.

"More *galaktoboureko*." Archie waved a fork at Cruz. "You have to have more *galaktoboureko*."

THERE WAS LITTLE doubt in Thumps's mind that Archie and Cruz would have sat in the restaurant for the rest of the evening, swapping war stories, if Archie hadn't been interrupted by customers who began coming in for dinner.

"So annoying." Archie stood, spread his arms in apology. "You open a restaurant because you like good food, and people come to eat your food, and then there is little time for stories."

"We'll come back," said Cruz.

"Yes, yes, you must come back," said Archie. "You must tell me what happened when you were lost in the Amazon."

Thumps stopped at the door. "You were lost in the Amazon?"

"It's a long story," said Cruz. "And it's complicated."

"Those are the best stories," said Archie.

Thumps held the door open. "Why don't you tell Archie about all the times you almost got me killed."

"Such a good time," said Archie. "We should hug."

Cruz tried to step away, but he wasn't fast enough.

"So many stories." Archie gave Cruz an extra squeeze. "So little time."

32

Thumps walked to the car. Cruz followed.

"Was any of that true?"

"What?"

"Your stories." Thumps tried a stern frown. "Machu Picchu? The Amazon?"

"All my stories are true."

Thumps tried incredulous. "Whatever. You seem to have made a friend."

"He can skip the hugging."

Thumps jerked to one side, as though he was hit by a taser.

Cruz yawned. "Cellphone?"

"Cellphone." Thumps fished the annoyance out of his jacket, stared at the screen. "Office."

"They solve the case?"

"Not sure we have a case."

"Gage is missing."

"Seems to me, that's *your* case." Thumps worked the keypad, held the phone out. "Hey, Cooley, what's up? . . . Really . . . He did . . . Yeah . . . Okay . . . We're on our way."

Cruz leaned on the cruiser. "So, we're on our way, are we?"

"We are." Thumps pulled the door open. "Watch your head."

Deanna and Cooley were sitting at the desk, deep into a game of Jenga. Thumps stood and waited.

"You know, this *is* a sheriff's office."

Cooley didn't look up. "It's the game for the championship."

Deanna waved a hand at the percolator and the file cabinet. "Bag's over there."

Cooley pulled a Jenga piece out. The tower trembled. Then it shuddered. And then it collapsed.

Deanna raised her hands in victory. "The once and future king."

Thumps strolled over to the bag, gave it a gentle kick. "Brian Little Horse brought this in?"

Deanna swept the Jenga pieces back into the box. "When they cleaned out Greeley's rental, they put all the trash in the bag. Would have tossed it out, but they missed the dump run."

"Then Brian figured you might want to see the trash," said Cooley. "You know, maybe there's a clue in Greeley's junk that will crack the case."

"You mean like a note," said Cruz. "Something with an address that tells us where Gage is being held?"

Deanna was unfazed by the sarcasm. "Won't know until you look."

"Not much of a bag." Thumps took a pair of gloves out of his pocket.

"The big question," said Deanna, "is whether to sift or dump."

"I vote for dump," said Cooley. "Nobody sifts anymore."

"Not sure Duke will appreciate trash all over his floor," said Cruz.

"No worries about Duke," said Deanna. "He's busy at the hospital."

Thumps stopped working the knot. "Hospital?"

"Not the real hospital," said Cooley.

"Wild Rose Pet Clinic," said Deanna. "Seems Howdy decided to snack on a bag of Cheetos."

"Cheetos?"

"The spicy version."

"*Dios mío*," said Cruz. "That stuff will kill you."

"Duke was pretty upset," said Cooley. "You want to wait to check the sack until he's here?"

"Going through trash could provide a pleasant distraction," said Deanna. "Take his mind off the dog."

"Dog going to live?"

"Bad diarrhea." Cooley tried to keep the smile off his face.

Deanna didn't bother. "It's not funny. And then, it is."

"You know the joke about the farmer," said Cooley, "who drives a monkey and a constipated pig to town in his pickup?"

"Let's look," said Cruz. "If we find something interesting, we can always put it all back in the sack and do it again, so Duke doesn't feel left out."

THERE WAS A CERTAIN satisfaction in dumping the contents of the bag all over the floor of the sheriff's office. Thumps remembered knocking over garbage cans in the trailer park with Howard Doyle.

That was fun.

Picking all the stuff up, putting it back in the cans, apologizing to the neighbours one by one, was not. He never discovered who ratted them out. Mrs. Upton, whose son Rollie was in the army or in jail, depending on whom you talked to, was a good choice. But it could just as easily have been Mr. Ford, who liked to sit in his La-Z-Boy and watch everyone through his front window with his binoculars.

"Course," said Deanna, "we don't know that all of this is Greeley's. Sort of depends on how good a cleaning job the rental folks did in between customers."

"Not that it matters." Cooley held up a Skippy's burger wrapper and an empty bag of ketchup potato chips. "Don't see a clue in the lot."

"Well, there should be one," said Deanna. "In every cop show, where there's a bag of trash, there's always a clue somewhere in the rubbish."

Cruz gestured to the pile. "Is that a 3 Musketeers bar?"

"Just the wrapper." Deanna touched the pile with her toe. "With a diet like this, it's a wonder Greeley lived as long as he did."

"Couple of empty cigarette packs," said Cooley. "Dead man walking."

"Passing judgment on a man's bad habits is fun," said Cruz, "but it doesn't help us find Gage."

"Here's what I don't understand," said Deanna. "Why would someone bother to hire Greeley?"

"He didn't seem all that smart," said Cooley.

"Not what I mean," said Deanna. "I looked Greeley up on the internet. Most of his business was finding people. Missing relatives, deadbeat dads, runaway kids."

"Probably did cheating husbands as well," said Cruz. "So what?"

"So, he wasn't hired to *find* Gage," said Deanna. "That envelope Cooley found at the car rental? Greeley already had her photo. He already had her address."

"And the sniper rifle?"

"Did Stan Greeley strike you as sniper material?" Deanna tapped the side of her head. "And if he was looking to shoot Gage, why didn't he have the rifle with him when you guys found him that night?"

"Okay," said Cruz, "what are you suggesting?"

"Not suggesting anything," said Deanna. "Just pointing out that not much of this melodrama makes a lot of sense."

Thumps was beginning to feel like an elementary supply teacher at recess. "How about we concentrate on finding Nora Gage and Sorin Dalca?"

"Sorin who?" Deanna put her hands on her hips. "How about we back up and share *all* the information with *all* the children."

"It's a federal matter," said Cruz.

"Try again," said Deanna.

"Too bad we're out of doughnuts," said Cooley. "Doughnuts tend to encourage co-operation."

Thumps wasn't sure whether Cruz decided that having four people working on the matter was better than having two people running around in circles, or if he was just tired and hurting from being shot. Whatever the reason, the man from Pie Town spent the next half-hour patiently going over the salient points of the case.

"Operation Black Ice?" Deanna snorted. "What the hell? You got a bunch of twelve-year-olds making up names?"

"Operation Enduring Freedom," said Cooley. "Operation Noble Eagle. Operation Tapeworm. My favourite is Operation Urgent Fury."

"The invasion of Grenada," said Cruz. "Look, I don't make up the names."

Thumps shuffled over to the filing cabinet and checked the doughnut box. Just in case.

Deanna shook her head. "So, Black Ice was basically a bunch of government white guys messing with a bunch of corporate white guys?"

Thumps licked his fingers. "That's about it."

Deanna grunted. "And we wonder why the country is so fucked up."

"You're forgetting the part about good versus evil." Cruz cleared his throat. "Do you want to hear my 'we're all in this together' speech?"

"Not really," said Deanna.

"I wouldn't mind," said Cooley.

Thumps yawned. "How about we give it a rest, get a good night's sleep. Hit it hard tomorrow."

"No can do," said Cooley. "Tomorrow's the tournament."

"Breakfast at Shadow Ranch," said Deanna. "Then we follow Wutty around the course, encourage him on to victory."

"Team Wutty," said Cooley. "Don't forget your T-shirt."

Cruz looked at Thumps. "You hearing this?"

Thumps shrugged. "We don't have any good leads on Gage or Dalca."

"That's not the point," said Cruz. "You don't take time off a case for a golf tournament."

"We can work on the case as we walk the course," said Deanna. "You got current photographs of Gage and Dalca, right?"

"We do," said Thumps.

"So, send them to our cellphones," said Deanna.

Cruz was smiling, but it was not a happy smile. "What? You're going to show them around at the tournament? Hey, have you seen this woman? How about this guy?"

"It's called canvassing," said Cooley. "The cornerstone of police work."

"Beats sitting around the office, eating doughnuts, playing Jenga," said Deanna.

"I'm going home," said Cruz.

"So far as I can tell," said Deanna, "you don't have a home."

"Holding cell is booked," said Cooley. "I'm on graveyard, so Scoop is coming in with dinner."

"Room at the Tucker?" said Deanna. "Seeing as you're on the government teat."

"Too expensive."

"The Wagon Wheel?"

Cruz grimaced. "Rather sleep on the street."

"Shadow Ranch is booked up 'cause of the tournament," said Cooley.

"Not a lot of choices left." Deanna turned and smiled at Thumps. "Strangers and good friends."

"No way," said Cruz. "Pancho has two man-eating cats, and he hasn't got cable."

"He finally broke down," said Cooley. "Got Netflix as well."

"Or you could bunk with Duke and Howdy," said Deanna. "You want me to call?"

Cruz waved her off. "The cats and cable."

"Just so we're clear," said Thumps. "I didn't invite you."

"Tell me you have the sports package."

CRUZ COMPLAINED ALL the way home. Thumps pulled up in front of his bungalow, left the engine running.

"You'll need to feed the cats."

"Where are you going?"

"Sheriff's business," said Thumps.

"I don't feed cats."

"Half a cup of dry food in each of their dishes. Feed Cookie first. Otherwise, he'll try to eat Freeway's food."

"I'm not cleaning kitty litter."

"Give them a couple tablespoons each of the wet food. It's in the refrigerator."

"Do I look like a cat concierge?"

"And," said Thumps, as Cruz got out, closed the door, "they like to watch *Pick a Puppy*. It's on channel forty-two."

WILD ROSE PET CLINIC was on the southern edge of Chinook, just before the town disappeared and the prairies took over. It was a prefab. A sky-blue aluminum rectangle with a large, fenced-in dog run at the back.

The parking lot was deserted. Except for Duke's sedan. The

sign in the window said they were closed, but if the sheriff was still here, then Thumps imagined that getting in wouldn't be a problem.

He tried the door. Locked. He pressed the doorbell and waited.

It was a young woman who came to the door. Thumps held up his badge, smiled, rocked on his heels, did what he could to make himself smaller and less menacing. An older uncle. A younger grandfather.

"You with the sheriff?"

"I am."

"I'm Dr. Zabner. Appreciate it if you could talk to Mr. Hockney."

"Dog okay?"

The smile was equal parts hope and consolation. "Maybe explain that we closed an hour ago. I'd like to go home."

"Okay."

"Husband? Two little girls?"

THE SHERIFF AND the dog were in a small, dark room. Howdy was stretched out on a large cushion. Duke was on the floor next to him.

"Hear he ate a bag of Cheetos."

"Macy was crazy about them," said Duke. "I forgot they were there."

"Guess they're not good for dogs."

"I'll tell you what's not good for dogs." Duke's eyes were dark and wet and baggy. "You know those laundry detergent pods? The ones you just drop into the washer? After he ate the Cheetos, he had a bunch of those for dessert."

Thumps wrinkled his nose, breathed through his mouth.

"Yeah, the farts are pretty bad," said Duke. "You should have seen the puke and the diarrhea."

"Doctor said you could take him home."

"Sure," said Duke. "But what happens if we get there and he takes a turn for the worse?"

Howdy was lying on his side, looking mournful. The orange mist around his mouth and muzzle added to the effect. But then most dogs looked mournful. Or happy. There wasn't much in between.

"Don't imagine he likes it here."

"Hospital," said Duke. "No one likes to be in a hospital."

"How about I follow you home, help you get Howdy settled?"

"Big dummy." Duke leaned over, ran a hand along Howdy's flank. "You know you could have been killed. And you're not even my dog."

Thumps stood, nodded. "Yeah," he said, "he knows."

33

It was well after midnight before Thumps was able to walk out the front door of Duke's bungalow. On the way home, Howdy had had a small accident in the back seat, and it had taken some effort to clean it up. Then there was the hour or so that the three of them spent in the backyard while Howdy got everything out of his system that there was left to get. After which Duke made a bed next to his bed, so the dog wouldn't feel abandoned.

Thumps wasn't sure if this effort was for Howdy or for Duke. Or the both of them. Not that it mattered.

What mattered was that, by the time he got back to his house, he was beyond tired, and no matter how the rest of the night went, he was not going to get his required eight hours. The good news was that Freeway and Cookie were not hogging the bed. In fact, the cats were nowhere to be found. Thumps imagined that they had crawled in with Cruz and were annoying him.

No way he was going to rock that boat.

A night without the cats squirming around on the bed, curling up next to his neck, purring at decibels above the legal limit, breathing their fishy cat breath in his face, was a gift horse that he was not going to look in the mouth.

He didn't bother to undress. He simply lay down on the bed, shoved a pillow against his side, tucked the other one under his head, and dragged the quilt over his body. He was debating whether or not to take off his shoes when sleep took him.

CRUZ WAS WAITING at the breakfast table the next morning when Thumps came into the kitchen. Cookie and Freeway were nowhere to be seen.

"Where are the cats?"

"Asleep," said Cruz. "They had a hard night."

Thumps went to the refrigerator, opened the door.

"They spent half the night trying to bite my toes." Cruz beat his fingers on the table, as though he were playing a drum solo. "The other half of the night was dedicated to prime-time wrestling."

Thumps closed the door. "We're supposed to be at Shadow Ranch for the tournament."

"You can buy me breakfast," said Cruz.

"I'm not buying you breakfast."

"I should charge you for cat sitting."

"I should charge you for a room."

Cruz stood, put on his jacket. "You know, when I make my report, I'm going to blame you."

• • •

THE PARKING LOT at Shadow Ranch was full, with cars driving around in circles like a flock of vultures in search of a carcass. Thumps pulled into the loading zone, put the sheriff's card on the dash.

"I see you've settled into the job."

"You want to walk in from Idaho?"

"You're actually going to watch a golf tournament?"

"We got any leads on Gage or Dalca or Para Bellum?"

Cruz got out of the cruiser, took in the herd of people milling about the clubhouse and the first tee.

"Looks like the cattle drive in *City Slickers*."

Thumps stood by the rear fender, seriously considered returning to the office, braving Duke's coffee, enduring a round of Jenga.

"There you are." Archie popped out of the roundup, a paper bag in his hand. "Youngbeaver had an early start. He's probably on the sixth tee by now."

"We haven't eaten," said Cruz.

"You can forget the dining room." Archie handed the bag to Thumps.

"Skippy's?"

"Of course not," said Archie.

"It says 'Skippy's,'" said Cruz.

"Yes, it's a Skippy's bag," said Archie, "but inside is *biftekia*."

"Sure," said Cruz. "Nothing like a bif . . . bife . . .bifeka . . . for breakfast."

"*Biftekia*," said Archie. "It's a Greek hamburger."

Thumps opened the bag, brought it to his nose. "Any octopus in it?"

"Lamb," said Archie. "And spices. And onions. And tomatoes. And tzatziki sauce."

"Which is?"

"Strained yogurt, cucumbers, garlic, olive oil, of course."

"Of course."

"Salt, dill, mint, parsley, thyme, and lemon."

"Strained yogurt?" Cruz looked in the bag. "Wait. There's only one."

"I didn't know you were coming," said Archie. "You two will have to share."

"And one cup of coffee?"

"Share." Archie grabbed Thumps by the arm, began dragging him through the crowd. "Share."

Thumps had never lived in large cities, cities such as Salt Lake, or Denver, or San Francisco, or Los Angeles, cities where people and traffic and the racket of living came together in a gridlock of impatience and exasperation. He had lived in smaller towns such as Roseville and Eureka and Chinook, towns where, if there happened to be a traffic jam, you knew who it was.

"Come on, come on." Archie plowed ahead, moving people out of the way.

"How's he doing?"

"Not bad." Archie dodged around a group of men laughing and spilling beer on each other. "Two under after the fifth."

"What you should do," said Cruz, "is fire a couple of shots in the air. That should part the Red Sea."

"More like the white sea," said Thumps.

"Point taken."

The golf course was a freeway at rush hour. Thumps was rear-ended and side-swiped, run over by several large SUVs in walking shorts, overwhelmed by the fumes of humanity packed into too tight a space.

"Over here." Cooley Small Elk, in his red and gold Team Wutty shirt. "Kinda amazing, ennit."

"Where's Deanna?"

"Holding down the office," said Cooley. "We played Rochambeau for who got to come to the tournament."

"Rochambeau?"

"You know, rock, paper, scissors."

"And you won."

"No," said Cooley. "I lost."

Archie was frowning. "The ninja assassin ate your *biftekia*."

"I was hungry." Cruz licked his fingers. "I didn't get breakfast."

"And he drank your coffee."

Cooley fished his phone out of his pocket. "The photos you sent me? I've been showing them around."

"Any luck?"

"Lots," said Cooley. "Most everyone I asked thinks they saw Gage."

"Let me guess," said Cruz. "They saw Dalca as well."

"At the concession tent," said Cooley. "Or in the merchandise pavilion. Or having coffee in the resort. Couple of people were pretty sure they saw the both of them at the water park, coming down the Aqualoop."

"So, a big bunch of nothing," said Thumps.

"About it," said Cooley. "People just want to be helpful."

"Come on," said Archie. "We need to get moving."

"I haven't had breakfast," said Thumps. "I'm diabetic. My blood sugars are dropping."

"Don't you carry sugar pills for an emergency?"

"I'd rather eat something healthy. Like bacon and eggs."

"Sure," said Archie. "But in the meantime, eat the sugar pills."

"Rest of the gang is waiting at the fifteenth hole," said Cooley. "You guys remember the chant?"

MAKING HIS WAY through the crowds reminded Thumps of crossing a swollen river. The trick was to start above where you wanted to go and let the current take you down and across.

Until you were washed up on the far shore.

Stas Black Weasel, Alvera Couteau, Jimmy Monroe, Russell Plunkett, Ora Mae Foreman, Dolores Cardoza, Beth Mooney, Gabby Santucci, Fancy Whelan, and several other people Thumps recognized but couldn't put a name to were standing in a cluster in their Team Wutty shirts.

Jimmy waved a finger at Thumps. "Where's your shirt?"

"On duty."

"What about him?"

"*No hablo inglés*," said Cruz.

"Did anyone bring food?" said Thumps.

"You mean like a breakfast burrito?" asked Al.

"Yes," said Thumps. "Like that."

"Nope," said Al. "Don't tell me you didn't eat before you came."

"I didn't eat before I came." Thumps turned on Cruz. "There *was* a Greek hamburger and a cup of coffee, but he ate it."

Fancy held out a large bag. "Would a doughnut or two be on the approved menu for a diabetic?"

"It would not," said Beth.

"I'll pretend it's a veggie burger," said Thumps.

"There's a food tent near the thirteenth hole," said Ora Mae. "Wutty's group won't be here for at least two hours."

"Two hours?" said Cruz. "You have to be kidding."

"Golf is four to five hours," said Stas. "American football is three hours. Baseball is two and a half. Basketball is just over two."

Going back to the thirteenth hole meant making his way back through the crowds. Staying where he was meant living off sugar pills.

Cruz pushed up against his side. "I'm coming with you."

"Why are you whispering?"

"Keep your voice down." Cruz put a finger to his lips. "Soon as Team Whatever figures out that we're heading for the food tent, we'll be taking orders."

Thumps could see the golfers on the tee now. Par threes were fun. The chance of hitting the green. The chance, however remote, of getting a hole in one.

"Okay," said Thumps. "Wait for it."

"Wait for what?"

The man on the tee took a long, smooth swing. The ball rocketed into the sky, arched out over the fairway, landed on the green, took two hops, then spun back toward the hole. In an instant, a thunderous roar erupted, and the ground shook as the onlookers surged forward.

"Now," said Thumps.

THE FOOD TENT had six lines. Six long lines.

"What the hell." Cruz rubbed his head with both hands. "We could starve before we get to the front."

"You already ate."

"It was a small burger." Cruz looked around. "How about you put your badge to good use?"

"As in, ordering a burger and a beer is official business?"

"As in."

"I'm not going to flash my badge. You get into one line, I'll get into another. First one to the front gets the food."

"You know, the food is going to be expensive and disappointing."

"Go for the hot dogs," said Thumps. "The hamburgers will be dried out."

THE LINES MOVED like a slow dance. One step, one step, with long pauses in between. Certainly not the skippy freedom of a Fred Astaire and Ginger Rogers number.

Thumps won the race, carried the hard-earned spoils to an empty patch of ground next to a utility building.

"Pizza?"

"It's all they had."

"What the hell is on it?"

"Supposed to be pepperoni."

Cruz took a bite. "It's not pepperoni."

"I think it might be Spam."

"Thought that stuff was illegal." Cruz took another bite. "You're right, it does taste like Spam."

"Pork and ham meat, lots of salt, water, potato starch, lots of sugar, lots of sodium nitrate," said Thumps. "Cleverly concealed in a blue and yellow tin."

"As opposed to emulsified meat trimmings, lots of salt, spices, MSG, celery powder, various fillers, and artificial additives all cleverly concealed in a tan little skin."

"Spam and hot dogs." Thumps took another piece of pizza. "The foods that made America great."

"Don't forget Froot Loops."

There was little to recommend the pizza. It wasn't even hot. Still, it was food. Thumps tried to imagine early man, off to bag a woolly mammoth, stumbling across a pizza. Would he have eaten it or left it by the side of the trail? And what would have been the evolutionary consequences of such a decision?

"I'm going to have gas," said Cruz.

"Thanks for the update."

"Don't tell the cats," said Cruz. "It will be my surprise."

TEAM WUTTY WAS WHERE Thumps and Cruz had left them. Cooley was on his tippytoes looking out over the crowd.

"I can see Wutty's foursome," he sang out.

"Where did you two go?" said Archie. "You almost missed the big moment."

"Food tent," said Cruz. "He was hungry. I made sure he didn't get lost."

"You ate food from a food tent?"

"A Spam pizza," said Cruz.

"Why would you do something so foolish?" said Archie. "Something so dangerous to your health."

Thumps shrugged. "They had run out of hot dogs."

"Wutty's on the tee."

Team Wutty surged forward, pushing through the crowd to the ropes. Sure enough, in the distance, Thumps could see Wutty talking to Chintak Rawat, consulting his yardage book, trying to figure out where he wanted his ball to land.

Jimmy and Russell began a low chant of "Wutty, Wutty, Wutty, Wuuuuuttyyy."

The fifteenth green was long and narrow, sloped from back to front, left to right. There was a bunker at the near corner with long, cigar-shaped bunkers on either side. Hit the tee shot long and you'd wind up in the underbrush at the back. Hit it short with spin and the ball would roll off the false front and trickle onto the fairway, eighty yards from the cup. The bunkers at the front and on the right were okay, but the bunker on the short side presented the golfer with an impossible shot. Hit the ball too softly and it would catch the lip of the bunker and stay in the sand. Clear the lip and the ball would land on the downslope, roll out with no chance of stopping anywhere near the flag.

Cooley held up a hand. "Here we go."

In the distance, Thumps could see Wutty settle his feet into the grass on the tee box, grip and regrip the club, check his line. And then slowly, almost leisurely, he took the club back and brought it through in a graceful arch.

As the club struck the ball, Team Wutty exploded.

Wutty hit a high fade. The ball curled in from the left, hit the green above the hole, took a skip, rolled back down the slope, settling at the front of the green.

"Uphill putt," Archie shouted. "They're the best."

"Mr. Wutty is not near hole," said Stas.

"But it's an uphill putt," said Archie.

Russell and Jimmy switched from the Wutty chant to "Birdie, birdie, birdie, biiiiirrrrdieee."

Cruz leaned into Thumps. "Can we go now?"

"Not before he finishes the hole."

“You do know this is embarrassing,” said Cruz. “The shirts. The singing . . .”

“Chanting.”

“Whatever. Any minute now, your Greek buddy is going to pull out a handkerchief and start dancing.”

The other golfers in Wutty’s foursome hit their shots. Two in the sand trap to the right. One on the green closer to the hole than Wutty’s ball, but hole high with a nasty right to left break.

As Wutty strolled down the fairway, he raised his club over his head, and Team Wutty broke into another round of chanting.

Thumps didn’t hear it over the cheer, but he felt it. An annoying buzz against his thigh.

“That your phone?”

Thumps let it buzz.

“You’re not going to answer it?”

Thumps took the phone out of his pocket. “You answer it.”

“Do I look like I answer phones?”

Thumps looked at the screen. Deanna.

“DreadfulWater.”

“I should hope so,” said Deanna, “because that’s who I called.”

Thumps waited.

“What’s all that noise?”

“Wutty’s on the fifteenth green. Team Wutty is cheering him on.”

“How’s he doing?”

“Uphill putt. Fairly straight with a left to right at the end.”

“You want to call me back?”

Wutty and the other golfers reached the green. Chintak Rawat put the bag down and began pacing out the putt, walking the slope.

"What's up?"

"Remember that woman we were looking for?"

Thumps stood up straight. "Nora Gage?"

"The same," said Deanna. "Appears we found her."

Thumps paused before he asked. "Alive or dead?"

The two guys in the bunker both got their balls out. Neither was a great shot, but they were on the green. Wutty was next. Jimmy and Russell raised their hands over their heads and began chanting.

"In the hole! In the hole! In the hole!"

"What was that?"

"Team Wutty."

"Sounds like someone is having a good time."

"Gage?"

"Alive," said Deanna. "Not in showroom condition, but alive."

34

Thumps put the phone back in his pocket.

"Who was that?"

"Deanna," said Thumps. "We found Gage."

"And?"

"She's at the hospital," said Thumps.

"But alive."

"Little worse for wear."

"Details."

"Quiet," said Thumps. "Wutty's about to putt."

"You're joking."

"He's putting for a birdie."

"What about Gage?"

"She's not going anywhere."

Thumps wasn't close enough to see the exact contour of the green, but if he was attempting the putt, he'd put it to the high side and let the ball drift back to the hole. Everything would depend on line and speed.

As it always did.

"You're going to stand here and watch a putt?"

"I am."

Cruz turned away. "I'll meet you at the hospital."

"You don't have a car."

"Shit."

"So, stand still and shut up."

Wutty took his time. He paced the green, squatted down so he could see the grain, walked off the green for a long look, and then went back to his ball.

"You think he might do something by the end of the week?"

"This *is* the end of the week."

Wutty took his stance over the ball, relaxed, took a breath, let it out. The stroke was smooth. The ball rolled out, leaning into the high side, curling back at the end. The speed was perfect. The line was good. The ball settled less than a foot from the hole.

At which point, Team Wutty burst into a cheer.

"Why are they cheering? He missed the putt."

"It was a good putt," said Thumps.

"Yeah, but he missed."

"Hard par three," said Thumps. "And he got a par."

"That's average, right?"

"It's par."

"Who gets excited over being average?" Cruz started back. "Can we go to the hospital now?"

GINA TUCCI WAS sitting in front of a monitor. Something on the screen was making her smile.

"Morning, Gina."

Gina ran a hand through her hair. "Just so you know," she said, "I'm married."

"Good to know," said Thumps.

"Not for you," said Gina. "For him."

Cruz flashed a smile. "I'll keep that in mind."

"See that you do." Gina moved the mouse. "Cat videos. They always cheer me up."

"Working emergency must be exciting," said Cruz.

"Sure," said Gina. "Kids with snotty noses. Guy who puts a drill bit through his finger. Broken nose from walking into a door." Gina rolled her eyes. "Wink, wink, nudge, nudge."

"Domestic abuse?"

"And not the first time."

"Husband? Boyfriend?"

"Does it matter?" Gina smiled at Cruz. "Are you married?"

"Not at this point."

"I'll keep that in mind."

"Deanna brought a woman in?"

"Nope," said Gina. "Highway patrol did. I called Deanna when I saw her name."

"We need to talk to her."

"She's pretty dopey," said Gina. "And she needs a bath."

"Serious injuries?"

"More like rough handling." Gina shook her head. "Think suitcases at airports."

"You going to give us a room number?"

"You going to give me your phone number?"

"You want it?"

"Naw," said Gina. "Cat videos are all the excitement I can manage."

• • •

Nora Gage was in room 204. Her eyes were closed, and there was an IV in her left arm. The right arm had an angry welt at the wrist, and there was a bruise forming up nicely on her cheek. Other than that, she looked fine. Which meant nothing. Thumps had seen dead people without a mark on their body, and he had pulled a guy out of a bad car wreck covered in blood from a minor head wound.

"She awake?" Cruz moved to the side of the bed.

"Yes." Gage kept her eyes closed. "She's awake."

"Good to see you again, Nora."

"Fine job you did protecting me."

"I got shot."

Gage opened her eyes, looked at Thumps.

"It's true," said Thumps, "he did."

"Maybe there is some justice in the world."

Cruz smiled, but Thumps didn't feel any warmth behind it.

"How about you tell us what happened?"

Gage tried to come to a sitting position. "A little late for explanations."

Cruz shrugged. "Humour us."

Gage tried to clear her throat. "First, I need a cold drink. Water will do, but I'd much prefer an Orange Crush or a Pepsi. You think one of you strong lads can manage that?"

Cruz picked up the water thermos from the bedside table, poured a glass, handed it to Gage.

"There's a flexi straw in the drawer."

"You were at Shadow Ranch," said Thumps. "Why don't we start there."

Gage took her time with the water, small, slow sips. "Warm," she said. "Hardly worth the drinking."

Cruz nodded. "The villa?"

"Sorin hired that detective."

"The investigator from Great Falls? How do you know?"

"Told me," said Gage. "Wanted to spook me."

"So, it was Dalca at the villa."

"I went out to watch the golfers practise. Have you seen some of those guys? They're huge. More like basketball players."

Cruz dropped his voice. "You were supposed to stay put, out of sight."

"I know." Gage rolled up on her side, winced. "When I got back, Sorin was waiting for me."

Thumps leaned against the wall. "So, he knew where you were hiding."

"That's what I want to know." Gage's face hardened. "How did he know where I was?"

"You're asking me?"

"You were supposed to keep me safe."

"No," said Cruz, "I was supposed to help you get out of D.C., get you settled out here. And that's what I did."

"And yet Sorin had no trouble finding me. What does that suggest?"

Thumps crossed his arms. "Someone told him where to look."

"Duh."

Cruz helped himself to the chair. "Take us through it. From the beginning."

"You think you're going to catch Sorin?"

"Sounds like a plan," said Cruz.

"Well, you can forget it," said Gage. "Sorin is dead."

Cruz settled in the chair. "From the top. Take your time."

GAGE HAD COME back from her outing. She walked into the villa to find Sorin Dalca sitting on the sofa, a gun in his hand. He forced her into the bathroom, injected her with something.

"A sedative?"

"That would be my guess," said Gage. "I don't remember a thing until I woke up in a house. Actually, it was a safe room. The must-have room for rich paranoids. All the amenities, no windows, so I couldn't see out. But I could hear water, a river. Guessed I was back in Ironstone River Estates."

"You were. Same development, different house."

"He handcuffed me to the toilet." Gage held up the injured wrist. "Chain was long enough to allow me to move around the room. Could get to the refrigerator, but not to the door. I did some yelling. For all the good it did me."

Cruz picked at a fingernail. "What did Dalca want?"

"Me," said Gage. "What did you think he wanted?"

"As in the Vault?" said Cruz. "The access code?"

Gage closed her eyes. Somewhere in her body something hurt. "Sorin was the only one who had the code."

Cruz nodded. "So, why grab you?"

Thumps was impressed. Cruz had started out with the obvious question and quietly looped his way around to the critical question.

"Para Bellum," said Gage. "Bastard sold me to Para Bellum."

"Question still stands," said Cruz. "If you didn't have the access code, why would Para Bellum want you?"

Gage sagged back onto the pillow. "Could I get that cold drink now?"

Cruz shifted in the chair. "Thumps will get it for you."

"I'd rather you get it for me," said Gage.

"You don't trust me?"

"I trusted Dalca," said Gage. "Obviously, I'm not a good judge of character."

Cruz stood, stretched his back. "She tries to get out of that bed, shoot her."

Cruz was gone longer than Thumps would have supposed. When he finally reappeared, he had a can of soda in one hand and a glass of ice in the other.

"Took you long enough."

"Big hospital." Cruz set the can and the glass on the overbed table.

"Club soda?" Gage made a face. "You must be kidding."

"It was either that or tonic water."

"You couldn't find a Pepsi?"

"That shit will kill you." Cruz eased himself into the chair. "So, what did you two talk about while I was gone?"

"I've done enough talking," said Gage. "I'm tired."

"Why do you think Dalca's dead?"

"Tired," said Gage. "Time for you two to leave."

"What did Para Bellum want with you?"

Gage rolled over on her side, buried her face in the pillow. "And take your fucking club soda with you."

• • •

THE DAY WAS bright and high. Thumps took his time walking to the car, enjoying the perfect prairie moment. Cruz hadn't said a word since they left the hospital and Gage.

"If we hurry, we might be able to catch a late breakfast at Al's."

"Does she make pizza?"

"No."

Cruz opened the door, got in the car. "Excellent."

"How's the leg?"

Cruz rubbed his thigh. "Who doesn't like club soda?"

"You were gone a long time."

"Had some business."

"You find the doctor who looked after Gage when she was brought in?"

Cruz smiled. "Damn, Pancho. Don't nothing get by you."

"How did you get around patient confidentiality?"

Cruz patted his breast pocket.

"You badged him?" Thumps made a right turn on Main. "And what? Told him it was a matter of national security?"

"Dr. Kazem is a patriot."

"Kazem? That's a Middle Eastern name."

"I guess."

"Don't tell me you threatened him?"

"Her," said Cruz. "And no, I didn't threaten her. *Cabrón*, you watch too much television."

Thumps did a U-turn in the middle of the block, pulled into a loading zone, put the police placard on the dash.

Cruz smirked. "Look who's badging who."

"Whom," said Thumps.

"Do you want to know what the doctor told me or not?"

"I'm guessing she didn't tell you much of anything."

"Superficial bruises. Dehydration. Raw wrist from the handcuffs. Kazem ordered a tox screen."

"So, Gage wasn't tortured."

"Like Gina said. Bags at an airport." Cruz opened the door. "Let's eat."

Al's was empty. The door was open, but Al was nowhere to be seen.

"Grill's still on," said Thumps. "That's a good sign."

Somewhere a door opened and closed.

"Must be my lucky day." Al came out of the back, wiping her hands on her apron. "I hope you don't want breakfast."

"We want breakfast," said Thumps.

"All we've had to eat," said Cruz, "is a crappy pizza at a golf tournament."

"He also ate my *biftekia*."

"Jesus," said Al. "That sounds worse than the pizza."

"So, we're hungry."

Al went to the grill. "All right, I'll make you breakfast while you fill me in on the tournament."

"You were there."

"Yeah," said Al, "but I couldn't stay. Café don't run itself."

"Not much to tell," said Cruz.

"Wutty hit the green on the par three fifteenth," said Thumps.

"But he missed the putt," said Cruz.

Al waited. "And?"

"That's it," said Cruz. "Thumps got a phone call from the office, and we had to take off."

"You watched one hole?"

"It was an exciting hole."

"So, did Wutty win? Did he lose?"

Thumps wondered if he could look up the results of the qualifying round on Google. Probably.

"So, I know as much about the tournament as you two do. And for this, you want breakfast?"

"The usual," said Thumps.

"Two usuals," said Cruz.

35

Thumps left the cruiser in the loading zone, and the two of them walked down the street to the office.

"Woman makes a mean breakfast."

"She does."

"You google the tournament results?"

"No." Thumps stepped over each line in the sidewalk. "We'll hear soon enough."

"My sister used to do that," said Cruz. "Step over the lines. Had a jingle to go with it."

"Step on a crack, break your mother's back?"

"That's the one." Cruz stepped over a line. "I used to step on every one, just to annoy her."

"We're going to have to go back, talk to Gage again."

"Let's give her enough time to make up a convincing story."

"You don't trust her."

Cruz smiled. "I don't trust anyone."

• • •

Sheriff Duke Hockney was sitting behind his desk, looking as though he had never left. Deanna had rearranged the furniture. Now the computer and monitor were sitting on a separate desk against the far wall.

Howdy the dog was squatted down next to the file cabinet, staring up at the box of Dumbo's doughnuts.

"Watch out," said Deanna. "The mutt's crazy for pastry."

"Turns out," said Duke, "he's a real police dog."

"Deputy Dawg," said Deanna.

"Who is a cartoon character," said Duke. "But points for being clever."

"He ate one of Duke's chocolate cakes," said Deanna. "Right off the desk."

"Better than snacking on detergent pods."

Howdy whined, his body twitched, his tail beat against the floor.

"He's getting ready to make another try," said Deanna.

"Fourth time," said Duke. "You think he'd learn."

"We had to move the coffee pot." Deanna took out her cellphone, aimed it at the cabinet. "His first try almost took it out."

Howdy's body began to quiver and shake, and then the dog exploded off the floor, hit the side of the filing cabinet, yelping, as he tried to claw his way up the side.

"*America's Funniest Home Videos*," said Deanna. "Howdy's sure to make the finals."

"Got one paw over the edge this time," said Duke. "You got to admire his dedication."

Cruz walked to the cabinet, opened the box. "If you were a human," he said to the dog, "you wouldn't have to jump."

Duke waited a beat, waited until Cruz had the doughnut in hand. "Wouldn't do that if I were you."

Howdy didn't waste any time. As soon as the doughnut cleared the box, the dog was on Cruz like a bun on a burger.

"Hey."

Cruz was quick, but he wasn't quick enough.

"He took my doughnut!"

Duke turned to Deanna. "Did you get that?"

"I did," said Deanna. "And it's better footage than the cabinet leap."

Howdy quickly disappeared into the back area with his booty.

"Jesus." Cruz shook his hand. "Dog snot!"

"Welcome to my world." Duke swung around in the chair. "Hear we found your woman."

"Not my woman," said Cruz.

"Kidnapped, beat up, dropped by the side of the road?" Duke cocked his head. "All on your watch?"

"I got shot."

"Right," said the sheriff. "That too."

"Point is, *she* wasn't shot."

Deanna took a file out of the drawer. "Nor was she dropped by the side of the road. She was left at the far end of the airport parking lot. Statement and photos."

"Still on your watch," said Duke.

Cruz went to the doughnut box. Stopped, looked around to make sure Howdy was not in the room.

"That it?" Cruz took a bite of the doughnut. "Statement and photos?"

"Okay, maybe this will help." Deanna turned to the monitor. "Remember that list of names you wanted me to research?"

"You found something?"

"A bunch of somethings, actually." Deanna ran her fingers over the keyboard. "First up, Sorin Dalca is dead."

"Except he's not," said Cruz.

"George Banks, Sarah Croce, and José Martinez are also dead." Deanna worked her way down the screen. "Jing-Quo Lee went back to China. Living in Hong Kong. Namis Chodosh is teaching at the University of Florida. Dano Kolar is in Los Angeles doing special effects for movies. And Connie Lansky bought a ranch in Arizona."

"Good work."

"Para Bellum and Porter Kincaide are a somewhat different story," said Deanna. "Appears the company is doing poorly. They invested heavily in AI technology that isn't working out as well as expected."

"AI," said Duke. "Assholes Incorporated."

"Artificial intelligence," said Deanna. "The wave of the future. But it seems that the wave they were hoping for hasn't come ashore just yet."

Thumps nodded. "And Kincaide?"

"Nothing definitive," said Deanna, "but if I were a betting woman, I'd make book on his being sick."

Cruz stopped eating the doughnut. "Sick?"

"Nothing definitive," said Deanna. "Rumours. According to several articles, he's been to the Institut Gustave Roussy in Paris and Sloan Kettering in Manhattan."

"Hospitals?"

"Cancer centres," said Deanna. "Also checked on Nora Gage and Cisco Cruz."

"Wait." Cruz put the doughnut to one side, licked his fingers. "You had her run a check on me?"

"I did," said Thumps.

"First thing I would have done," said Duke.

"It seems Mr. Cruz is a ghost," said Deanna. "Motor vehicles, nada. Social Security, nada. Birth records, nada. I found more on Duncan Renaldo than I found on the ninja assassin."

Duke frowned. "Duncan Renaldo?"

"He played the Cisco Kid in the TV series."

"Oh, right."

"So," said Deanna, "we're dealing with Cisco Nada."

"I can't believe you guys ran a check on me." Cruz went back to the doughnut. "You need to leave this alone."

"Or what?" said Thumps. "Extraordinary renditions? Offshore black sites? Santa's naughty list?"

Duke sat up straight. "A tax audit would certainly have me curled up by the chimney with care."

Cruz closed his eyes. Long, exasperated sigh. "Does anyone know what happened at the tournament?"

Deanna turned around in her chair. "Do you care?"

"Not in the slightest," said Cruz.

"So, you just want to change the subject."

"Please."

"Wutty shot four under."

Thumps waited.

"Unfortunately, the winning score was eight under. Wutty came in seventh."

"That's pretty good," said Thumps.

"And there's a big party for the conquering hero," said Deanna. "Out at Moses's place. This evening. Everyone is invited."

"For a guy who finished seventh?" Cruz shoved his hands in his pockets. "What am I missing?"

"Community," said Deanna. "You're missing community."

Thumps's phone went off. There it was again. That sudden startle, as though someone had hit him with a defibrillator.

"DreadfulWater . . . Yeah . . . Great, when? No, not a problem. Yes, I'll tell him."

Thumps put the phone back in his jacket. It was barely mid-afternoon and he was ready for a nap. Maybe give the holding cell a try before someone else beat him to it. That is, if the dog wasn't using it.

"That was Gina at the hospital."

Cruz looked at the ceiling. "Don't tell me. Gage?"

"Gage," said Thumps.

"She get kidnapped again?" said Deanna.

"You know," said Duke, "we might have to start giving her the sheriff's discount for search and rescue."

Deanna smiled. "We have a discount?"

"Let me guess," said Cruz. "The minute we left, she took off."

"Took a bit to find her clothes," said Thumps. "Then she left."

"And we don't know where she went."

"*Au contraire*," said Thumps.

"That's French," said Duke, "for 'on the contrary.'"

"This time," said Thumps, "she was good enough to leave a forwarding address."

Howdy wandered out of the back area, his tongue hanging out, his eyes limpid and sad.

"Don't forget the party," said Deanna. "Share in the glory."

• • •

GAGE HAD LEFT word with Gina that she would be checking into the Tucker. Hot bath, clean clothes, room service, cable television.

"The Tucker?" Cruz made a disparaging noise. "Government sure as hell isn't paying for that. If they were, I'd be staying there."

The Tucker House was a Chinook landmark, a limestone structure that had once been the tallest building in the town. The hotel opened for business in 1876, about the same time that George Armstrong Custer attacked an encampment of Lakota, Cheyenne, and Arapaho along the Little Bighorn River.

There was no other connection between the hotel and the event other than the band that George Tucker hired for the grand opening, which contained the same number of musicians as Custer's regimental band, who played "Garryowen" as the good general rode off into Montana history.

"You think she's actually there?"

"Only one way to find out."

"If I have to chase her down again," said Cruz, "I might think of killing her myself."

In 1890, the Tucker lost its top floor to fire. Through that winter, marked by the massacre of Big Foot's band of Lakota at the hands of a revitalized and well-armed Seventh Calvary, the hotel remained vacant. But by the summer of the new year, the hotel opened with fanfare and two new floors.

After the First World War, the Tucker fell into disrepair. Over the next eighty plus years, it was a hospital, a general store and warehouse, a theatre, a library, and a roller-skating rink. Then in 2002, a conglomerate out of Dallas and Los Angeles bought the property. The limestone was blasted and coated with a sealant that helped bring out the veining. Brass railings, stone steps at the entrance, and a deep-red all-weather carpet were added, and the Tucker House was once again an upscale hotel.

"Did you have your deputy do a background check just to annoy me?"

"What aren't you telling me about Black Ice and Nora Gage?"

"We going to spend the rest of the day accusing each other?"

"I'm the sheriff," said Thumps, "so I get to do all the accusing I want."

"You're a photographer who is filling in for a man who lost his wife."

Thumps stopped on the stone steps of the Tucker House. "And exactly what are you?"

"You going to let me read the incident report?"

Thumps handed Cruz the folder. "Report reminds me of you. Thin and vague."

"*Pendejo*, I'm not thin. I'm wiry."

THE YOUNG MAN at the front desk looked as though he had been detailed by a full-service salon. "Adrian," according to the gold name tag. Every hair on his head was in place. His skin was glowing. His nails buffed and polished.

Thumps felt like workboots standing next to a pair of Ferragamo loafers. Even the man's voice had a musical ring to it that only comes with practice.

"Good afternoon, gentlemen." Adrian smiled, so you could see all his teeth at once. "How may I be of service?"

"Nora Gage," said Cruz.

"Ah, yes. Ms. Gage said she was expecting visitors."

"We're them," said Thumps, and immediately regretted the grammar. Or was it the syntax?

"Names?"

"Why?"

"And your email addresses," said Adrian. "If you don't mind."

Thumps kept his tone under control. "Why would you want our email addresses?"

"We'd like to send you a survey. So you can share your Tucker House experience."

"Pass," said Cruz.

"There's a draw at the end of each month," said Adrian. "Some very nice prizes."

THE ELEVATORS HAD been renovated since the last time Thumps was at the Tucker. The dark wood interior had been replaced with western murals and a brass railing.

Cruz pressed the button for the third floor. "I'm still not used to guys with earrings."

Thumps yawned. "I remember when long hair and miniskirts were an abomination unto the sight of god."

"Were you ever tempted to get your ears pierced?"

"Nope."

"Nose? How about tattoos?" Cruz leaned against the railing. "Is it me or was Adrian wearing eye makeup?"

ROOM 346 WAS AT the end of a long hall. There was a Do Not Disturb sign on the doorknob.

Thumps gave the sign a tap, watched it swing back and forth. "I suppose you want to be bad cop?"

"Why don't we both be bad cop," said Cruz. "That always confuses the hell out of suspects."

"And exactly what do we suspect Gage of doing?"

Cruz pressed the buzzer. "How about we start with lying to sworn officers of the law and go from there."

36

Nora Gage came to the door in a bathrobe. Her hair was wet. Water was dripping down her cheeks.

"You two can't read?"

"I figured it was a suggestion," said Cruz.

"I just got out of the bath. Why don't you run around the block a couple of dozen times."

Cruz held out the incident report, weighed it in his hand. "Temporary Sheriff DreadfulWater. Does this seem a tad light to you?"

"Very light," said Thumps.

"You mind if I get dressed?" Gage turned, went back into the room. "Give me time to tie a couple of sheets together, rappel down the side of the building."

Cruz crossed the room, helped himself to the sofa. "Knock yourself out."

While the elevator had been given a western mural theme, the suite Gage was in had been redone in New York cool. Hard edges. Blacks and whites.

A one-bedroom, one-bath refrigerator with furniture.

There was a party platter on the coffee table. Enough finger food to feed a family of four.

"Nice." Cruz shook the thermos, poured himself a cup. "Wonder where they got the watermelon."

"Is THAT A brownie?"

"You're diabetic," said Cruz. "Eat the cheese."

Gage did not escape out the window, but she did take her time.

"I see you two made yourselves at home."

"We did."

"Let's get to it," said Gage. "I don't plan to stick around."

"And where are we going?"

Gage squeezed a bit of moisture out of her hair. "We are going home."

"D.C.?"

"No point staying here." Gage helped herself to a piece of ham. "Didn't I tell you, Sorin is dead."

"You told us," said Cruz, "but you didn't tell us how you know."

"As in, did you see him die?" said Thumps. "Man has a habit of rising from the dead."

"Not this time," said Gage. "And no, I didn't see him get killed. I heard it."

"That's not in the incident report," said Cruz. "So, why don't we start from the beginning."

Gage picked up the thermos. "May have to order more coffee."

Thumps held up fingers. "We've got the bullet points from the time you worked for Black Ice to Sorin Dalca showing up at your place and threatening you, and you taking off with me riding shotgun out to the wide-open spaces. Got the part about renting the McMansion and Stan Greeley showing up to spy on you. And we know about the move to Shadow Ranch and the phony Italian villa with the crappy canals."

"Don't forget about me getting shot," said Cruz. "And having a good pair of pants ruined."

"Right before you disappear again," said Thumps.

"And what is it you don't understand about 'kidnapped'?"

"Good," said Cruz. "Let's start there."

"I told you, Sorin was waiting for me."

"And he forced you to go with him."

"That's right."

"And he took you to the house in Ironstone River Estates. The one with the safe room."

"Where he handcuffed me to a toilet and gave me microwave pizza to eat."

"Couldn't have been any worse than the pizza we had to eat at the golf tournament."

"What?"

"Never mind." Cruz took a couple of grapes. "What happened next?"

"I'm not sure."

"And we were doing so well."

Gage resettled herself in the chair. "I heard voices downstairs. Loud voices. Sorin. Three, maybe four other men."

"No signs of an assault in the house," said Cruz. "Just the chain around the toilet and the leftover pizza in the safe room."

"What did they say?" asked Thumps. "These voices."

"I couldn't really hear what they said."

"And then?"

"One of the guys came upstairs. Had on a ski mask. Strong. Precise. Guessing military. Put a bag over my head, carried me downstairs, put me in a van."

Thumps tried to imagine the scenario. "Where was Dalca?"

"In the van with me," said Gage. "I didn't know it at first. I couldn't see anything, but then I heard him moaning."

"You try to talk to him?"

"No," said Gage. "Honestly, I was terrified. I thought they were going to kill the both of us."

"Dalca try to talk to you?"

"Once," said Gage. "He called my name, and one of the men hit him. Told him to shut up."

"Would you recognize their voices?"

"That was the only time I heard any of them speak in my presence."

"What about smells?" said Thumps.

"When you think you're going to die, you don't much worry about smells."

Cruz held up a hand. "So, you're in the van. Where did they take you?"

"We drove around for about an hour," said Gage. "Near the end, there were railway tracks and a stretch of rough road. No idea where they took us. I was put in a room that smelled of mildew and solvent. Nasty carpet on the floor."

"They ever take the bag off your head?"

"No." Gage made a face. "Could hardly breathe."

"And Dalca?"

"He was somewhere else." Gage wrapped her arms around herself. "But I could hear him scream. Went on for hours. Then two gunshots. And no more screaming."

Cruz leaned back, closed his eyes. For a moment, Thumps thought the man from Pie Town had gone to sleep.

"But they didn't kill you."

Gage held out her hands, palms up. "Evidently not."

"Because?"

Gage shrugged. "I'm guessing they got what they wanted."

Cruz nodded. "The Vault. And the access code."

"Paranoia got him killed," said Gage. "He was afraid that if he tried to withdraw the money from the Vault, he'd be arrested."

"So, he tried to make up his loss by selling you to Para Bellum." Cruz looked at his hands. "Only it backfired."

Thumps straightened his jacket. "But the government didn't know how to access the money, did they?"

"No," said Cruz, "we didn't."

"Then he could have been a very rich man," said Gage. "All he had to do was to stay dead."

"Still doesn't explain why Para Bellum left you alive. What's one more body?"

"You sound disappointed." Gage got out of the chair, walked to the door. "Now you know everything, and now it's time to say goodbye."

Cruz stayed on the sofa. "They find out you talked to us, what's to keep them from coming back?"

"I've got nothing they want."

"Kidnapping is still a federal offence." Thumps stood, helped himself to a slice of cantaloupe. "Dalca may be dead, and we may never find his body. But so long as you're alive, you're a loose end. You could testify against them."

"Testify to what?" said Gage. "I never saw their faces, and my memory of the events is fuzzy at best. It's probably the trauma."

"Withholding evidence is a crime."

"Are you going to arrest me, Mr. DreadfulWater?"

"Temporary Deputy Sheriff DreadfulWater," said Thumps. "Is there a reason I should?"

"Gentlemen." Gage held the door open. "Enjoy the rest of the day."

CRUZ WAS QUIET on the elevator ride down. Thumps waited until they were on the street.

"Would you have left her alive?"

"Nope."

"You remember that game, truth or dare?"

"What am I? Twelve?"

"Truth," said Thumps. "You didn't bring Gage to Chinook to protect her from Dalca. You brought her here to draw Dalca out, and because you think she might know more about the Vault than she's telling."

"Suspect."

"Truth," said Thumps. "So, when Dalca died, you . . . and the guys back east . . . began watching Gage."

Cruz looked up at the sky. "An hour out. Railroad tracks. Rough road. Place that smells like mildew and solvent. An abandoned manufacturing facility of some sort. Anything come to mind?"

"I'm the wrong person to ask," said Thumps. "But I know someone who might know."

The Aegean was Chinook's one and only authentic bookstore. If you wanted scented candles or slippers or gift cards or throws and pillows, you went to the Barnes & Noble in Great Falls. If you wanted books, you came to the Aegean.

Archimedes Kousoulas was sitting behind his desk, staring at his monitor.

"Are you here to kill me?"

"Not today."

"We need some information," said Thumps.

"You always need information," said Archie. "Every time you come to town, you need information."

"We're looking for an abandoned building, probably a factory of some sort, hour drive from here. Railroad tracks. Rough road."

"You know which states have the most abandoned factories?" Archie ticked each place off on his fingers. "Indiana, Illinois, Michigan, Ohio, Pennsylvania."

"How about Montana?"

"You looking to set up a black site?" Archie peered over the top of his glasses. "Extrajudicial rendition? Sensory deprivation? Torture?"

"Not this trip."

Archie sat back in his chair. "There's Burke, Idaho, but that's a long drive from here."

"Nothing in the state?"

"We're known more for ghost towns, abandoned mines, and Bureau of Land Management functionaries."

"Okay," said Cruz. "*If* you were going to set up a black site, where would it be?"

"Glasgow Air Force Base," said Archie. "Place is mostly abandoned. But it's more than a two-hour drive."

"Nothing else?"

"You want to be more specific?"

"No."

Archie folded his hands across his stomach. "You two coming to the party?"

"Party?"

"For Wutty. At Moses's place. I'm just heading out now."

"Don't think so," said Thumps. "Someone has to watch the office."

"Suit yourself," said Archie.

"There going to be food?" said Cruz.

"Lots of it," said Archie. "I'm bringing some of my lamb pilaf."

"Okay," said Cruz. "We'll be there."

Thumps frowned. "*You* want to go to a party?"

"All work, no play."

"And what about Gage?"

"I'm done. Case solved. Go to the party. Go home."

"Sure," said Archie. "You can come to the party. But you have to promise not to shoot anyone."

37

Thumps stood outside the Aegean and waited for Cruz to explain.

"Nothing to explain," said the man from Pie Town. "Good bet that Gage is right and Dalca is dead. Good bet that Para Bellum got what they wanted and killed him. I doubt we'll ever find the body. So, I might as well go to the party."

"And then home?"

"And then home."

"Which is where, exactly?"

"Here and there," said Cruz. "Here and there."

"Gage?"

"Gage hasn't done anything illegal. She can come and go as she pleases. She gets herself killed, that's on her."

"Let's say I don't believe you."

"You are one suspicious gringo."

"What about the Vault? What about the money?"

"Gone," said Cruz.

"Maybe Gage has the code. She probably helped Dalca set up the Vault."

"You think we didn't look at that?" Cruz hooked his thumbs in his jeans. "We've been watching her since Black Ice was shut down."

"What about Para Bellum? They killed Dalca."

"Except Dalca is officially dead." Cruz started for the car. "And the only person who has actually seen him alive is Gage. You see the problem?"

"The guys who killed him saw him."

"And they're not going to mention that to anyone, are they?"

"So, we have a dead private investigator . . ."

"Natural causes."

". . . and a dead Black Ice operative . . ."

"Who was supposedly already dead."

". . . a former Black Ice operative who isn't going to help bring her colleague's killers to justice."

"You mean the same colleague who was going to sell her to the guys who killed him?"

". . . a wounded ninja assassin."

"Yeah." Cruz rubbed his leg. "That part sucks."

"The party will cheer you up. With any luck, there'll be doughnuts."

Cruz stooped at the car. "On second thought, how about you drop me at the house?"

"You're going to pass on a party? Free food? Good company? No dead bodies?"

"I'm tired," said Cruz. "My leg is throbbing. I'm grumpy. I wouldn't be good company."

"You're always grumpy. You're never good company."

"I'll just grab a hot shower, relax, watch television."

"Can you feed the cats?"

• • •

It was after five when Thumps turned off the main road and started down the side of the coulee to Moses's place, easing the car in and out of the ruts that had started to form. He had once asked Moses if there was a difference between coming down through the ruts and just driving off the cliff, and the old man had told him that coming down the road was slower.

In the distance below, Thumps could see a large jumble of cars jammed up against the trailers. He didn't think that all of Chinook was here.

And then again.

There were several tables stacked with food and coolers. Al was working the grill of a makeshift barbecue. Someone had a portable CD player going, and Dolores Cardoza, Gabby Santucci, Beth Mooney, and a mismatched cast of couples were dancing under two large cottonwoods that had been strung with lights. Deanna and Cooley had brought the Jenga tower along, had it set up on a stump.

Duke was off to one side, throwing sticks for Howdy, who lay on his belly, content to watch them sail off into the grass.

Moses Blood was sitting in a lawn chair by the firepit. Claire Merchant was sitting next to him.

"Ho." Moses held out his wrists. "The law is here. You'll never take me alive, you dirty mouse."

"Rat," said Claire. "Dirty rat."

"You're a nice surprise," said Thumps.

"You sure it's not a mouse?" said Moses.

"As well as a nice party."

"I'm too old to go to a party," said Moses. "So they brought the good times to me."

"More space out here." Claire shaded her eyes. "And it's going to be a beautiful evening."

"Where's Ivory?"

There was an explosion of shrieking downriver by the big S bend.

Claire smiled. "Wutty is showing the kids how to hit a golf ball."

"Do you know," said Moses, "that golf balls don't float?"

"I do."

"And do you know that golf balls are also good at hiding in plain sight?"

"I do."

Moses shook his head. "I'm embarrassed to say that I did not."

Claire stood, brushed off her jeans. "You want to go for a walk or you want to eat?"

"Walk," said Thumps.

"Right answer," said Claire. "Let's go upriver."

"Because Wutty and the kids are downriver?"

"And people think you're just a photographer."

Claire didn't take Thumps's hand, and she didn't take his arm. She walked by his side, close enough so he could feel the heat of her body. Thumps followed her down to the river.

"You hear that?"

Out of the coulees on the far bank. A thrilling, raspy scream, sharp and brittle.

"Red-tailed hawk," said Claire. "Probably a male. Warning us off. We're in his territory."

"Maybe he's just happy to see you."

"Or maybe he's just trying to scare up a meal."

Thumps picked up a flat stone. "How was Alberta?"

Claire nodded. "Good. I got to see relatives I haven't seen in years. Cousins. Couple of uncles. A crazy auntie. Ivory was a big hit. Everyone took turns spoiling her."

"Any news?"

Claire took a deep breath. "No. We saw the specialist. Have a date for a bunch of tests. Everything is still up in the air."

Thumps skipped the stone across the water.

"You're probably wondering what we're doing back here."

Thumps tried his best red-tailed squawk. "Me and the hawk are happy to have you back."

Claire tried her best not to laugh. "God," she said, "that was awful."

Thumps picked another stone. "Everybody's a critic."

"And who taught you to skip stones?"

"I'm a good stone skipper."

"You're average," said Claire. "A good skipper gets at least four skips out of a stone. You only get two."

"And you can do better?"

"Certainly." Claire bent down, searched the riverbank. "First thing you have to do is find a good stone. That's half the battle."

Thumps held a stone out. "Like this one?"

"Too heavy," said Claire. "And too thick."

"This one?"

"Better," said Claire.

Thumps waited.

"The adoption hasn't been finalized. You knew that. And as it turns out, that's a good thing." Claire fired the stone into the river, five skips before it sank. "That's how you do it."

"So, she's a Canadian citizen."

"Alberta resident, as it turns out. Her legal address is with her uncle in Calgary. Means she has access to the health care system there."

"Better than here."

"Anywhere is better than here."

"So, when do you go back?"

"It's getting cold." Claire put her arm around Thumps's waist. "Maybe you'd like me to hold you."

"What's that red-tailed going to think?"

"We're not going back." Claire put her head against Thumps's chest. "Not right away. Not until the tests. And then we'll return."

"Okay."

"This is our home. Our friends are here. Here is comfortable. Took me a couple of days to figure that out."

"You missed all the excitement."

"You mean the dead private investigator and the kidnapped secret agent? Duke and the dog?"

"Howdy."

"Did Howdy really eat detergent pods?"

"Roxanne fill you in?"

"Deanna," said Claire. "Cruz okay?"

"It was just a flesh wound."

"Which is the general definition of a bullet tearing a hole in your body." Claire took a breath. "Do you know who shot him?"

"Not yet."

Claire stepped away, picked up a stone, flipped it out across the water. "Ivory missed you. Duke asked her if she'd like a dog, and she said she already had one."

Thumps tossed a stone into the river, where it sank immediately.

"So, you'll go back and forth to Alberta as needed."

"That's the plan," said Claire. "And when we do, I'm hoping you'll come with us."

"Is this where I find that horse to ride to the rescue?"

"I missed you as well." Claire gave Thumps a quick squeeze. "But I'm hungry. We had breakfast in Lethbridge. Probably time I ate again."

"Maybe the hawk and I could find you a rabbit."

"My hero."

AL WAS SQUATTED next to the stump with the Jenga tower. Ivory was standing at her side.

"You're supposed to make it fall down," Ivory was telling Al.

"Don't think that's the idea," said Al.

"But it's fun." Ivory pulled out a block from the centre, and the tower collapsed. "See."

"Hi, sweetie."

"Mom!" Ivory skipped across the yard, leaped into her mother's arms. "Hello, Dog."

It was impossible, but it seemed as though Ivory had grown in the time she had been gone.

"Did you miss me?"

Thumps smiled. "I did."

"Mom missed you."

"I missed her."

"Are you going to stay with us?"

"I think we better get your mom something to eat."

Al started putting the pieces back on the stump. "All this reunion is sweet, but maybe you can help me set this back up."

Thumps held up his hands. "Don't know how."

"I'm thinking there's a moral in here somewhere, but damned if I can find it."

"What's on the grill?"

"What you'd expect," said Al. "Grilled stuff."

Thumps caught Duke and Howdy coming back from their game of fetch.

"What kind of dog doesn't chase sticks?"

"Smart kind?"

"Very funny. Where's the ninja assassin?"

"My place. Recovering."

Duke snorted. "From what? He didn't do anything. Except screw up."

"He did get shot."

"Oh, yeah." Duke gave Howdy a vigorous rub. "That."

Howdy rolled over in the grass, moaning. Duke bent over and rubbed him some more.

"He's got his appetite back," said Duke. "Ate one of my workboots. Not going to miss the big dummy."

"You're taking him back to the shelter?"

"You know how many times I've had to clean my side window after he finished licking it?"

"You can't take him back to the shelter."

"You want him back?" Duke waited. Waited some more. "Then it's the shelter."

"Sheriff DreadfulWater." Brian Little Horse and his uncles, Elmer and Elroy, came out of the merriment with hamburgers and soft drinks.

"It's Temporary Deputy Sheriff DreadfulWater," said Duke. "You guys want a dog?"

Elmer bent over, picked up a stick, tossed it into the prairie grass. Howdy was up and off like a shot, hitting the stick almost before it landed.

Elroy nodded. "That's a good dog."

"Except we already have two," said Brian. "Now, if it was a horse . . ."

"Your dogs lick car windows?"

Brian smiled. "It's really gross, isn't it? Like hard lard. Remember that car? The one that belonged to that detective?"

"Private investigator," said Duke.

"Side window was a real mess."

"You ought to see mine," said Duke. "Side windows, rear windows. Likes to hang his head out and lick the side mirror."

"The trick," said Brian, "is to start with a razor blade. Get as much as you can off that way, before you hit it with glass cleaner."

Thumps turned to a sudden clamour. Wutty Youngbeaver was coming back from the river, dragging a troop of kids behind him. Jimmy and Russell, Stas and Rawat were sheep-dogging the perimeters, as the kids leaped about and ran off in all directions.

"Wutty, Wutty, Wutty, Wuuuuuttyyyyy!"

Rawat arrived out of breath. "Such a day. So exciting."

Thumps nodded. “Hear Wutty did pretty good.”

“Three birdies in the first seven holes,” said Rawat.

“Then par, par, par,” said Stas. “Then bogey, bogey, bogey.”

“The fourteenth hole.” Rawat shook his head. “So close.”

“But Mr. Wutty does not listen to caddy,” said Stas.

“The 7-iron,” said Rawat. “I suggested the 7-iron.”

“The fourteenth hole,” said Stas. “Was Dostoevsky short story.”

“The 8-iron was not enough.” Rawat sighed, his eyes sad. “So, I will say no more about it.”

Moses was sitting alone, a blanket over his shoulders.

“In the old days,” he said, stretching out a hand, “there would be tipis and horses. Now there are trailers and cars.”

Thumps sat down next to the old man. “Times change.”

“People are much the same. Babies grow up. Children become adults. Old people die.”

“You want some tea?”

“If I could live again, I think I’d like to be a tree. A cottonwood. So I could live by a river.”

“You already live by a river.”

“Is Claire going to forgive you?”

“For what?”

Moses shrugged. “We try hard, but we always wind up doing something wrong.”

“We?”

“Men,” said Moses. “We’re not as smart as we think we are.”

Claire appeared with Ivory and two hot dogs. “Anyone hungry?”

Moses grinned. “Is that for me?”

“If you want it,” said Ivory. “The other one is for Dog.”

“Good,” said Thumps. “Because I’m starving.”

“Mom tried to eat it.”

Claire rolled her eyes. “We should get going. This one needs to be in bed.”

“Do not,” said Ivory. “Is Dog coming home with us?”

“If he wants,” said Claire.

Thumps took a large bite of the hot dog. “Yes,” he said, “he does.”

38

Ivory insisted on riding home with Thumps.

"Don't read anything into it," Claire told him. "She's just looking for a fresh audience."

Thumps wasn't sure whether all seven-year-olds had eidetic memories. Maybe it was simply a matter of space. At this point of their lives, there wasn't much in the garage that they couldn't find quickly and with ease.

"There was Auntie Celeste and Auntie Easter and Auntie Ona and Uncle Melton and Uncle Billy and cousin Martin and cousin Pam and cousin Wilton and somebody named Andrew Shoots."

"Must have been nice, meeting all your relatives."

"I didn't know them."

Thumps smiled. "But now you do."

"Do you like needles?"

"Depends."

"That's what Mom said." Ivory picked at a thread on her shirt. "Mom says you don't like to be called Dog."

"I don't mind."

"That's what she said you'd say."

"It's a good nickname. Maybe we should get you a nickname."

"Something's wrong with my brain," said Ivory. "They're going to put me in a big machine, so they can see my brain, but I won't remember, because I'll be asleep."

There were any number of things on which Thumps had no opinion. Children in hospitals was not one of them.

"I don't want to go back to Alberta. If we go back to Alberta, Mom will take me to that hospital, and they'll give me needles."

"Maybe the doctors will make you better."

"I don't want to be better," said Ivory. "I want to stay home."

Claire beat them home, had the lights on in the house, was waiting for them at the front door. There was a warmth and a welcome to the still life. Even the Russian olive in the driveway seemed alive and happy to see him.

"Mom's worried I'm going to die," said Ivory. "But I won't."

"No," said Thumps. "You won't."

"Are you going to stay overnight?"

"Would you like me to stay overnight?"

"Mom would," said Ivory.

Claire stood at the door, her arms hugging her chest. "You two have fun?"

"Dog doesn't like hospitals. Or needles."

"What about hot chocolate?"

Ivory took Thumps's hand. "He likes hot chocolate."

• • •

Ivory didn't want to go to bed. "It's early."

Claire gestured to the window. "It's dark out."

"Dark isn't late. Dog's not going to bed."

"Thumps will go to bed later."

"I want to sleep with you."

"We'll talk about that later."

Ivory turned to Thumps. "That means no."

"You have your own bed, young lady."

"I'm not a young lady," said Ivory. "I'm a baby."

Claire dropped her head. "Remember what I said about having a second shot at raising a child?"

Thumps retreated behind his cup of chocolate.

"I may have been overconfident."

"I'll only go to bed if Dog reads me three stories."

"One story," said Claire.

"Two stories," said Ivory. "And I get to pick them."

"What about it, Dog?" said Claire. "That work for you?"

Thumps knew he had made a tactical error as soon as he stepped into Ivory's room and saw the bookcase with its dozens of books. Big books, small books, picture books, word books, picture *and* word books.

Ivory sat down in front of the books and began going through them, as though she were perusing a menu at a Chinese restaurant.

"Hmmmmmm," she said, making a noise like an engine that wasn't about to start anytime soon. "Which ones to pick?"

Thumps took the skinniest book he could find. "How about this one?"

"Dog," she said, "I'm seven."

Ivory continued searching the shelves, taking out a book, putting it back. Thumps didn't think about checking the time, but he was sure she was able to waste fifteen to twenty minutes making a decision.

"You need to choose something."

"All right." Ivory pulled two books off the shelf. "These."

Getting conned by a seven-year-old was somewhat embarrassing. "This one is sixty-five pages. And this one is seventy-two. That's too much. How about I read a chapter from each?"

"Six chapters from each."

"Two chapters."

Ivory sagged against the shelves. "You're just like Mom."

CLAIRE WAS WAITING for him at the kitchen table. "And how did you enjoy playing Scheherazade to her Shahryar."

"As I recall, Scheherazade stopped the story in the middle, so she could keep her head for another night."

"Your point?"

"What happened to short books for children?"

"When negotiating with a seven-year-old," said Claire, "you have to be specific."

"You're enjoying this, aren't you?"

"Yes, I am," said Claire. "Can you stay?"

"I can."

"I'll make a bed for you on the sofa," said Claire. "She's seven, but she's still four. She'll be in bed with me before the night is out."

"No problem."

"And Cooley called. Evidently, Cisco Cruz has set up shop at the sheriff's office. Cooley says he's using the office computer and the office phone and sleeping in the holding cell."

"Cooley say why?"

"Don't think he knows. You want to call him back?"

"Did he want me to call him back?"

"He was sweet," said Claire. "Asked if he had called at a bad time. 'Awkward' was the word he used."

Thumps went to the sofa, stretched out, tried to strike a languid pose. Claire stayed at the table.

"I take it you want to know about Alberta?"

"I do."

"Ivory's going to have an MRI. They did one in Helena, but they want to do another in Calgary."

"You want help with the driving and the talking?"

"I do."

"No problem."

"What about Duke?" Claire paused. "How's he taking Macy's suicide?"

Thumps sat up.

"Word gets out," said Claire. "I might have done the same thing. He's not going to do something stupid, is he?"

"He's got a dog. And there's Deanna and Cooley. They'll help look after him."

"Archie?"

"The Greek grief counsellor," said Thumps. "Yeah, Archie finds out, Duke won't be able to keep him away."

"Still," said Claire, "he's your friend. What if he needs you?"

"You and Ivory need me."

Claire stood, came to the sofa. "You look like a man who wants to cuddle."

"I'm that man," said Thumps.

"What about Cruz? It could be important."

"If it can't wait until morning," said Thumps, "Cooley will call again."

"That sounds like a man who is hoping for something more than cuddling."

"It's been a while."

Claire eased herself onto the sofa, snuggled up against him, put her back to him, so he could hold her.

"Yes," she said, "it has."

IVORY WAS UP at least six times in the night. Cooley didn't call back. Around three o'clock, Claire left the sofa and went to the bedroom. Thumps looked in early in the morning. Claire was on one side of the bed. Ivory was lying sideways, draped across her mother.

He dressed quietly, carried his shoes to the door. He was just about to open it when Claire appeared.

"Sneaking away?"

"Figured I'd let you guys sleep. Probably should get in, see what Cruz is up to."

"And check on Duke."

"Absolutely."

"I could make you breakfast." Claire smiled. "That should strike fear in your heart."

"No," Thumps lied. "Sounds good."

"Liar."

"Should I come back tonight?"

Claire brushed the hair away from her face. "Yes," she said. "I suppose you should."

39

Claire was right.

Thumps *had* lied about breakfast.

The thought of her making breakfast *did* strike fear in his heart. Most times, Claire started her day with a bowl of sugar-coated cereal or a jelly-filled cardboard wedge that you dropped into a toaster. If the two of them did wind up living together, he would have to be mother.

Al was just unlocking the door when Thumps got to the café.

"You're early. Again." Al tossed a towel over her shoulder. "I sure as hell hope you don't start making a habit of it."

"What about the early bird and the worm?"

Al took a tray of potatoes out of the refrigerator, set it next to the grill.

"I like to sneak up on the day. Get the mouse report from Lucy. Have a cup of coffee by myself. Maybe listen to the news on the radio."

Thumps settled on his favourite stool. "What's this?"

"What does it look like?"

"It looks like Jenga."

The tower was sitting on the counter. Someone had started a game. There were holes in the structure, with the blocks that had been removed piled on top.

"Borrowed it from Deanna," said Al. "Damn thing is addictive."

Thumps reached out, gently pushed on a block.

"You knock it over, you set it back up." Al dropped a wad of potatoes on the grill, drizzled oil over them. "You missed the speeches."

"Speeches?"

"Last night. At the party. Wutty Youngbeaver, conquering hero. Wutty Youngbeaver, the Tiger Woods of Chinook." Al wiped her hands on her apron. "I figure he's earned the moment. Putting himself out there like that."

Thumps pushed his coffee cup to the edge of the counter.

"That some kind of hint?"

"It is."

Al brought the coffee pot over. "You left with Claire and Ivory. Are we supposed to read something into that?"

"No comment."

"Christ, DreadfulWater, you're not running for office."

Thumps pushed another block out. The tower trembled but held.

"Good thing I'm not the curious sort." Al cracked a couple of eggs in a bowl. "How's Ivory?"

"Great."

"You know what they call a single word that forms a sentence?"

Thumps touched another block. Saw the danger.

"A sentence word," said Al. "Look it up."

"Okay."

"Or it might be an imperative sentence, so long as the single word is the imperative verb. And 'okay' can be a verb, adverb, noun, or an adjective. But there's not much meat on that bone, if you get my meaning."

Thumps brought the cup to his lips. No doubt about it. The next person to remove a block was going to bring the tower down.

"So, you might consider tossing a few compound or complex sentences into the conversation, sentences that contain information and emotion. That is, if you want breakfast."

"I want breakfast."

"Then let's try again. How's Ivory?"

"Don't know. She's going to have an MRI in Calgary. Claire is waiting for a call from the doctors."

Al put the eggs in a pan, started stirring them.

"And Duke?"

Thumps shrugged.

Al stopped stirring.

"There's the dog . . ."

Thumps was trying to figure out exactly how he was going to finish that sentence when Wutty and Jimmy and Russell banged into the café, followed closely by Chintak Rawat and Stas Black Weasel.

Wutty was wearing a bright red blazer and an enormous smile. "Coffee for everyone."

Jimmy and Russell grabbed their usual seats. Rawat and Stas took stools on either side of Thumps.

"We tried to find Mr. Wutty a green jacket," said Rawat.

"But all they have is red," said Stas.

"The Masters already has a lock on green, anyway," Jimmy shouted from his stool. "Red's more appropriate."

Russell raised his coffee cup. "The Indigenous Tiger Woods."

Jimmy held up a manila envelope. "Signed photos of Wutty in action. Only five bucks each."

Al arrived with Thumps's breakfast. "Better grab one quick before he has to make more."

"Wutty's going to be giving lessons out at the Ranch," Russell called out. "Slots are filling up fast."

"Perhaps you should sign up for a lesson," said Rawat. "Improve your short game."

"Producer called." Wutty raised his arms, rocked back and forth on the stool. "They want me on *Wake Up Montana*."

Al leaned on the counter, lowered her voice. "Next he'll be doing ads for car lots and reverse mortgages."

Thumps couldn't help himself. He slid another block out.

"Bad choice," said Al.

A tremor ran through the tower. It shivered, leaned slowly to one side, and collapsed.

"You do understand," said Al, "that if you pull out the wrong piece, the whole thing falls apart."

One moment, the thought wasn't there. The next, it was. Thumps straightened up on the stool, stared at the Jenga piece in his hand.

"It's no big deal," said Al. "Easy enough to put it back together."

Thumps scooped up the rest of his eggs. "I have to get to work."

"You going to leave me with this mob?"

Thumps slipped the block into his pocket. "I am."

"And running off with part of the game?"

"I'll bring it back."

Al picked up Thumps's plate. "Tell Duke I said he should keep the dog."

THUMPS MADE IT out the door and onto the sidewalk without having to buy an autographed photo of Wutty swinging his driver.

And just in time.

More people began arriving, and in a blink, Al's began to look like an extension of the party the night before. Through the plate-glass window, Thumps could see Wutty soaking up the congratulations and the accolades like a sponge in water.

And why not.

Playing in a qualifying round of the U.S. Open was a major accomplishment. And Wutty had done well. One bad hole. Just like life. Sometimes it came down to one bad hole.

And a piece of wood.

DUKE WAS AT his desk, Howdy the dog curled up at his feet. Deanna was at the new computer station. Cooley was standing at the filing cabinet, looking as though he had lost a game of musical chairs.

"There aren't any doughnuts," said Duke. "New regime for a healthier sheriff's department."

"It won't last," said Deanna. "I give it two weeks. Tops."

"I miss them already," said Cooley.

"Cruz is in the holding cell," said Deanna. "Your buddy pulled an all-nighter."

"You won't believe what he was able to do," said Cooley.

"Seems he has friends in high places," said Duke. "And now, we have access to a shitload of databases I didn't even know existed."

"DMV, credit card transactions, cellphone records, flight manifests." Deanna patted the monitor, as though it were a favourite pet. "IRS, Social Security. We even have satellite maps and real-time imaging."

Thumps started toward the back area. "He tell you why?"

"Remember that list of names you gave us? We're running them again through all the new toys."

Duke shifted in his chair. Howdy raised his head for a moment. "You want to know who really killed JFK? Aliens in Area 57?"

"It's Area 51," said Deanna.

"Doesn't seem right," said Cooley. "A sheriff's office without doughnuts."

CRUZ WAS ASLEEP in the holding cell. Thumps thought about locking the door and walking away.

"Wakey, wakey."

In romantic comedies, when the hero is asleep, someone generally douses them with cold water. Thumps wasn't sure if it was all that funny, but considering the problems that Cruz had created for him over the years, it was tempting.

"Don't even think about it."

"Good," said Thumps. "You're awake."

"You throw cold water on me and I may shoot you. By mistake, of course."

"Get up," said Thumps. "I think I figured it out."

Cruz groaned, rolled over, slid the quilt off his face. “Should I round up all the suspects?”

“No need,” said Thumps.

When Thumps and Cruz came into the office, Howdy was chasing wadded-up paper balls that Duke was tossing across the room.

“See what you can find on the Valentich disappearance,” said Duke. “Or the signal from the UVB-76 radio station.”

Cooley kicked one of the paper balls back toward the sheriff. “How about the fourth code on the *Kryptos* sculpture?”

Howdy stopped in the middle of the room, began barking.

“Don’t tease him,” said Duke. “You’ll just get him upset.”

“What the hell,” said Cruz. “You understand that’s not Google you’re playing with.”

“It’s better,” said Deanna.

Cruz stood next to the monitor. “And?”

“And you were right,” said Deanna. “Porter Kincaide is sick. In fact, according to his confidential medical records”—Deanna lowered her voice—“that no one is supposed to have . . . he’s dying.”

“How bad?”

“There’s something worse than dying?”

“And Para Bellum?”

Deanna hit a couple of keys. “Para Bellum has lost about twenty percent of its value in the last quarter. Company is in deep shit.”

“What about the names?”

“More information on everyone,” said Cooley, “but no revelations.”

"Don't mind me," said Duke. "I'm just throwing paper balls to a dog."

"Jesus," said Cruz. "Do you guys ever solve crimes?"

"Don't normally have that many to begin with," said Duke. "Until you come to town."

"George Banks, Sarah Croce, and José Martinez are all definitely dead." Deanna handed Thumps a printout. "The rest of the Black Ice gang are alive and don't have a dog in this fight."

Cruz nodded. "Dalca?"

"Here's where it gets interesting," said Deanna. "It appears that our Mr. Dalca was skimming."

"Skimming?"

"So far as I can tell, Mr. Dalca set up a shell company out of Nevis. Outfit called Island Consolidated. It appears that Island Consolidated was our man's piggy bank for good times and fun things."

Cruz watched the computer. "Show me."

"Had a thing for French Polynesia," said Deanna. "Here's a summary of the company's expenditures for the last three years. Luxury hotels in Papeete and Moorea. Restaurants. Airline tickets. Just before Dalca flies to Tahiti the last time, the company buys a 1987 twenty-four-foot Pacific Seacraft Dana for $48,000 and rents it back to Dalca for next to nothing."

"And then he sails off into the sunset." Cruz took a moment. "And the storm?"

"Tropical cyclone." Deanna pulled up a different screen. "They're rare, but it looks like he got caught out."

"No wreckage, no body?"

"The really good part is that Island Consolidated is the same outfit that paid for Stan Greeley's plane ticket, his motel room, and his car."

Howdy brought one of the paper balls over to Cruz, dropped it at his feet.

"He wants you to throw it," said Duke.

"Yeah," said Cruz. "That's going to happen."

"Least you can do is kick it," said Duke.

Howdy dropped down flat, began whimpering, low, anxious sounds, overflowing with pleasure. Cruz squared the ball up, flicked his foot, sent the ball sailing. The dog was off the floor and airborne in one motion, catching the ball in a graceful snatch, before crashing into the file cabinet.

"*Perro loco.*" Cruz shook his head. "I didn't get breakfast. I need to eat."

"That's why we should keep doughnuts in the office," said Cooley. "For emergencies."

"Let's go, Pancho." Cruz headed for the door.

"I already had breakfast," said Thumps. "And we need to talk."

"*Sin comida, sin hablar.*"

"Which means?"

Duke tossed a paper ball at Thumps, bounced it off his chest. "I think it means you're buying."

40

Cruz was limping down the block, moving along like a broken-down cowpoke on his way to a gunfight. Thumps had to hurry to keep up.

"Al's is the other way."

Cruz kept walking.

"The Quick Claim? You kidding? High prices, bad food?"

"It's quiet, and it's got nice booths."

The Tucker had been hard hit by the initial COVID surge, and while it had recovered, the coffee shop had stayed closed. Then it opened. And then closed again. Thumps hoped it was still closed so he could suggest someplace else for a late-morning meal. He had already been to Al's, but given the difference in prices and quality of food, he was willing to make a same-day return appearance.

As well, there was Dumbo's. Surely there were one or two recommended food groups in a cup of coffee and a doughnut.

Adrian, of the buffed and polished Adrians, was not at the front desk. Today, it was Allison, Adrian's fraternal twin.

"Gentlemen."

"Food," said Cruz.

"Absolutely," said Allison. "The Quick Claim is across the lobby and to your right."

"So, it's open?" said Thumps, not trying to hide his disappointment.

"It is," said Allison. "It's been remodelled. And there's a new menu."

THE QUICK CLAIM *was* open. No salvation there. And it had been remodelled. Thumps could smell the snap of fresh carpet and wet paint. He couldn't remember the old version, and the new version wasn't much better.

"You ever wonder why we call them 'fraternal twins'?"

"What?"

"I mean, that only makes sense if both the kids are boys. But what if it's two girls, or a girl and a boy? Clearly, they're not brothers. Why don't we call them sororal twins, or familial twins?"

"A booth," said Cruz. "I want a booth."

PETER WAS THEIR SERVER, and clearly not related to either Adrian or Allison. Dark, swarthy, twice-a-day shave required, receding hairline, gleaming face and neck, as though he had jogged to work in a light rain.

"Coffee," said Cruz. "Leave the pot."

Now that Thumps thought about it, Peter reminded him of the guy who played Adrian Monk in the TV series. What was his name? Tommy? Tony?

Cruz put his menu to one side. "We could ask Peter."

Thumps frowned. "About?"

"Twins." Cruz turned to Peter. "My friend here is interested in the different kinds of twins."

"No, I'm not."

Peter cleared his throat. "The number most frequently cited is eleven, though depending on how you organize them, you can have a few more or a few less."

"You hear that," said Cruz. "Eleven different types."

"Everyone knows about identical twins and fraternal twins. But you also have semi-identical twins, polar body or half-identical twins, mirror-image twins, mixed chromosome, superfecundation, superfetation, parasitic, twinning, and vanishing."

Thumps opened his menu.

"I'm pre-med," said Peter. "And there are four sets of twins in my family."

THE NEW QUICK CLAIM menu was larger than the old Quick Claim menu, more the size of a tanning reflector. Cruz held it open on his lap, so the selections could shine on his face.

"How much do you think two chickens would cost?"

"A lot less than the two-egg omelette," said Thumps.

"Yeah, but it comes with toast, potatoes, sausage or bacon, and a fruit cup."

"And a flower," said Thumps. "The last time I was here, they put a pansy on my plate."

"Quit complaining," said Cruz. "I had to spend an evening in your holding cell."

"You could have stayed at the house."

"Sure," said Cruz. "Where I would have been assaulted by Mom and her two-ton son."

"Wait. If you weren't there, who fed them?"

THE BREAKFAST PLATES arrived. Cruz poked at the eggs with his fork. "No pansy."

"Liars don't get flowers." Thumps took the Jenga block out of his pocket, set it on the table.

Cruz put some jam on his toast. "Are you waiting for me to ask you what that is?"

"I am," said Thumps.

"It's a block of wood."

"It's a Jenga block."

Cruz cut the sausage into pieces. "You think they have ketchup in this place?"

"This is the piece that you don't want to pull out. This is the piece that holds the tower together. You pull this piece out, and the whole thing falls down."

Cruz sighed. Put his knife and fork to one side. "This piece got a name?"

"Sorin Dalca." Thumps sat back. "This piece is Sorin Dalca."

Cruz wiped his hands on the napkin, smiled, began a slow clap.

"Shit." Thumps could feel the exasperation overtake him. "You knew, didn't you."

"That Dalca *is* dead? That he *had* been killed in a sailing accident in French Polynesia?"

"You knew that all along."

"Suspected," said Cruz. "We suspected that he was dead. How about you? Lucky guess?"

"Car windows," said Thumps. "Greeley's rental. The side windows were covered with dog slobber. The same dog slobber that Howdy slops all over Duke's car."

"Dog slobber?"

"Greeley didn't have a dog. I'm guessing that Gage used the car to pick up Howdy from the shelter, and then left it at the airport for Greeley."

"Not something you could take to court."

"There's only one reason why Gage and Greeley would be sharing a car."

"You jumped from dog slobber to Dalca being dead?"

"Not right away. But it got me thinking. And if Dalca is dead, he couldn't have shown up at Gage's place."

Cruz sat back, a smile on his face.

"Which is why we're having breakfast here." Thumps turned toward the lobby. "I'm guessing, after we eat, you're going to arrest Gage."

"She's already left."

"What?"

"Took off last night. Just after we talked. Roughed up the room a little. Even spread some blood around this time."

Thumps nodded. "So it would look as though Para Bellum came back for her."

"The blood was a nice touch. Left everything else behind. Clothes, purse with all her ID, half-eaten room-service dinner."

Thumps could feel the exasperation fade and exhaustion take its place.

Cruz checked his watch. "She drove to Great Falls and is about to catch a flight to Denver. From there, she's going to New York. New York to London, London to Dubrovnik, Dubrovnik to Podgorica."

"Podgorica?"

"It's in Montenegro," said Cruz. "Nice place. No extradition treaty."

Thumps spun the Jenga piece on the table and started kicking himself. There it was. Clear and complete. He should have seen it sooner, but he hadn't.

"Dalca and Gage."

Cruz nodded. "So, you're not just a pretty face."

"They set up the Vault together. Gage must have known about the shell company in Nevis as well."

Cruz nodded. "When Dalca died, Gage saw her chance. She had the code. She just needed the right opportunity."

"Use Dalca as the bogeyman." Thumps leaned back from the table. "Coming out here to get away from Dalca was a ruse. Gage hired Stan Greeley to suggest that she was in danger. She used Island Consolidated to rent the motel room and the car. She put the sniper rifle in the trunk for show, faked the kidnapping."

Thumps took a breath. "It was all theatre."

"A miniseries," said Cruz.

Thumps ran through the scenario one more time to make sure all the pieces fit. "Does Gage know you know?"

"Not sure," said Cruz. "I guess we'll find out in the next little bit."

"Because?"

"She left the room in a mess to suggest another kidnapping. The storyline is supposed to read that Para Bellum is tying off loose ends. Gage is snatched, killed, and her body dumped along with Dalca where we won't find it. In the meantime, Gage sneaks out the back door with the keys to the Vault."

"And if she can pull off being dead," said Thumps, "no one is going to go looking for her. She doesn't have to live the rest of her life in some Third World backwater. Maybe some plastic surgery, a new identity, and she can live where she pleases, in comfort and luxury."

There was a strawberry on Cruz's plate. Thumps reached out and speared it with his fork.

"Hey."

"That's for keeping me in the dark."

"You would have just given the game away."

"Speaking of which." Thumps put the Jenga piece in his shirt pocket. "Doesn't it bother you that she's getting away?"

Cruz went back to his breakfast. Ate the rest of the sausage. Finished off the fruit cup. Thumps would have expected the ninja assassin to be more animated. But there he sat, as though he was on vacation.

"Except she's not getting away, is she?"

Cruz gestured with his fork. "We may be meeting her plane in Denver."

"And by 'we,' you mean . . . ?"

Cruz smiled, picked up the coffee cup. "You think they have any pie?"

41

The Quick Claim did have pie. A choice of pies, in fact. Cruz went with the chocolate cream.

Thumps stayed with coffee. "You know it's not going to be real cream. It'll be that junk from a spray can."

"The irony," said Cruz, "is that Gage will probably not spend any time in jail. Most likely, she'll make a deal with the feds."

"That's not an irony," said Thumps. "That's a travesty."

"Life in the fast lane." Cruz took a bite of the pie. "You're right. It's not real cream."

"Gage knew she was being watched. She knew that as long as she was alive, she couldn't access the money."

"It's probably Reddi-wip."

"Plan A was to fake her death, buy a new identity, disappear somewhere nice with a shitload of money."

"Or maybe Cool Whip."

"Soon as her plane lands," said Thumps, "she'll know that Plan A is a bust."

Cruz licked his fork. "Which takes us to Plan B."

"She gives up the Vault and the code in exchange for an immunity deal."

"More or less," said Cruz.

"Island Consolidated." Thumps rubbed his forehead. "If Dalca and Gage set up one holding company to help hide the money from the Vault, they probably set up a dozen."

"Which means?"

"Gage will give up the Vault for the deal, but she'll hold back a couple of the shell companies."

"A good supposition."

"Plan B is a bust as well."

"Yes, it is," said Cruz. "The guys back east will assume that she's held something back, and they'll sit on her like a frog on a lily pad."

"All of which leaves Plan C. Run far, run fast, get a nice place in Pod . . . Poda . . ."

"Podgorica."

". . . with a ton of money and the inconvenience of corrupt authorities, power outages, and TV game shows in a foreign language."

Cruz put his fork to one side. "Plan B is her best option. She doesn't get the money, but she doesn't go to jail."

"Even though she should."

Cruz pushed the pie away. "She didn't kill anyone."

"Stan Greeley."

"Not her fault."

"She shot you."

"She was just trying to hit the car."

"Jesus," said Thumps. "No wonder the country runs a deficit and has lousy health care."

• • •

Peter brought the bill.

"You notice how you get roped into the tip?" Cruz opened the leather folder, looked at the bill. "Used to be you gave ten percent if the service was good. Fifteen if you were feeling flush. Now the choices on the machines start at eighteen and go up to twenty-five. You can't do fifteen unless you enter it manually."

"Just leave cash."

"Cash?" said Cruz. "Who the hell carries cash anymore?"

"People still carry cash."

"I'll need your card."

"I'm not paying for a breakfast I didn't have."

"You had coffee," said Cruz.

"Why don't you get Island Consolidated to pay for your breakfast?"

Cruz smiled. Then he chuckled. "Pancho, every so often you come up with a fine idea."

"I was kidding."

Cruz picked up the pen. "You remember Gage's room number?"

"No."

"You think a twenty-five percent tip is too much?"

Duke was at the office when Thumps returned.

"Where's your buddy?"

"Dropped him at Stas's garage," said Thumps. "From there, he's on his own."

"Lover's quarrel?"

"Deanna and Cooley?"

"Deanna's on patrol," said Duke. "Cooley's got the rest of the day off."

"Where's Howdy?"

"Don't get excited. He's with Deanna. He likes to ride in cars, and Deanna said she could use the company. Said Howdy was better company than most of the men she knows."

"Little harsh."

"Ourselves excluded, of course," said Duke.

"Of course."

Duke rocked back in his chair. "I'm doing a little better. Getting some sleep."

"You keeping the dog?"

"Don't think so," said Duke, "but I'll give it some time and see. What about you?"

"What about me?"

"Hear you and Claire are back together." Duke waited. "Guessing you're going to try and quit again."

"Expect I will."

"Go back to photography?"

Thumps spotted a Dumbo's doughnut box on the filing cabinet. "Any reason to hope?"

"Fancy dropped by bearing gifts," said Duke. "I'm going to take her on a ride-along tomorrow, show her the wonderful world of peacekeeping."

"So, the doughnuts are back. What happened to the healthier regime?"

Duke grinned. "We're going to eat them slower."

Thumps settled in the chair. "You want me to keep you company? I could regale you with tales of shadowy government agencies, white-collar criminals, secret bank accounts, and corporate conspiracies."

Duke went to the coffee pot, poured himself a cup. "Or," he said, "we could watch the football game on the flat-screen in the holding cell."

"Who's playing?"

Duke cradled the cup in both hands. "Who the hell cares?"

FREEWAY AND COOKIE were waiting for him, full of complaint. There was water, but no food, and Thumps had to hold both cats off with his foot while he filled their bowls.

"Not my fault," he explained. "Cruz was supposed to feed you."

Thumps felt the motion before he heard the voice.

"They can be pretty insistent."

Nora Gage. Nora Gage with a gun.

"I don't keep animals. Too much responsibility. Too much hassle."

"Howdy?"

"That was for Greeley," said Gage.

Thumps nodded. "You knew he was watching the place, because you hired him. You figured that Howdy would find him. You'd call the cops. Help, help, intruder alert. They'd arrest him, and it would raise the curtain on the play."

"Didn't mean for the big dummy to knock Greeley off a cliff. But that's what happens to plans. FUBAR, FUBAR, FUBAR."

"And you didn't know that Porter Kincaide is terminally ill."

"It did take the edge off the Para Bellum angle."

"Why are you here?"

"You mean, why am I not in Denver in handcuffs?" Gage motioned with the gun. "Why don't we go to the living room. Get comfortable. Have a little chat."

The living room was dark. Thumps reached for the switch.

"Leave the lights off," said Gage. "Cozier in the dark."

"So, the reservation to Denver was more theatre."

"You mean the Great Falls to Denver, Denver to New York, New York to London, London to Dubrovnik, Dubrovnik to Podgorica?"

"Except you didn't go to Great Falls."

"Let's start with what Cruz knows."

"He knows you shot him."

"That was his fault," said Gage. "I was just trying to add a little jeopardy to the mix. How was I to know that he would panic and hit the gas?"

"He knows that Dalca is dead," said Thumps. "I think he knew that all along."

"Yes," said Gage, "I was afraid of that."

Freeway came into the living room, jumped onto his lap, began purring loudly.

"Hell of an attack cat," said Gage.

"You ought to see Cookie," said Thumps. "Heart of a lion."

"The small refrigerator?" Gage smiled. "I guess you could get crushed if he fell on you."

"As soon as Cruz figures out that you weren't on that flight, he's going to come looking for you."

"Back to business." Gage raised the gun. "What does Cruz know?"

Thumps shrugged. "Cruz doesn't tell me shit. He lies to me all the time. I think he does it just to stay in practice."

"What. Does. He. Know?"

"He knows about Island Consolidated."

"Island Consolidated is a throwaway," said Gage. "It was Dalca's personal debit card."

"He suspects that there are other such shell companies. Companies set up to move monies from the Vault to more secure locations." Thumps ran a hand over Freeway. "But it doesn't matter what I tell you. You're not going to believe me. You can't afford to believe me."

Gage sighed. "You're right. So, it's back to the lesser of the plans."

"Run away to a non-extradition country?" Thumps snorted. "Why not make a deal with the feds? Give up a bunch of the companies, keep a couple for your retirement. Doubt that the government wants a public scandal over a secret government agency helping themselves to corporate bank accounts."

"Hardly seems fair," said Gage, "after all the work we did. Why should I have to give up any of it? You think the government is going to let me walk away? You've been living in the West too long. All these wide-open spaces and fresh air have gone to your head."

"So, what's the plan?"

"I'm afraid you're going to have to disappear."

"Kill me?" Thumps rolled Freeway over on her back, so he could pet her stomach. "That's not a plan. That's a major felony."

"I'm not going to kill you. Unless I have to."

"Ah," said Thumps. "You want Cruz and the gang to waste their time looking for me."

"Better than having them waste their time looking for me." Gage pulled several books off a shelf. "We could kick over some furniture, break a few dishes. I'd appreciate it if you would cut yourself, bleed a little."

"I like my plan better."

"There is no *your* plan." Gage pushed the floor lamp over. "On your feet, Mr. DreadfulWater. We're going to walk out the door to your car like the old friends we are. I'll have the gun in my jacket pocket, and if you do something ill-advised, I'll shoot you."

"That'll wreck the jacket."

"Yes," said Gage, "I imagine it will."

Cookie was sleeping on the kitchen table. Evidently, eating had worn him out.

"Cat's not supposed to be on the table." Thumps reached out and smacked the big cat's butt. "Off."

Cookie rolled up on his side, pulled his front paws up around his chin.

"He's cute," said Gage, "if you like cats."

Thumps stepped out onto the porch. Evening was on its way. The bright of the day turning to dusk. Next door, the house was quiet. Pops wasn't on the porch, which was just as well. If his neighbour had been home, Dixie would have wanted to talk, and Pops would have wanted to come over to play with Freeway.

All of which would have made explaining Gage and her gun somewhat of a challenge.

"And now we walk to the car and get in." Gage poked Thumps in the back. "I'll sit in the back. You drive."

Thumps had seen any number of movies where the heroes disarmed the bad guys. It was, he recalled, a matter of letting them get close. He was trying to remember just how close that was and what you were supposed to do when the shouting began.

Thumps didn't hear what was being shouted, but suddenly there were loud voices.

And Cisco Cruz.

Standing behind Thumps's car, gun drawn. At the same time, Cooley and Deanna and Duke along with Howdy the dog appeared from both sides of the house.

"Put the gun down." Cruz leaned on the hood of the car, steadied his aim.

Thumps could feel Gage stiffen.

"Don't think so," she said. "I think you want to put your gun down and step away from the car."

Two more men with guns, whom Thumps didn't recognize, appeared at the side of Dixie's house. The sheriff took a step forward. "Not happening."

"I'll shoot your friend."

"Excellent," said Cruz. "Then I can charge you with the murder of a police officer."

"I can drop her," said Deanna.

"I'd listen to her," said Cooley. "She had great scores at the academy."

Thumps turned, held out his hand. "You're not that stupid."

Gage sighed, brought the gun out of her pocket slowly, handed it to Thumps. "No," she said, "I'm not."

Howdy padded over, wagging his tail, leaned into Gage, began licking her hand. She reached down, gave him a scratch.

"Big dummy."

42

The office was warm and inviting. There was a fresh pot of coffee on the boil and a large box of doughnuts on the filing cabinet. Duke took the swivel chair behind the desk. Cooley grabbed folding chairs from the storage room, set them up in a semicircle.

"Sort of like an old-time longhouse," he said. "Except not so smoky."

Howdy was asleep on the floor next to the sheriff, the confrontation having worn him out.

"He was a bit of a disappointment," said Duke. "Fraternizing with the enemy."

Deanna tossed the dog a paper ball. "Does he have a 'kill' command?"

"He has an 'eat' command," said Duke. "I put food in his dish and tell him to eat and he does."

"Dogs aren't killers," said Cooley. "Humans on the other hand . . ."

Cruz stood by the cabinet, trying to blend in with the shadows. Thumps was having none of it.

"You used me as bait."

"No I didn't."

"You knew that Gage hadn't gotten on that plane."

Cruz shrugged. "Maybe."

"So, you knew she was still in town."

"Suspected."

"He called us right away," said Cooley. "Plus the two FBI guys."

"Pretty cool," said Deanna. "My first armed confrontation."

"You should be thanking me," said Cruz. "I brought the calvary, saved the Indian."

"Seems to me," said Deanna, "that the Indians saved the Indians."

"Enough glory to share," said Duke.

"You could have gotten me killed," said Thumps. "Again."

"You didn't feel good about her just walking away," said Cruz. "Now we have her on assault and kidnapping charges. She won't be walking away from that."

"And the Vault? The money?"

"Worry about that when the time comes," said Cruz. "Who wants a doughnut?"

"There's fresh coffee as well," said Duke.

"Pass," said Cruz.

"Pass," said Thumps.

"Don't be like that," said the sheriff.

"Pass," said Deanna.

"Pass," said Cooley.

• • •

THE CELEBRATION, IF that's what it was, was short-lived. Deanna had to get back on patrol. Cooley and Scoop were going to take in a movie at the drive-in. Duke and Howdy were going to watch *One Hundred and One Dalmatians* on the flat-screen in the holding cell.

"His turn," said Duke. "I chose last time."

Thumps tossed a paper ball at Cruz. "Stas fix your car yet?"

"Paint has to dry." Cruz threw the ball back. "Probably stay in town for a few more days. Might try my hand at golf."

"Thought you didn't like golf."

"Don't like to watch it," said Cruz. "Wutty has offered to give me a couple of lessons."

"You got a place to stay?"

"Depends."

"On?"

Cruz fished a doughnut out of the box. "I hear you might be moving out to the reservation?"

"Maybe."

"Then I can stay at your place," said Cruz. "Friends helping friends."

"And you'll wash the dishes, feed the cats?"

Cruz sighed. "Yes, I'll feed the cats."

"Not like last time."

"*Pendejo*," said Cruz, "I was busy saving your life."

• • •

IT WAS DARK by the time Thumps got on the road, the night black in a moonless sky. Living in a city, even a small city, made you forget how dark a night could be, forget the difference a full moon could make.

Under a full moon, he would have been able to see the Ironstone as it snaked its way across the prairies. Tonight, it was lost in the deep shadows, the only illumination coming from the throw of the car's headlights.

He hadn't called ahead to see if he would be welcome. Claire had certainly hinted that he was. Still, she could have changed her mind, decided that living alone was not such a bad arrangement after all. Or maybe she was waiting for him to make a decisive move.

The alpha male. King of the jungle. The *capo di tutti i capi*.

He certainly wasn't going to say any of that out loud. It sounded bad enough in his head.

At the top of the rise, he stopped the car, rolled down the window, let in the night. In the distance on the flat below, he could see Claire's place, the lights from the house turning the Russian olive into a blaze of silver.

He'd park the car next to the tree, walk onto the porch. Maybe he would knock, wait for Claire to come to the door.

Or maybe he would simply walk in, as though he were coming home.